After the Game

Norman C. Chastain

PublishAmerica
Baltimore

First printing

ISBN: 1-4137-8083-0
PUBLISHED BY PUBLISHAMERICA, LLLP
www.publishamerica.com
Baltimore

Printed in the United States of America

Dedicated to

Ansley, Andrew, and Ally

Acknowledgements

If an author's success was measured by the number of people who wish you to succeed and are willing to help you do so, then I *am* a successful and fortunate writer, no matter how many copies of this book sell. Encouragement from family and friends keeps me writing when giving in seems easier than digging in. This book would be unfinished bytes in my hard drive without the eager support from a few individuals I wish to recognize.

My brother, Bill Chastain, serves as my personalized writing forum, stokes smoldering embers when doubt threatens the creative flame, and remains my true friend always. His baseball knowledge and sports writing experience added authenticity to *After the Game*.

When I need a boost, a laugh, a fast idea, or a…title, I rely, and often, on John Fowler's sound judgment, quick wit, and amazing way with words—he writes as good as he paints! I owe Doris Booth and Susan Malone for their advise, wisdom, and kindness. Thanks to Greg Weydert for ripping my first draft and caring for it like it's his own. I appreciate Bill Middleton's willingness to waste photographic talent on my mug shot. To Ruth, Melissa, Carole, and Jackie—the Pre-published Manuscript Society a.k.a. the "Murder Girls"—patio conversations and writing friendships nurtured the will to improve and press on.

Most of all, I thank my family. They put up with me when I can't, believe in me when I don't, and love me when I'm hard to love. Ally's optimism and fascination with life give me endless hope. I envy Andrew's quiet resolve, temperament, and poise. Ansley, my wife and dearest friend, keeps me focused on what *is* important, and inspires me with her strength, faith, courage, and love.

Chapter One

Quarterflash. Queen. He alphabetized compact disks. His sweaty fingers stuck to the lining of the yellow rubber gloves. Smashing Pumpkins before the Supremes. He restored order—absolute order.

He shuffled the Backstreet Boys and the Beatles with a collection of Beethoven's best, then shrugged. To rank Margaret Gordon's diverse music accumulation by achievement invited subjectivity, an imperfect touch he could not accept.

It was after three in the morning. His eyes blurred on the next two plastic cases. He inserted Al Jarreau in the slot behind the Indigo Girls. He nabbed Jethro Tull's *Thick as a Brick* between his index finger and thumb. The inept, the sloppy, thought Jethro Tull played flute, sang lead, and often categorized the artist in the 'T' section. Any half-wit knew Ian Anderson played flute for Jethro Tull, the rock band—filed under 'J.'

Two disks remained. He grinned, satisfied, and jammed Aerosmith and ABBA—the Swedish cornerstone of any alphabetized music compilation—into reserved slots at the front of the flimsy CD rack.

He stood from one knee, smoothed the depression in the shag carpet with the toe of his shoe, and walked through the living room of her small house. The quaint two-bedroom home, a short walk from Bayshore Boulevard, befitted a teacher's modest earnings. He hesitated at the bedroom door, gazed into the yellow light, and strolled forward.

Margaret's golden hair fanned out on the shoulder of a cream nightgown and shimmered in forty-watt lighting. She lay atop the print comforter, her delicate fingers interlocked. Asleep forever, a bloody halo blemished the angelic portrait. He had bathed her and brushed the tangles from her hair. Deep red blood clotted in a pool on the pillow.

He stared at Margaret's peaceful features. His eyes followed her sharp cheekbones. Margaret's long eyelashes entombed hazel green eyes. Her passionate sparkle dimmed for eternity. Remorseful, he sighed, "I didn't mean to." He had wanted to make love with Margaret, not murder her.

His other victims were convenient. A pantyhose run, a lipstick-smeared tooth—grating annoyances pushed him beyond sanity's vague boundary. Margaret was different. He loved her. Why didn't she listen? He told her, "Not tonight." She pleaded with him to drop by after the game. He knew better. He should have remained steadfast, strong. He surrendered to lustful temptation, thinking this time he could banish the demons for Margaret.

Wrong. Demons never back down.

He pinched the bridge of his nose. The hours since the baseball game seemed like a decade in hell. Jorge Alfonzo's bloop-single down the right field line ruined a routine ninth inning and condemned Margaret. When the Devil Rays' second baseman scored the tying run, extra innings followed. The Braves rallied to overcome the flawed ninth and won in twelve innings. Three innings too long. Three innings of chaos. Three innings for the demons to rant, revolt, and mash his brain against his inner skull. Alfonzo's base hit only loaded the gun. The blame spread elsewhere—even to Margaret.

He drove away from Tropicana Field and aimlessly roamed unfamiliar streets, sucking in salty air to relieve his volatile intolerance for imperfection. Through open windows, the Tampa Bay breeze soothed his rage like a car's rhythmic drone on a screaming toddler. He entered Margaret's house for the first time, calmed and willing to leave the extra inning game in the past.

Books, magazines, newspapers and mail covered every countertop. Dust clung to heaped bookshelves. Filthy plates and utensils towered from the sink, begging for lemon-scented detergent.

Margaret giggled when the wine bottle slipped through her hands and shattered on the linoleum kitchen floor. Cabernet on white linoleum is no laughing matter. This exquisite woman defied structure, shunned cleanliness. His fragile balance between tolerance and retaliation teetered and crumbled.

The first blow had stunned her. Her wide eyes flickered and lips quivered between muffled screams. He battered the arm she flailed at him, her feeble defense against his lethal swings. Margaret's kind face formed a collage of betrayal and total disbelief. The gruesome barrage lasted only a few seconds. Margaret rested in peace. Sated demons reveled in the vicious outpour. And her house sparkled and shone like never before.

He tugged on the yellow cleaning gloves he had found beneath the kitchen sink. Adoring her tranquil pose, he debated deep within his mind. *Which had required more elbow grease, the red wine or the bloodstained tub?*

He bent over her. His breath streamed over her ashen cheeks. "Would you like me to vacuum?" He paused. "Of course I don't mind. Where do you keep the vacuum cleaner?"

He straightened his back, cupped his hands on his hips, and waited as if Margaret's answer would burst open the window and flutter on windblown curtains.

"You rest," he broke the eerie silence. "Don't you worry, I'll find it." He kneeled beside the bed. His warm lips brushed her tepid forehead. "Goodbye."

Charlotte climbed creaky stairs. She tilted, her right side weighted down by six point two pounds of processor chips, RAM, and hard drive gigabytes in a scratched leather case. Along with power cords, audit files, and her leather-bound organizer, the bundle gouged her collarbone. She dragged a collapsible aluminum luggage cart up one agonizing stair riser at a time. An inkjet printer, tethered to the cart, and the laptop dangling from her side contorted her spine. The virtual remote office in two-inch pumps was home. Wasn't progress great?

She reached the landing, balanced the load, caught a breath, and fumbled with a fist full of keys. Searching the hallway shadows for Jack the Ripper's descendants, she crammed a single key into the cylinder deadbolt. Tumblers clicked. She turned the knob and leaned into the door.

"Damn."

Charlotte released the cart handle and lunged at the swollen door. The doorjamb popped and the seal parted. She stumbled inside, her shoulder throbbing from the collision.

Cool air rushed to her. Without looking, she flipped the light switch. The cart wheels rattled over the aluminum threshold. She lowered the laptop from her shoulder and shoved the door closed. She turned and gave the apartment a reacquainting glance. The unfamiliarity saddened her. She paid the rent, bought the couch, chairs and lamps, yet little connected her to this place.

She had conducted a physical inventory at a Brownwood copper cable manufacturer for a week, followed by two weeks in Midland on the Energco audit. She hadn't set foot inside her Dallas apartment for almost a month. A big paycheck and potential with the Big Four public accounting firm had surpassed her ambitious expectations. She chugged along the firm's fast track, managing Texas audits, and envisioned a Payne, Wyman & Bradford partnership within five years.

She was destined to five more years barreling along stark Texas highways scrutinizing others' credits and debits. She cringed. Despite the dismal sneak preview of the future, she wasn't a hostage to accounting. The job gave her an escape hatch from marital captivity and freed her from material dependence on anyone ever again.

"What now?" she whispered. "Wine…if I didn't drink it all."

She tossed her suit jacket on a chair back, loosened the skirt waist button, and walked out of her pumps. She massaged her toes, imprisoned in navy leather since before sunrise, in the shag carpet. Her feet spread to their natural shape. She entered the kitchen, turned on the light, and reached for the refrigerator handle.

"Kendall Jackson. My dear friend," she spoke to the Chardonnay bottle. "You never disappoint."

She grasped the bottle's neck and ransacked a utensil drawer, looking for a corkscrew. A blinking light underneath the wall-mounted phone annoyed her. The answering machine persisted for her attention.

Who could have called? She had cleared her messages around eleven, waiting to board a puddle jumper in Midland. Whoever called this late could wait until morning.

Charlotte wrestled with the bottle and corkscrew. Cork crumbs rained on the counter. She glowered at the emerald reminder flashing from the recording device between twists and tugs.

"I refuse to listen." Her voice startled her. She let go of the corkscrew and glared at the answering machine. "What's wrong with this picture? I'm conversing with seven hundred and fifty milliliters of Chardonnay." She nodded at the amber bottle. "A good listener, I should add. I'm in a heated debate with an electronic gadget, and I'm ducking messages from real, live, breathing human beings.

"I surrender!" She jammed the play button and renewed the bout with the stubborn cork.

The tape rewound and beeped before it played the first message.

"Charlotte, this is James. It's midnight and I'm all by my lonesome. Your e-mail said that you'd be home around two."

The cork popped from the bottle. She listened to James Houston, her managing partner and discreet lover, while flooding her wine goblet with Chardonnay. The lofty figureheads at Payne, Wyman & Bradford frowned upon fraternization, so extracurricular relations remained under the linens.

"I've missed you," James continued. "Why don't you drop by when you get home? I have a surprise for you."

"A silk sheet pup tent," Charlotte quipped.

"You have a key. Let yourself in. I'm sure I'll be *up* for your visit. See you soon. Bye." The machine clunked.

A tense wrinkle etched over her brow. She contemplated the twenty-five-minute drive into downtown Dallas to pardon James from his self-imposed abstinence. She ran fingers through her fine walnut hair and wiped a thumb over her oily cheek. Her feet ached, and at the moment, she would rather smack him than smooch him. After all, he had hurled her into the bowels of Texas. She would see him tomorrow, when she was refreshed and amorous after a good night's sleep—alone.

The beep interrupted her reclusive thoughts.

"Hi, it's me."

Charlotte smiled. Her sister's cheery voice drew her toward the machine like a post-hypnotic suggestion.

"Are you out counting little doggies again?"

"Oil rigs, not cattle."

"If I sound happy, joyful, exuberant, hyperactive and a bit dizzy, it's because I am! I met a guy, Charlotte. He's wonderful. 'Yeah, yeah, right,' you say. 'Here we go again, my idealistic spinster big sister and Prince Charming waiting to fall off his steed.' Not this time. Did I say that he's wonderful? He's my dream come true. I might be moving. He's a—"

A soft knock in the background of the recording interrupted her sister.

"Got to go, Charlotte. He's here. Call me when you get in. It's one fifty. I'll be up, unless... Well, you know about unless. Love you."

The answering machine shut off and reset.

"Well, well, in love again." Charlotte smiled and tipped her glass toward the phone. "To you, big sister."

Charlotte admired her sister's steadfast adherence to ideals amidst life's neutrality. She was altruistic, enthusiastic about her meaningful career, and a tireless romantic. Money, power, and instant gratification weren't enough for her sibling, a flower child wandering among the "me" generation.

She mused over what kind of man survived her sister's stringent gauntlet of idealistic expectations. He must be a special man—a literature professor from University of South Florida, a poet waiting tables to fund his artistic quest, or an environmentalist crusading to save the Florida panther from extinction. Charlotte's imagination sketched the man's scraggly beard, wire rim spectacles, maybe a pipe, and, of course, shiny armor.

Why should I fret over inaccurate conjecture when I can go right to the source? She lifted the phone from the cradle, punched the number, and smirked. *Unless.*

Up and back, up and back, the vacuum tracks overlapped, shaping shag mountain peaks and acute carpet valleys. He admired the precise angles.

He had lingered much too long, but Margaret's house needed extra attention. Considering the circumstances, the least he could do was leave her home in perfect order. Of course, he also scoured the house to expunge all traces of his presence. A fallen hair, clothing fiber, or haphazard fingerprint would be catastrophic. And imagine the ensuing media frenzy.

He squatted next to the vacuum cleaner, unzipped the bag holder, and twisted the dust-stuffed bag off the output nozzle. He folded and creased the top of the used bag.

The telephone rang.

He flinched, jerked his head toward the chirping phone, and braced a hand on the floor to maintain his balance. His neck arteries pulsated. His heart pumped, rushing blood to feed the sudden anxiety. He breathed deep until the machine answered the call on the fourth ring.

"Hi! I am Margaret's machine. You know what to do after the beep. She looks forward to speaking with you. Have a wonderful day!"

He listened to an encore of Margaret's sweet voice.

An electronic tone prompted the caller.

"Hey, Margaret, it's Charlotte. It's about two fifteen—three fifteen in Tampa, I guess. I got your message. I'm so happy for you. I can't wait to hear about Mr. Wonderful. I'll be home tomorrow. Call me anytime, unless," Charlotte cleared her throat, "you're busy. I can't wait to talk to you. Goodbye. Oh, I love you, too."

Charlotte Gordon. Margaret had boasted with tireless adoration about her sister in Dallas. A CPA with a Big Four firm. Smart, independent, strong, and Margaret's best friend. He glanced at the terracotta picture frame on the oak end table.

Earlier he had wiped the grimy glass until his reflection stared back. He studied the photograph. Margaret's Kodak companion must be her sister, not quite as tall and her hair a shade darker. The two women hugged and laughed beneath a palm tree canopy as an ocean breeze tossed the women's hair. Spontaneous, uninhibited smiles of elation. Smiles of joy. Smiles of love.

Oh, well. Precious memories, Margaret's gift to her survivors.

He turned to the vacuum cleaner. The harmless phone call shot volts of reality through his senses. He needed to leave, and soon, with a corpse in the bedroom. It would take days to clean Margaret's house with the meticulous attention he had become accustomed to. However, if he fled before he attached a clean vacuum bag the omission would grate at him for days, like squirrels dashing on attic girders.

Chapter Two

What can I say to him? Across the screened-in pool, Charlotte watched her father, silhouetted against the horizon. Adler Gordon gazed at a fiery orange sun plummeting through the salmon-streaked sky above Tampa Bay.

She walked around the crescent-shaped pool and lowered her eyes to the chlorinated water. Sunset reflected on brilliant aqua ripples, stirred by a steady evening breeze. Her eyes traced the fuzzy stairs below the pool surface, and grasped for a glimpse of her sister in the fountain of youthful memories.

Marco...Polo, visions of childhood games echoed in her mind. Swimming lessons, birthday parties, and skinny-dipping in the dark while their parents played bridge at a neighbor's house transformed treasured recollections into anguishing reminders of how much she longed to see Margaret.

Charlotte traversed the small backyard over a stone path implanted in the dense St. Augustine lawn. The whiny screen door slammed shut behind her. She stepped onto sturdy pressure-treated planks, bolted to timber pilings, and joined her father on the dock. Her distorted image, like a funhouse mirror reflection, rode the windblown tide in the channel below.

Dredged shell and sand formed the small peninsula, shaped like a hand. Saltwater channels separated the fingers that extended into Tampa Bay. The streets were named for literary legends—Longfellow, Dante, Dickens, and Homer—and the bayside neighborhood became known as the Poet Fingers. Her parents bought the house on the tip of the Dickens finger before she turned two. This was home.

Charlotte slid her arm around his waist and laid her head on his shoulder. He wrapped his solid arm around her.

Perspiration speckled his balding scalp and trickled down his scorched face. Sweat soaked the starched white shirt he had worn to the funeral. He had stood here and stared at the bay since the funeral parlor limo brought them home.

"You're sunburned," Charlotte said. "You should wear a hat."

Adler pulled her close.

"How's your mother?" he asked in a crusty voice.

"Asleep. I gave her the sedative Dr. Ferguson prescribed. I stayed with her until she drifted off."

"I'm worried about Libby. No mother should have to bury her child. Thirty-three years your mother talked to Margaret every day. Maybe she missed one here or there, but I'll bet you can count the days they didn't gossip on two hands. I'm not sure she'll ever accept the notion that Margaret won't call again."

A twinge of guilt in her reply, Charlotte said, "She was so good about staying in touch. I'll call more often, Daddy."

"Your mother would like that." He licked chapped lips. "Me, too. I'm sorry, sweetheart. I didn't intend to make you feel like you haven't done your part. It's just…just those two were wired alike. When your mother told a story Margaret could jump in without skipping a beat. Before you knew it, you couldn't remember whose story it was. Telepathic soul mates, you know?"

"I know."

"Kind of like you and me, Charlotte. We're the tough ones, the realists, the skeptics. Libby and Margaret are kind and trusting…dreamers—"

"Romantics," Charlotte finished his thought. "Then it's up to us to make sure Mother copes. I'll call every day and I'll fly home whenever my schedule allows."

He exhaled and squinted at the sunset.

"It's not right." Adler grimaced. "Margaret was the cautious one. When she was a baby she didn't take her first step until she could scoot across the room. Careful, calculating, not like you. One speed—full throttle. Your bike, your car, scuba diving with sharks, and men. Lord, some of the men. I was always worried about you until I recognized the resilience within you. Do first, damage control, and bounce back stronger from the experience…but not Margaret. It's not like her."

"Mother said Margaret never told you his name?"

"Never," her father confirmed. "She invited us to dinner for the night after… Libby is sure Margaret intended to introduce us," he slammed his fist on the railing and gritted his teeth, "to Prince Charming."

"They'll find him." Charlotte looked up to him. His bloodshot eyes were distant, a look she'd never seen from her father. Was it anger, failure—vengeance?

"I hope so. I do hope…so…"

A mullet shot up and splashed in the channel.

"What can I do to help before I go back to Dallas, Daddy?"

"With the investigation and all the arrangements to make, I didn't even ask. How long will you be home?"

"I start an audit in San Angelo next week. I can stay through the weekend. Two more days of me and you'll pack my suitcase, shove me on the plane, and strap me in."

"Don't count on it," he answered, his sense of humor deflated. "Enjoy your visit. Be with your mother."

"Why don't I pack up Margaret's personal things at her house?"

"A million dawns will pass before Libby ever sets foot in there again. We'll do it together."

"Mother needs one of us," Charlotte said. "Jeb will help."

"You'll have to get him off the golf course first."

"Daddy," she snapped. "Most sportswriters work at night."

"Work, ha! Since when is writing about baseball work?"

"Be nice."

"If I have to. Margaret gave us a key. It's in the kitchen drawer somewhere. Like I said, 'your choice in men.' Remember, he's married and has a new baby."

"We dated twelve years ago. We're just friends, Dad."

"Whatever you say." Her father's eyes filled with the sudden horror. "Please be careful, Charlotte."

"I read the paper." Jeb Owens turned left onto Bayshore Boulevard and shifted the Corolla into third gear. "Tell me what really happened—that is, if you want to talk about it."

"Don't you believe what you read in the newspaper?" Charlotte asked.

"Never. And neither should you. Take it from an expert. I know the guys that write that drivel. Can't trust a one of them."

"Hmm," Charlotte smiled. Jeb had come over as soon as she called. His company afforded a pleasant diversion from the morose day. "Can't trust reporters. Now, there's a novel idea. Of course, then how can I believe the journalist who tells me not to trust reporters?"

"I'm hurt." He covered his heart and swerved into the left lane.

They laughed.

Charlotte looked out the window and gazed beyond the bay at Davis Island's twinkling lights. "Is Beer Can Beach still there?"

"There's a blast from the past. I haven't thought about Beer Can Beach since Plant High. Go Panthers, rah! Too bad we graduated to dorm rooms and apartment sofas. Necking on cramped vinyl seats required such ingenuity. Hey, want to relive our adolescence?"

"Not a chance I'm climbing in that rat's nest." She pointed to the backseat, cluttered with newspapers, coffee cups, and file folders. "My dad warned me about you."

"Adler never did like me. Still doesn't, I presume?"

"He detests anyone that comes between him and his darling daughter. By the way, does Gretchen know you're with me?"

"What she doesn't know won't hurt her."

"Nothing like an honest relationship."

"Come on, Charlotte, give me a break. You're an old friend. You would've been disappointed if I said, 'No,' when you asked me to help. Right?"

"I suppose."

"And I could've told Gretch I was going with you, and driven her nuts thinking I'm romancing an old flame while she's stuck changing junior's diapers. One little white lie, and no one gets hurt."

"You darted out at dinner time with the baby screaming his lungs out. What did you tell the poor woman?"

"Breaking Devil Rays news. Gretch hates sports and would never think of reading the sports page. And if by some remote chance she scanned the *Trib* sports, there's always some trivial tidbit by yours truly during baseball season."

"Logical. Deceitful, but logical."

"Pure genius. I'm gushing with the stuff. Now that we've determined I lie and would cheat if I aroused you in the least, I should change subjects before I do something stupid. What did the cops tell your family?"

"Off the record?"

"Of course," Jeb answered, indignant at her innuendo.

"Never trust a reporter, right?"

He flipped the blinker and turned left at South Willow. "You learn quickly. Don't worry, nobody believes a word I say unless I'm writing about earned run averages, runs batted in, or outrageous Major League salaries."

"They don't know much." Her words were almost inaudible. Jeb shut off the radio. "With the message she left me and no signs of forced entry, they're certain she knew the killer. Probably this *Mr. Wonderful* she mentioned. I miss her."

Tears filled her eyes. Jeb extended an arm. She clutched his hand.

"The bastard beat her with…with an object hard enough to shatter her skull. 'Blunt force trauma,' they called it. Could have been a piece of pipe or a crowbar, the detectives aren't sure." Her despair transformed into anger. "Then he bathed her, dressed her, and laid her out on the bed like some north Florida redneck strapping a trophy buck on a goddamn pickup truck for the whole world to gawk at!"

"A real sicko." Jeb pressed the brakes and pulled the Toyota against the curb. "No leads?"

"The discussion with the detectives is kind of foggy. Like a dream I can't wake up from. I couldn't believe I was talking to the police about my sister's murder." She sniffled. Facing the car window, she looked at Margaret's darkened house. "They came up with zilch in the interviews with her friends and the other teachers at Grady. No one knew about this guy. She had so many false starts with men. She must have been gunshy, embarrassed to share her relationship with friends until she was sure it would last.

"Her phone records showed nothing unusual. No recent transactions on her credit cards. I wasn't surprised. She hated debt and paid cash most of the time. I think the detective mentioned the possibility of DNA match-ups if they identify a suspect."

"That's what the newspaper account indicated," he said. "The article read like clues seeped from every crevice."

"Then it couldn't be true." A smile cracked dried tear trails on her cheeks.

"That's my girl." He grinned. "Never pass up a chance to stick it to good ole Jeb. I suppose next you'll tell me the biggest mistake I ever made was dumping you."

"I broke up with you."

"Thank the Lord! All these years I just thought I was a dumb-ass."

Charlotte touched his cheek. "You're sweet, Jeb. Thanks."

She watched him open his door. Harsh light flooded the car interior.

"Sweet, huh? Let's go inside before those cobalt eyes of yours make me stoop to my real self."

Charlotte and Jeb crossed the small front yard, blackened by dense oak shadows. Homey lamplight had shone from the windows on her previous visits to Margaret's house. Tonight, the porch became an unlit cavern between the fieldstone columns and the front door.

"It's so dark," Charlotte whispered.

She felt Jeb's arm ease around her shoulders. They ascended the concrete stairs. "Lions and tigers and—"

She slapped his arm. "Quit it."

Underneath the porch ceiling, Jeb groped for the screen door handle. He pulled the door open. The hinges squeaked.

"I'm glad the key isn't on a key ring, I'd never find it," Charlotte complained while she probed for the deadbolt. "Got it."

She jiggled the key until the ridges aligned inside the ancient lock. The edge of the key dug into her fingers. She released the key, afraid it would snap off in the lock. "It won't open."

"Let me try," Jeb offered.

The lock didn't budge. He lifted on the doorknob and drew the door tight against the doorframe. The lock plug spun free and he pushed the solid core door open.

"There's a lamp over here," Charlotte remembered from her summer visit. She waved her left arm to find the lampshade and any unanticipated obstacles by touch. She crept in baby steps along the front wall.

A creak from within the house halted her advance. She turned to Jeb, her heart thumping. "What was that?"

"Old houses settle."

A floor joist groaned.

She backtracked down the wall and bumped into Jeb. "That's not settling."

"We'll come back tomorrow when it's—"

Bright beams blinded them. Outside, the yard burst into brilliant blue strobe light.

"Police! Reach!"

"We have a key," Jeb yelled. He stepped sideways, shielding Charlotte, his hands above his head. "I'm Jeb Owens, *Tampa Tribune*. This is Charlotte, Margaret Gordon's sister."

Footsteps pounded on the porch stairs.

"Step forward, Miss Gordon," a baritone voice ordered.

She looked around Jeb, her hands on his shoulders. The flashlight beam hesitated on her face, then vanished in a deluge of incandescent illumination.

"What are you doing here? This is my sister's house! You have no right!"

A slender man holstered his weapon while a heavyset man with a thick black mustache entered the living room from the kitchen.

"I'm Detective Foster Sanders. And this is my partner, Luis Menendez. Sorry we frightened you, ma'am." Sanders's pearly grin contrasted with his dark brown skin.

"What are you doing here? My God, don't you have any respect for the dead? Her family? Get the hell of here! Now!"

Uniformed officers, ready to pounce, tightened the circle surrounding them so close Charlotte smelled stale coffee and spearmint gum.

"Want to call off the stormtroopers before someone, namely me, gets hurt?" Jeb said.

"Who's he?" Sanders nodded at Jeb.

"He's my friend," Charlotte answered. "Now get out!"

"Button it up, Luis," Sanders said to his partner.

Menendez mumbled orders into a handheld radio. Uniformed policemen receded to the porch.

"Again, I apologize," Sanders said.

Charlotte's eyes shifted from the detective to the bookshelves behind him.

"Your father gave us permission."

"Permission," she repeated. Her eyes roamed. "Permission for what?"

"A stakeout."

"You thought he'd come back?" Charlotte was drawn to the bookshelves. She wiped a ledge and held up the finger. "Who cleaned the house?"

"He ain't coming back now that our op is blown," Menendez fumed.

"The newspaper," Jeb said. "There's no evidence, is there? Nothing for DNA analysis? Charlotte, we triggered their snare."

"No dust," Charlotte said, enamored with the tidy shelves.

"Proactive strategy. We hoped disinformation would rattle him," Sanders answered Jeb. "Plant an acorn of uncertainty, nurture it with media sensationalism, and grow a live oak of doubt. Make the killer wonder what he left behind. If he remembered a flaw, it's possible he'd attempt to correct it."

Charlotte ignored the detective and darted into the kitchen, brushing Menendez.

"What's with her?" Menendez shot a look toward the kitchen.

"You! Menendez. How do you spell it? My cohorts at the city desk would love an eyewitness account how TPD treats a victim's survivors."

The bridge of Menendez's nose scrunched.

The irate detective stomped in Jeb's direction. Sanders squeezed between them. "No need for that, Mr. Owens. We're just trying to do our job."

Jeb fired back, "Then catch criminals instead of frightening—"

"The kitchen is spotless." Charlotte barged into the living room. "There are no piles. No dust." She swiped the end table with a hand and opened her palm near Sanders's face. "See, no dust."

"Yes, ma'am," Sanders said and tilted his head.

"Don't patronize me, Detective. Can't you see it?"

"See what, ma'am?"

"Margaret was a sloppy housekeeper. She stacked everything, including dirty dishes." Charlotte waved at the shelves. "Those bookshelves haven't been that clean since the day she bought them. Look, look at the books.... They rise in ascending order from paperbacks to the taller hardbacks, and the CDs are arranged alphabetically."

"I do that myself, Miss Gordon," Sanders interjected. "Helps me find the music I want to hear."

"You don't understand! The kitchen floor looks like a Mr. Clean commercial, not my sister's. She hated cleaning her room as a child and never acquired the discipline as an adult. Who cleaned my sister's house?"

"Nothing's been cleaned since the victim was found. Only TPD and the crime lab techs have been allowed in here," Sanders said. "Let me get this straight. You're suggesting the killer cleaned her house?"

"A tidy home wasn't important to her. She wasn't good at it when she tried," Charlotte added.

"Must have hired a maid," Menendez offered.

"Come off it," Jeb scoffed. "An elementary teacher can't afford a domestic servant."

"No way the scumbag hangs around after offing—"

"Luis," Sanders hushed his partner.

"Yeah, yeah, yeah." Menendez inhaled through his nose. In a rehearsed professional tone, he continued, "Waiting for the perpetrator to arrive, the victim must have straightened her home in anticipation of his visit. It's common activity."

"Not Margaret," Charlotte insisted.

"Then you're saying with a dead body in the bedroom, and an appointment on death row if he gets caught, the perp mopped the floor and dusted the furniture. No way…ma'am," Menendez huffed.

Sanders scribbled notes in a small pad.

Charlotte glared at the skeptical detective. "Think what you want. Margaret didn't clean this house."

"It could explain the lack of evidence." Sanders shoved his pen in a shirt pocket.

"Not you, too." Menendez grimaced.

"Miss Gordon, I've noted your observation and thank you," Sanders said. "Even if the killer cleaned the house, it doesn't give us much to go on. A sense of invincibility, deliberate and confident enough to rub out any possible link to his visit—maybe, the profilers will see something that is escaping an old flatfoot like me."

Her shoulders slumped before she collapsed on the loveseat. The framed snapshot stared at her. St. Thomas—their last vacation together. Good times together gone forever, she cherished the memory.

"Are you through here?" Charlotte asked.

"Let's go, Luis." Sanders motioned to the door. "I apologize for the scare, ma'am."

His cordial attempt sputtered and slammed against Charlotte's silent indifference.

"Good night," Sanders said to Jeb, and he exited.

Jeb lifted the handle, leaned his shoulder against the heavy hardwood, and pushed the door closed.

Charlotte clutched the St. Thomas photograph and drifted away, siphoned into a time warp. Trade winds mussed their hair, they sipped coconut-flavored rum punch, and Margaret howled at the windblown toupee on the head of a divorced financial planner. Herbert Munson, sporting a Speedo swimsuit and sucking in his gut, had journeyed from Ft. Wayne, Indiana, on a wife hunt. Margaret and Charlotte egged him on, flirted, toyed with him, and ran up his bar tab, then giggled like schoolgirls when he turned his back. The mention of Herbie's name brought on immediate laughter thereafter. Yes, they'd been cruel, but what delicious fun, and Herbie Munson, the Virgin Islands lady killer, returned to the Hoosier state with bolstered confidence and exotic boasts of Caribbean conquests.

"How about some tunes to liven up this party?" Jeb asked as he studied the varied music.

Charlotte remained quiet, lost in the tropical mirage.

"Yes, Jeb, I'd love some music," Jeb spoke. His finger scrolled along the titles from classical to heavy metal. He selected a CD, slid *The Way It Is* into the player, and forwarded it to the title track.

Waves of Bruce Hornsby's keystrokes washed away the woeful silence. Charlotte disconnected from the surreal séance and turned from the picture.

"You okay?" Jeb asked.

"Sorry. I was somewhere else."

"I never could keep your attention. Anywhere interesting?"

She shook her head. She hoarded the vivid daydream as if sharing the vision would void a return trip.

"This is a nice place," Jeb said. "And this is a hell of a music collection."

"'Dark Side of the Moon,' Schubert's 'Unfinished Symphony,' and the 'Hokey Pokey.' Margaret loved anything with a beat, rhythm or melody." Charlotte glanced at the photograph again. "I'm not in the mood to box up her belongings. I feel like she's going to walk in here any minute, only her home is spotless." She looked up to Jeb. "The books, the music, the knickknacks, and the pictures are part of her. Would you mind if I just sit here and enjoy being among the little things that made her happy?"

"Not at all. You're the boss. I just came along for the ride."

"Thank you."

"I could spend hours snooping through these shelves." He pointed to an oversized brandy snifter, stuffed full of matchbooks. "What's with the matchbooks?"

"She collected them. Margaret believed she enhanced the spirit of each memory when she brought a piece of the experience home."

"Cool." He cupped the snifter in his hands, removed it from the shelf, and centered it on the coffee table near Charlotte. "A flammable scrapbook. Before it goes up in smoke, why don't we turn a few pages?"

Her uncertainty became an enthused grin. "Okay."

Charlotte leaned forward, extended her hands, then froze. Her smile melted.

"What? What is it, Charlotte?"

"He cleaned it, damn it! Look." A starburst of lamplight glistened in the cheap glass. "There's not a smudge, not a single fingerprint on it."

He stretched his neck and peered down on the snifter. "You really think the sicko cleaned the place?"

"I can't come up with another explanation. When we were little, Daddy would threaten to spank her if she didn't clean her room. She'd just fold her arms, stand there, and stare him down."

"Did he spank her?"

"And harm one of his little darlings? Never. She called his bluff and he folded."

Gazing at the matchbooks, Jeb said, "If it's any consolation, he didn't clean it all."

Her eyes joined his and inspected the snifter contents. "The matchbooks."

"Enough dust mites in this puppy to set off an allergy epidemic."

A layer of undisturbed dust coated the matchbooks. Bern's Steakhouse, Valencia Gardens, The Colonnade—local restaurants Margaret and Charlotte had frequented since their youth. She barely recalled riding in the backseat of the family Ford, dressed for bed, to the Colonnade's drive-in for a chocolate shake and a grilled cheeseburger. Years later, they razed the original Colonnade and upgraded its image to a seafood restaurant with a Bayshore Boulevard view. Despite the change, the Colonnade remained a Gordon family favorite throughout the years.

Fond memories swirled, opening a tunnel to her past. She lifted the Colonnade matchbook from the snifter. She studied the etching of the raised one-level building under a palm tree umbrella. The miniature drawing was familiar, crisp…clean.

Her eyes rolled to Jeb. "This one isn't dusty. Why would he dust this one?"

"Maybe she just added that one."

His words reverberated like a scratched compact disc. Charlotte widened her eyes.

"Last time I spoke to Margaret, she had eaten at the Colonnade with some teaching friends to celebrate the first week of school. Near the end of August." She stared down at the snifter. "She couldn't resist a matchbook, especially from new places." Charlotte slid from the loveseat to the floor, kneeled at the coffee table, and hovered over the matches. "If there is one without dust, there could be another."

Jeb dropped to his knees to examine the glass bowl.

Afraid to disturb the top layer, her eyes shifted side to side, seeking a hidden clue, evidence buried in her sister's quirky affection for matchbooks, a coincidental diary of Margaret's last hours.

Charlotte pointed a trembling finger. "That one!"

Like the remaining matchbooks would topple if he wasn't careful, he pinched it and removed the matches. No dust. He read it in silence, then turned the cover to Charlotte.

"Down the Hatch Pub," she read the block letters printed on a plain white background. "I've never heard of it. Have you?"

"I was there last night."

Surprised, Charlotte asked, "Why?"

"The Hatch is on my way home from Tropicana Field, just off Fourth Street in St. Petersburg. I covered the game last night, Devil Rays and the Yankees. When I first started with the *Tribune*, I covered the Tampa Tarpons. Tully Reynolds, a utility infielder with the Yanks, never forgot a feature story I hacked on him when he was with the Tarpons. I saw him after the game, and he invited me to join him for a few brews."

Charlotte raised herself from the floor, kicked off her sandals, and curled her legs on the loveseat. "What's this place like?"

"Like it sounds. Heavy drinking. Greasy patty melts and onion rings. Secondhand smoke so thick you wake up the next morning with nicotine withdrawal."

"Ballplayers, even utility players, make big money, right?"

"Obscene bucks," Jeb answered.

"Then why frequent a dive like..." she checked the name on the matchbook, "Down the Hatch Pub?"

"The owner, Phil Duggan, is an ex-ballplayer. Cardinals, I think, backup catcher in the late sixties. Autographed photos, jerseys, bats and pennants plastered on every square inch of wall space. You know the kind of place?"

"I suppose. Do the players go to fulfill an obligation to some baseball code of loyalty?"

"When it's convenient," Jeb said. "Don't get me wrong, these guys aren't saints. Far from it. Most teams that come into town to play the Rays stay at the Vinoy Hotel. It's only a few blocks from the Hatch. Close enough to stumble home.

"They pay these guys to play a game. The result is that many of them never grow up. They shower after the game, do their propaganda bit to the media, then slither into the underbelly of whatever city happens to be their host. Mostly high-end strip clubs. Mon Venus and 2001 in Tampa, The Cheetah in Atlanta... Well, you get the picture."

"Not an image I care to envision," Charlotte said. "By the way, why are you so well informed about strip clubs in Atlanta?"

Jeb dropped his eyes and mumbled, "People talk."

"So, what is the association between Mon Venus and Down the Hatch?"

"Duggan keeps his place open late. The players get liquored up, come back from Tampa after a couple of hours of lap dances, looking for a nightcap and a one-night stand. When the Rays are at home, the place is packed with gold diggers that will resort to anything, and I mean anything, to get their hooks into a Major Leaguer's bankroll."

"Pretty disgusting portrayal of the next generation's childhood heroes."

"And it's my privilege to be a part of the masquerade. Exposing the degeneracy is professional suicide. A short series of scandalous episodes, denial upon denial, and the ensuing blackball by every Major Leaguer. Baseball journalism without interviews doesn't sell."

"What happened to the first amendment and hard-nosed reporters in pursuit of the truth and righting the injustices of the world?"

"The truth doesn't buy diapers, Charlotte."

"I suppose not."

She rose from the loveseat, stepped into her sandals, and slung her purse over her shoulder.

"Where are you off to?" Jeb asked from his knees.

"Margaret didn't care much for baseball or any professional sport. Furthermore, unless she went batty since I last talked to her, she would never be attracted to a pro baseball player. I want to go there."

"Down the Hatch?" He bounded to his feet.

"Yes. I want to see it for myself. See why she would be in a place so unlike her."

"The Hatch is a dive."

"Are you going to take me? If not, you can drop me off and I'll drive Daddy's car."

"What if Margaret never went there?"

"She was there. It's against Margaret's rules to accept others' matches."

"Wait," Jeb pleaded and rushed around the loveseat. "We ought to tell…" he pulled the detective's card from his pocket, "Detective Sanders."

"I will, after I've seen it for myself. I don't want any of their watered-down, there's-nothing-to-it versions." She glared at Jeb. "Are you coming or shall I call my father and tell him you deserted me?"

"That'd make his day, wouldn't it? All right, all right, you win…like always. I'll drive you."

He opened the stubborn door for her. She started for the door, paused, and turned. She grabbed the St. Thomas photo from the end table and shoved it in her purse.

Chapter Three

Smoke billowed into a starlit sky from the Pinellas County side of the bay. Charlotte watched the light blink atop the Florida Power smoke stacks, warning aircraft of the candy cane painted structures impaling low altitudes. She looked north. The streetlights from Howard Franklin Bridge fused with the moonlight to coat Tampa Bay in a silver sheen.

Charlotte bounced in her seat when Jeb's Corolla rattled over the expansion joint connecting the bridge to the Gandy Causeway. They zoomed past mangroves, darkened boatyards, seafood shacks, and Derby Lane, St. Pete's greyhound track waiting for the tourists to flock south and squander hard-earned savings on trifectas. Jeb braked and veered into the left-turn lane. The traffic arrow lit, and he turned onto Fourth Street. They drove south, toward St. Pete, through a neon light and chain restaurant passageway. Urban sprawl transformed into unique apartment buildings, local eateries, and the glassy office towers near the city's hub. Jeb turned left at Fifth Avenue North and glided into a curbside parking space.

Charlotte banged the door against the raised curb and squeezed out onto the sidewalk. A neon sign flickered, *DOWN THE HATCH PUB*, inside a grimy plate glass window. Plywood covered a matching window encasement on the opposite side of the solid door.

She crossed her arms over a sleeveless sweater and cast a wary look at Jeb. "Nice place."

"After you see the inside, you'll think the outside looks like the Don," he said, referring to the Don Cesar Beach Resort at St. Pete Beach.

He opened the door. Charlotte hesitated, then preceded him into the smoky cavern. Menthol smoke engulfed her. Her eyes stung and adjusted to the low light. She peered at the shattered glass and splintered furniture beneath the plywood-sealed opening.

Jeb placed a gentle hand on her elbow and guided her to the bar. Ripped vinyl padded the metal barstools. Charlotte's stool wobbled as she rested her elbows on the bar counter.

"It's not very crowded, Jeb."

"The Hatch is always slow when the Rays are on the road," the nosy bartender said. A gold stud pierced his left ear lobe. *MY WIFE RAN OFF WITH MY BEST FRIEND AND I SURE DO MISS HIM* was airbrushed on his sleeveless black T-shirt. "What can I get ya?"

Jeb ordered two beers.

"I was scheduled to travel with the Devil Rays, but I swapped trips with David Ronin when I heard about Margaret's death. So what do you think about the Hatch?" Jeb said.

"Charming."

Memorabilia touting baseball greats—Mantle, Musial, Seaver and Ripken—stared down from dime store picture frames. Two gray-headed drunks, around the bar corner, chased whiskey shots with foamy drafts. An entwined couple demonstrated amplified foreplay in a dark corner booth.

"Ever seen a coupla dogs get stuck. I'll separate 'em with a hose before they start shedding outer layers." The bartender set down their bottled beers. "First time in the Hatch?"

"Is it that obvious?"

"Most women that come in here are bimbos. You ain't one." Alabama, South Georgia, maybe northern Florida, his accent had a Deep South twang. "You ain't trying to impress no one, which, if those bimbos could figure it out, is what impresses men most."

"Thank you…I think."

"Yeah, sure." He smiled. "Let me know if I can get ya anything."

As he turned, Charlotte said, "Well, there is something you might be able to help us with."

He snapped around. "Name it."

"Did you work last Friday night?" Jeb asked.

His eyes flittered from Jeb to Charlotte. "You cops? Phil doesn't want me talking to cops. No, you ain't cops. Lady cops are harder than you and wouldn't be ruffled by a joint like this since they seen worse. And you," he spoke to Jeb, "you was in here last night pounding down brewskis with Tully Reynolds and those two Bronx floosies."

Jeb blushed.

"Sorry, sport," the bartender said. "I didn't figure you two was together."

Charlotte trained a harsh look at Jeb and growled, "We're not."

"Good. Thought I stepped in dog stuff for a second there." The bartender paused. "Yeah, I was here Friday. I'm here most nights since Phil took me in. I washed out with the Blue Jays." He formed a wing and rotated his right arm at the shoulder. "Ninety-five-mile-an-hour fastballs, then *pop*, the next thing I know I'm slinging Budweiser."

"Rotator cuff?" Jeb asked.

"Yep. Surgery never took."

"I'm sorry," Charlotte said.

"What the hell. At least I had a shot at the bigs." He lifted their coasters out of habit and toweled moisture from the counter. "Friday night..." he pondered, "that was the night Torch busted up the place."

"Torch Traynor?" Jeb recognized the name.

"The one and only."

Bewildered, Charlotte asked, "Torch who?"

The bartender's face formed a condescending scowl. He looked at Jeb. "Doesn't follow the game, huh?"

"Not a lick." Jeb shook his head. He took a long sip of beer and turned to Charlotte. "Earl Traynor, a.k.a. the Torch. He's the Braves' closer, and probably the best relief pitcher in baseball."

"Not that night," the bartender said.

"You got that right," Jeb agreed. "He blew up in the ninth after Alfonzo chipped one into right field. Braves won it in twelve. What set him off?"

"He was stone drunk when he came in. He slammed down cold ones like Kool-Aid. Some of the Braves said he goes psycho after a blown save. He bounced around like a pinball, grabbing bimbos'...rears, then he finally takes a load off next to a lady sitting at the bar." He hesitated and examined Charlotte's face. "Couple of beers later, she asked for a phone, insists on paying for her wine while Torch is flashing hundreds, then she bolts.

"All hell broke loose. He yanks her stool off the floor, winds up, and slings the dang thing like a damn Olympic hammer thrower. Torch's got a helluva arm. The window busted into a bazillion pieces. People ducking and screaming, drinks spilling everywhere. He nabs another stool and starts bashing tables until a couple of the Braves strong-armed him. It took forever to sweep it up. Over there's what's left after Torch went berserk." He pointed to the wrecked furniture pile.

"I didn't hear about an incident." Jeb sounded skeptical.

"Nobody hurt. Braves are cutting a deal to reimburse Phil. And baseball sidesteps another black eye."

Jeb gave her a like-I-was-saying glance.

"So he performs poorly, he gets mad at this woman, pitches a tantrum, destroys private property, and walks without so much as a slap on the wrist?" The story irritated Charlotte.

"You got it." The bartender squinted and peered at Charlotte.

"What?" His gaze made her uneasy. "What is it?"

"Must be that déjà vu stuff. I could tell the Hatch wasn't her kind of place. The players hit on her and she wouldn't give 'em the time of day. She weren't no bimbo either. If I didn't know better, I'd swear that lady and you were kin."

Charlotte spun on the stool and knocked her beer with an elbow. Jeb lunged forward to catch the teetering bottle. She reached inside her purse and retrieved the photograph.

She revolved back to the bar. Her bony elbow grazed Jeb's cheek. She thrust the St. Thomas picture toward the bartender. "Is that her?"

"I'll be damned. Yep, that's her."

Charlotte returned from the quiet corner. She patted Jeb's back and gave him his cell phone. "Thanks."

"Did you get Detective Sanders?"

"I left him a lengthy voice mail. The matchbooks, Margaret's visit to this...lovely place hours before she died, her run-in with Traynor, and his destructive rampage. I'm sure he loves messages from amateur sleuths."

"Another beer?"

She straddled the barstool. "Please."

Jeb signaled for the bartender and raised two fingers. He acknowledged with a nod and reached inside a cooler.

"Jeb, for the life of me, I can't comprehend why Margaret was here."

He waited until the bartender brought the fresh beers. "You're not going to like it."

"I don't like a lot of things you say, but it's never stopped you before."

"What are good friends for?" He clinked his beer bottle against the neck of hers. "I covered the games last week. The Braves came in Thursday for a four-game series. Is it possible Margaret's new beau was Torch Traynor?"

"Margaret and a hot-headed athlete. No. I just don't believe it!" She swallowed a sip of beer and inhaled. "Since the funeral, I've been wallowing around in a sorrow pit without a ladder to climb out. Now, I'm angry—make that mad as hell! I could have simply mourned with my parents until we found that damn bowl full of matchbooks. I won't back down until I find out why Margaret was here, until I understand what happened the night she died."

"You said Margaret wasn't the type to go cruising for shortstops. Why else would she be here? Let the cops take over from here, Charlotte." He patted her hand. "Let it go."

"I won't let it go! Accepting anything at face value is not my nature. I've made a career out of questioning others. A professional certified skeptic. When I walk on the job, the client understands until the audit is over that I am compensated to disprove everything they show me. Follow the documentation, question the process, never assume just because someone says it's so that it is indeed so. It's better to doubt and disclose an untruth than to accept an invalidated truth as fact. It's my job and I do it well. Shouldn't I put forth the same effort for my sister?"

She blotted tears with a cocktail napkin. "I'm tired of crying, damn it." She chugged beer. "I'm going to Atlanta."

"What! You're losing it. Why, Charlotte?"

"To fill gaps. It makes perfect sense." She leaned toward him. "This pitcher…Torch, even if he isn't Mr. Wonderful, could be the last person to speak to Margaret. She made the phone call with this ballplayer sitting next to her. Maybe he remembers the conversation."

"You're going to Atlanta to track down Torch Traynor?"

"Don't the Braves play in a massive city-subsidized stadium? He shouldn't be too hard to find."

"Turner Field. And you'll never get near him."

"I'll find a way."

"Still bullheaded, aren't you? Listen, if he is involved it could be dangerous. Hell, Traynor could be dangerous if he's not involved. Leave it to the cops."

"If he is involved, then I will leave it to the cops. I'm going, tomorrow."

He swallowed a sip of beer. "I know you well enough to know you won't listen even though I'm right…again. You married Igor despite my repeated warnings."

"His name was Rocky, and you whined until the processional began."

"Sorry, I confused my Neanderthals. Point is I was right. Regardless, I realize there's no way short of chaining you to Adler's dock that I'll persuade you otherwise, so…"

"So…" she mimicked him.

"I know I'll regret this." He snatched his phone off the bar. "So, I'll try to help."

She kissed his cheek.

"That'll get you everywhere." He smiled. "I have a few contacts in Atlanta. I know the *Journal-Constitution's* Braves writer. Pierce Pope. Good-looking guy. Maybe he can get you close to the Torch."

He glanced at the ball game on the television above the bar. The Braves were hosting the New York Mets.

Jeb dug a small address book out of his pocket. He flipped a few pages, found Pope's number, and tapped fluorescent yellow buttons. Nodding at the television, he said, "He's covering the game. I'll leave a message."

"Will he call back?"

"Reporters are curious. There's plenty of dead time during the game. If he picks up the message before it's over, he'll call. Let's watch the game. When it ends he'll be on deadline and I won't hear from him until later."

Charlotte tolerated the baseball game, drained her beer, and ordered another.

She looked at Jeb, absorbed by the game, making occasional commentary, hoping to lure her into the mounting drama. "What a great game. Abbott's homer ought to ice it for Atlanta."

"What's on the Weather Channel?"

"Chill, Charlotte. If you'd relax, watch a little baseball, and try to learn the game, you might actually enjoy the great American pastime."

"I don't dislike sports. I enjoy running, tennis, volleyball—healthy fun and exercise. What I despise is the media blitz, commercialization, and idolization of grown men playing a child's game for absurd money to participate in the *big game*. Otherwise responsible adults, addicted to the *big game* hype, revel in first downs and stolen bases while starvation and violence climb to astonishing levels. And you know what? When the *big game* ends, another always follows."

"Do you hate sportswriters, too?"

"Feed the beast. I suppose someone has to report the outcome of the *big game*." Charlotte watched ex-jocks peddle low-cal beer on a commercial. "How much longer?"

"Braves lead six to three through eight innings. Unless the Mets rally in the top of the ninth it's over. Traynor will probably pitch the ninth."

"I guess he's not going to call."

An advertisement for John Wayne week on TBS aired between innings.

"He must not have picked up his messages."

"I'm going to Atlanta with or without—"

The phone interrupted her.

"You want me to answer it?" Jeb grinned.

"Hello, Jeb. Pierce Pope, returning your call. You got the scoop on some hot trade news?"

"Your salary for mine," Jeb said.

"Put 'em together and we don't add up to the Major League minimum. It's a shame no one appreciates all the press box talent gathered to glorify the great American pastime."

Jeb laughed. "I've been watching the Bravos. How's it going?"

"Couldn't be better. Three-run lead. Story's done and ready to transmit."

Jeb heard the PA system announce a pitching change in the background. He glanced at the television and watched Traynor warm up. He touched Charlotte's shoulder, pointed at the screen, and whispered, "Torch."

"Shit," Pope exclaimed. "There goes my story. I'll be writing through the first edition. My deadline is quarter of twelve. With this bum coming in, I'll be lucky to submit before they put the final edition to bed."

"Give me a break, Pierce. Thirty-seven saves. Traynor's the best in the game today."

"That's sad commentary on the effectiveness of modern relief pitchers. Don't forget the five blown saves, including that disaster against your hapless Devil Rays last week. Give me Wohlers," he referred to the Braves' closer from the mid-nineties, Mark Wohlers, "bad control and all. At least he had an excuse and he was a nice guy."

For the first time, Charlotte's attention to the television heightened. Traynor tugged at his sleeves, smoothed his goatee, wiped sweat from his brow, and threw a curve for ball four.

"Geez. A curve on a three and oh count. See what I mean." Pope seethed. "The idiot walked the lead-off guy on four pitches."

"The Devil Rays sure could use him."

"I'd ship him out on the next flight if it was up to me. Give me a couple of passes to Busch Gardens and a Cuban sandwich, toasted, and he's yours.

"Damn, a hit. Two on, nobody out, tying run at the plate. Looks like Torch is about to screw up another night of sleep. What do you need, Jeb?"

Traynor fired a high fastball for strike one. He walked behind the mound, bent over, and fussed with his pants legs.

"I need a favor," Jeb said.

"I like people owing me. What is it?"

"A freelance friend needs a break."

"No," Charlotte whispered, protesting the lie.

The Mets' batter chased an outside curve ball for strike two.

He put a finger to his lips before he continued. "She wants to do one of those women's exposés. You know, the inner workings of a Major League club from a female perspective. Would you get her close to the Braves for a few days?"

"Why don't you give her the nickel tour of the Devil Rays?"

"Cause she wants to sell the article. No one gives a shit about a perennial cellar dweller. Everyone likes a winner. Now, a woman's view of America's team preparing for another jaunt to the playoffs has potential."

"I'll be damned," Pope quipped. "He actually struck someone out with runners on. Will wonders ever cease?" He paused, typed a sentence, and asked, "Is she cute?"

"Uh, yeah she's cute." Jeb winked at her.

Charlotte rolled her eyes, annoyed with the conversation.

On the screen, Traynor interpreted the catcher's signals, came set, and checked the base runner at second.

"What's her name?" Pope's voice became curt as the game intensified.

"Charlotte Gordon."

He delayed before he responded, "When should I expect her?"

"Tomorrow."

"Tell Charlotte Gordon I'll have credentials waiting for her at the press gate. I'll be there at four, sharp, or I'll have someone meet her if I'm swamped."

"Thanks, Pierce."

"I'll send you my due bill."

A scorching liner soared from the bat, kicked up clay and scooted to the shortstop. He flipped the ball. The second baseman nabbed the ball with his bare hand, pivoted, and fired the ball inches over the runner's head for a game-ending double play.

"Damn, he's the lucky sumbitch," Pope howled.

"Torch flickers, Braves win."

"Good lead. Mind if I plagiarize?"

"It's all yours, Pierce."

"What did he say?" Charlotte asked before he turned off the phone.

"Pick up your pass from the press gate at four. He'll have someone there to meet you."

"You told him I was a freelance writer."

"So I stretched the truth a tad."

"I'm an accountant, not a writer."

"Be nosy. Ask aggravating questions. Take a lot of notes. Lie. No one will ever know the difference."

Chapter Four

Charlotte had navigated I-85 from Hartsfield-Jackson Atlanta International Airport to the stadium, reading road signs and referring to directions she had jotted down from the Turner Field Web site. She parked the rental car in the near barren lot four hours before the first pitch.

The unfamiliar surroundings rattled her. *Am I actually in Atlanta, posing as a journalist, trying to pin my sister's murder on a professional ballplaye*r? *Was Jeb right? Am I losing it?* Her arm trembled when she checked the time.

Delta gouged her for four hundred and ten dollars to fly fifty minutes from Tampa. Almost five hundred dollars an hour. Crunching numbers settled her frayed nerves. She could earn a year's salary in a month at that rate—without overtime.

She hadn't slept much. Jeb dropped her off around one. She surfed the Web to book an airline ticket, find directions to the stadium, and reserve a hotel room. Since Jeb had cast her as a writer, she spent half an hour researching the Braves personnel; in particular, Torch Traynor. Whether it was the beer talking or Atlanta anxiety, once she laid her head on the pillow her mind had whirled, conjuring incoherent thoughts and disjointed dreams.

This is not an emotional knee-jerk reaction, she convinced herself, again. Charlotte craved fast answers to the out-of-character behavior her sister exhibited over her last hours. She would go bonkers waiting for law enforcement's methodical bureaucracy to resolve her intuitive concerns. The police didn't even know Margaret.

She regretted abandoning her distraught parents. Over morning coffee, she guarded her intent to dig into Margaret's murder. "Rash and irrational. Damn it, Charlotte! Here you go again," her father had denounced her plans, although she sensed he understood at a subliminal level. Her mother sobbed.

Her bloodshot eyes glared back from the rearview mirror. She combed her fine hair and painted Estée Lauder lipstick on dry lips. *Wimp or warrior?* She inhaled. *It will work. Right? Whether it works or not, I will not back down.*

I'm here for Margaret...and my sanity.

She battled the urge to crank the engine and flee, threw open the door and stepped out of the car. A delicate breeze welcomed her to the mild Atlanta afternoon. Enormous fluffy clouds softened the severe blue sky. She slung the laptop case on a shoulder, smoothed wrinkles from her black slacks, and started down the gentle slope toward Turner Field.

City crews were busy erecting sidewalk barricades while street vendors unloaded souvenirs to prepare for the pre-game bustle. During the peaceful stroll, she imagined fifty thousand fans descending upon the stillness. The empty parking lot to her right enshrined the demolished Atlanta-Fulton County Stadium. Plaques positioned at each base and the site of Henry Aaron's record-breaking home run would soon be buried under a blanket of sheet metal and vulcanized rubber.

She wandered south on Hank Aaron Drive. The Turner Field panorama engrossed her. The view of the stadium complex surpassed her expectations. Bronze statues glorified Georgia baseball legends—Phil Niekro, Henry Aaron and the Georgia Peach, Ty Cobb. A theater-size television broadcast the latest from CNN, embedded in a colossal enlargement of the ball Aaron hit to break Babe Ruth's career home run record. Games, activities, and concessions booths surrounded the billboard-sized photo. She caught a glimpse of the playing field between the ball and the Chop Shop, the onsite brewpub.

Stadium workers, dressed in Braves blue and red, and slumped-shouldered stragglers plodded to the stadium. Laptop cases deformed the men's posture. She arched her back, worried that her appearance mirrored the gawky, hunchbacked dribble of journalists clad in jeans and casual shirts.

She paused on Pollard Boulevard, near the southwest entrance, and peered at the toes of her two-inch heels. Wearing black slacks, a burgundy silk blouse and a cream blazer, an overdressed uneasiness flustered her as she joined the lazy press gate processional.

Lean, fat, short, tall, bald, and unkempt peppered hair—unenthusiastic reporters flashed credentials and secured passes from the guard. Just another day on the job.

She looked at her watch. Four o'clock. Nervous as a teenager buying Boone's Farm Strawberry Hill with a fake ID, she handed him her driver's license.

"You Charlotte Gordon?" the sagging-faced black man asked without looking up.

"Yes, sir," her voice cracked.

He slid two passes across the counter. "The red one gets you in the press box. The other gets ya in the locker room and on the field before the game."

"Thank you." Charlotte poked her head through the press pass necklace, hole-punched and strung with twine. "Do you know where I can find Pierce Pope?"

"Sports section, most mornings." The guard chuckled alone. "He's around somewhere. I let 'em in, but it's not my calling to keep up with 'em."

"He said that he would meet me here."

"Are you Charlotte Gordon?"

Charlotte turned her head.

The long-legged woman leaned against a brick wall. Pale green eyes glimmered when she smiled. She tilted her head and flung a long braid of bronze hair off her shoulder. She wore no make-up to soften a rugged, leathery complexion. In hiking boots, khaki shorts and a wrinkled vest, she lifted a gadget bag and approached. The woman extended her hand. "Liz Vanderwahl, *AJC* photographer. Pierce sent me to find you."

Charlotte shook her hand. "Nice to meet you."

Liz's eyes lingered on Charlotte's outfit. "First time at the Ted?"

"The Ted?"

"Mr. Turner's monument to his idol," Liz waved her arm.

"How could you tell?" Charlotte's eyes panned down. "I'm overdressed, right?"

"You look great. You've got television glitz written all over you. The guys will love it. Watch the stray hands. Come on, Pierce is down in the locker room."

Charlotte followed her to a stairwell. They showed their passes to a lethargic, ruddy-faced guard and descended.

"The guys will love what?"

"New blood. Dressed to kill. Boys of summer, good old boys, all one and the same. The players, the owners, the journalists... There's a chauvinist lurking behind every beer vendor. Women only have one purpose as far as good old boys are concerned. So beware."

In silence they continued down into the stadium's painted concrete catacombs.

Charlotte contemplated the subtle warning. "Do you cover baseball often?" she asked Liz.

"I shoot most of the home games, unless the desk needs coverage on breaking news. I usually do a couple of road trips, and the playoffs."

"Then...well, you're attractive, how do you—"

"Keep their hands off me?"

"Yes."

"They think I'm a lesbian." An awkward pause ensued. "I'm not. But if you betray my illusion, I'll claim you're a jilted lover seeking revenge." Liz laughed and beamed a brilliant smile.

Charlotte liked the gruff photographer.

They pushed through double doors and entered a well-lit tunnel at the bottom of the stairs. They followed the contours and ambled around to the first base side of the stadium. Whether her attire or bloated self-consciousness sharpened her awareness, Charlotte sensed the eyes of strangers.

"Liz," a voice behind them bounced off the tunnel walls.

She turned and frowned. "Oh, it's you."

A tiny man in a tailored gray suit came toward them. He had blond hair, not a strand out of place. He examined Charlotte, dwelling for an exaggerated moment on her cleavage. "Who's your friend?" he asked Liz.

"Charlotte Gordon," she introduced herself before Liz could answer. "Freelance journalist." The lie propagated.

"Not familiar with your work. Tad Smithurst is the name. I'm Special Assistant to the GM. Maybe I can be of assistance?"

"Charlotte's a business analyst," Liz said. "She's investigating allegations of nepotism and kiss-ass junior executives within the Braves' organization."

"Ha! Always with the sharp tongue, Liz." Smithurst took a dramatic glance at his watch. "No time to spar now. I need a favor. How about shooting a couple of first pitch candids for tomorrow's *Constitution*? Black lady sheriff from some Podunk county south of here. A little equal opportunity PR never hurts."

"Anything to promote the upstanding morals of Major League Baseball," Liz said.

"Splendid," Smithurst replied and faked a smile. "Got to run. A pleasure to meet you, Charlotte. I'll catch up with you once we get this game underway. I'd be honored to learn more about your work."

Charlotte nodded.

He pranced away in an arrogant gait.

Liz walked as she whispered, "'Want to see my etchings?' The twerp actually asked me that once."

Liz barged through double doors labeled *BRAVES CLUB HOUSE.*

Charlotte hesitated.

Standing in a long hallway inside the doors, Liz snickered. "Never been in a locker room either?"

"How do you know if they're dressed?"

"I don't."

A plump white man in a tight blue blazer inspected their passes, then they wandered down the hall.

"Better than a male strip club." Liz toyed with Charlotte. "And *AJC* pays me to ogle."

"Maybe I should wait outside."

Liz laughed. "It bothers the players more than it will you. The media is only allowed in at certain times, and even then our access is restricted to the locker area. You might get mooned by one of them trying to intimidate you, but as a rule they're pretty shy about exposing private parts."

They rounded a corner and stepped into the locker room at the end of the hall. Television lights reflected from the lavish paneling. Sports anchors and journalists interviewed Braves' players. One shirtless Brave showed off his taut upper body, while other players lounged in varying uniform layers.

The carpeted and illuminated locker room realigned Charlotte's preconceived image of Spartan quarters reeking of sweaty socks and jockstraps. The room formed a circle lined with large wooden lockers. Two open doorways led back to the showers and restricted areas the players frequented to dodge outside attention. The player names and numbers were attached to the top of the lockers.

Charlotte turned in a slow circle while pods of reporters jotted pre-game quotes from the National League East contenders. She spotted Traynor's locker two-thirds around the room. She drifted away from Liz to examine Traynor's possessions at a closer vantage.

The locker contents contradicted her vision of those belonging to an untamed drunk flailing barstools. Pressed jeans and a collarless dress shirt, starched, hung on wooden hangers. On a third hanger, black socks were folded on the crossbar. A uniform shirt and warm-up jacket dangled on the other side of the locker. Polished cleats glimmered underneath the uniform. Cordovan boots shone across the locker floor, as if a superstitious taboo prohibited baseball gear and casual wear to mingle.

His game hat, embroidered with a large 'A,' sat like a crown above the uniform on the locker shelf. A portable CD player, headphones wire coiled neat, and a plumb stack of country CDs lay near the hat. Black, Judd, Tritt, Twain, and Yearwood, in...alphabetical order. Left of the CDs, shaving cream, pump toothpaste, deodorant, cologne, and a small bottle of Advil were lined up by height.

Was she seeing more than she saw? Could there be a locker room attendant assigned to tidy up for the superstars? Had she confused the facts before her with conspiracy she longed to reveal?

"There you are." Liz's voice startled her. "You look white as a sheet. Are you sick?"

"No, no. Late night. I might be a little overwhelmed." Charlotte rubbed some color into her creamy complexion. "It's nothing, really."

A man stood at Liz's right. He offered his hand. "Hello, I'm Pierce Pope." James Bond handsome, in a blue blazer, a maroon and navy striped tie, and tan trousers, he stood at least six feet two inches. His smile sparkled under abundant ebony locks. His bedroom brown eyes locked with Charlotte's.

"Isn't that just like a reporter?" Pope went on. "Overdramatize the routine, and understate the exquisite. Jeb's adjective selection is grossly inadequate. Cute? I'd say, hmm..." he pinched his chin, "stunning. Of course, in Jeb's defense, on the Devil Rays' beat he spends most of his day searching for new ways to find a synonym for 'pathetic.' Welcome to Atlanta, Miss Gordon."

"Uh..." Charlotte stammered. "Thank you, Mr. Pope. And thank you for all your help."

"It's Pierce. Not what you expected?"

"Don't worry, Charlotte, he does this all the time," Liz said. "The coat and tie routine along with that face. Once you get to know him he's no different from any other hack."

He laughed. "How else can a humble journalist compete with a room full of naked athletes?"

"Humble, my butt," Liz jibed.

"Before the game I'll be busy with my game notebook and feature material for a Sunday centerpiece on Houseman's MVP candidacy. Your passes should allow you the freedom to piece together *a woman's perspective of the Braves*. Stick with Liz, or roam on your own. The press box dulls after the first few innings. Come join me, and I'll show you the routine."

"I'd like that," Charlotte replied.

"Then I'll look forward to—"

Microphones flew and cameras crashed to the floor. A human battering ram parted a gathering of reporters. Journalists staggered from the rampage's path. Flexed forearms pried open a gap in the crowd. A hateful grimace carved on his face, Torch Traynor lunged at Pope.

Not braced for Traynor's blitz, Pope stumbled, tripped and tasted the carpet.

"Son-of-a-bitch!" Traynor yelled above appalled gasps, and fretful cries. "You don't know shit!"

Positioned over Pope, fists clenched, he bellowed, "I pitch out of a jam and you tell the world it was dumb luck. *Torch flickers*, my ass!"

"The whole world," Pope fired back. "*AJC* circulation is soaring. And your so-called pitching birthed that jam you muddled through thanks to a couple of slick-fielding middle infielders."

Braves teammates pushed through reporters. Cameras and video equipment aimed to record the event, over the initial shock, the scent of big news brewing.

"You cynical smart-ass!" Traynor cocked his arm. "A mouth full of knuckles ought to teach ya not to bash Torch Traynor!"

A large black arm hooked inside Traynor's left-handed thrust, blocking the punch.

"Let go!" Traynor pleaded with Joe Robinson, the Braves' manager.

"That's enough, Torch," Robinson said.

Butch Crowder, a backup catcher, bear-hugged him and pinned Traynor's arms against his side. "Come on, Torch baby, he ain't worth it."

Traynor struggled to break free. Frank Houseman, the Braves' mammoth all-Star first baseman, grasped Traynor around the waist, hoisted him, and carried him toward the back of the clubhouse.

Robinson offered his hand to Pope and helped him off the floor. "You okay, Pierce?"

Pope wiped blood from the carpet burn on his chin. "Nothing a ten-game suspension won't fix. You might even increase that measly lead over the Mets without that moron in the bullpen."

"Come on. I'll get the trainer to look at that chin."

Charlotte watched Traynor. His belligerent outburst astonished her. Houseman set him down, drooped a muscular arm around the pitcher, and they vanished into their sanctuary. Her eyes drifted to Traynor's faultless locker, his belongings stowed with such meticulous forethought.

Chapter Five

Players huddled in the outfield and shagged soaring fly balls. Reporters bounced from player to player, sniffing for an exclusive or controversial quote behind the batting practice cage. At both ends of the dugout, star-struck kids, seeking autographs, thrust their baseballs at two Braves, who flashed obligatory Skoal-stained grins.

"There's so much going on at once," Charlotte said, enthralled with pre-game pageantry.

Liz smiled. "You like my office? It sure beats sitting behind a desk ten hours a day."

Charlotte meandered through the crowd on Liz's elbow. Liz squinted and formed a half square with her fingers, as if she framed each view, face, and background in her viewfinder.

"What are you looking for?" Charlotte asked.

"I shoot *AJC* file photos during pre-game, you know, player mug shots. If I'm lucky I might harvest a few freelance opportunities. Once the game starts, I have to concentrate on the action, and *AJC* owns my work."

Overcome by the stadium dimensions from field level, Charlotte said, "It's huge down here."

"Yeah. Kind of changes the nineteen-inch Technicolor perspective we tend to accept as life."

"The grass is so soft." Charlotte fluffed the turf with her foot. "The blades are uniform and bounce back like springs. How do they do it?"

"A little fellow spends all night with a finger nail clipper and ruler." Liz laughed, aimed her Nikon, zoomed in on Houseman in the batting cage, and fired three rapid shots as he swatted a belt-high floater. "Money, money, money, that's all it takes to sow the lawn of champions."

Pope emerged from the Braves' dugout, talking with the manager like old chums, a small butterfly bandage on his chin, the lone token of the clubhouse scuffle.

"Looks like he'll live to slice up Torch another day," Liz said.

"Does Torch explode like that every time a writer criticizes him?" Charlotte asked.

"No, that's the first time I've seen him go ape. Pierce and Traynor have been exchanging verbal blows since opening day. It's late in the season. During a pennant race the media analyzes every pitch under a microscope. I guess Traynor snapped."

"I can see how bad press upsets Traynor, but why does Pierce pick on one player? It's like a personal vendetta. I even noticed it when my friend, Jeb, spoke with him last night."

"Don't let Pierce's charm fool you. He's got the nastiest keyboard in Atlanta—he'll harass anyone that plays poorly. But I'll admit he does seem to have a passion for ripping the Torch."

They faced the dugout and watched Traynor exit the tunnel. He stuffed a jacket pocket with bubblegum and climbed the dugout stairs.

"Speak of the devil," Liz whispered.

Charlotte remembered Jeb's assessment of Traynor's ability. "Isn't Traynor one of the best relievers in baseball? While popular opinion praises Torch's performance, Pierce goes against the grain. It doesn't make sense. Why not join the love fest, snuggle up to the guy, and become the local advocate?"

"Hatfield agin McCoy. It's a feud. Does there have to be a rational reason to hate? Pierce has a great way with words. Have you read his any of his articles or columns?"

"Not yet."

"You need to. His words sing, grab you by the bra strap, and pull you into the page. But that's a gift, not a job. Pierce's job is easy. The Braves make it easy—perennial contenders, cooperative players, professional to a fault. Predictable as they plod along to the playoffs, every season mirrors the last with only modest adjustments to the routine.

"Then along comes Torch. He's the best in the business one night and looks like a green rookie the next. He's hotheaded raw potential with periodic and random lapses of inconsistency. You'll see Pierce work later, then what I'm saying will make more sense. Oil and water."

Liz turned when she heard her name. Tad Smithurst wiggled his index finger at her.

"Little Lord Suck-Up beckons," Liz bantered. "I'll be back in a minute."

As Liz squawked at Smithurst, Charlotte grinned, then swung her attention to Traynor.

Ball after ball, he scribed autographs. He tossed signed balls back and relished each child's smile. He answered the relentless chorus of "Torch, Torch," cupped each baseball in his right hand, the pen in his left, and scrawled illegible script between raised red seams.

I'm here to learn about you and expose you, Torch Traynor, she reminded herself. She sneaked a look at her watch. He seemed to enjoy the fans and took an exceptional liking to the younger children. His quick smile accompanied each autograph, imprinting an everlasting ballpark memory. His gentle rapport contrasted with the enraged maniac she'd seen moments earlier in the depths of Turner Field. His drastic mood swing puzzled Charlotte.

She edged toward him. Traynor was tan, healthy, without any visible wrinkles. In her opinion, only the trimmed goatee marred his otherwise kind face. His icy gray-blue eyes resembled a spirited Siberian Husky. His short blond hair was clipped above the ear. He looked like the All-American boy—with a tendency to attack writers and splinter barroom furnishings.

Houseman finished with batting practice and lumbered to the railing for a halfhearted encounter with his fans. Torn between a star relief pitcher's autograph and one from the probable National League MVP, Torch's admirers clambered to Houseman. Traynor finished his signature and returned the ball to an anxious boy shooting desperate looks of lost opportunity toward the mob swelling around Houseman.

Traynor grinned, turned left and rammed into Charlotte. She staggered and began to fall. His large hand caught her arm and kept her from crashing to the turf.

"Sorry, ma'am"

"My fault." Charlotte straightened her jacket.

The pitcher pointed to Houseman. "If I could only hit. The fans choose the home run hitter over a psychotic rag arm any day."

Inches from Traynor, she gulped.

"You were in the clubhouse," Traynor said.

Charlotte gazed at his wild eyes. "I was."

"I hate that you had to see that. I blew a gasket, but Pope had it coming. I haven't seen you here before." He offered his hand. "Earl Traynor. Most folks call me Torch."

His strong grip enfolded her fingers.

She cleared her throat. "I'm Charlotte Gordon."

He studied her press pass. "Who are you with, ma'am?"

"No one…I mean, I'm doing a freelance piece. You know, a feminine slant from inside baseball."

After an awkward silence, he said, "Well?"

"Well, what?"

"By now most writers would've fired off a half dozen zingers at me."

"Zingers?"

"This is the strangest interview I've ever done." He chuckled.

"I was just watching you. I heard ballplayers hate signing autographs, steer clear of the fans. You're good with the children. You looked like you were actually having fun."

He put a finger on his lips. "Shh. Might ruin my nasty boy ninth inning image. You want to know the truth? It's a rush to hear a bunch of kids holler your name and beg you to sign a ball. I remember when I was a half-pint like them, looking up to Major Leaguers like they were Thor or Hercules. The day I forget how I felt, forget those kids' dreams of doing what I do, is the day I leave the game."

"Torch!" a chubby coach hollered. "Quit your yakking and stretch."

"Yeah, yeah," he barked back. "Hey, I gotta go. See ya around."

He stepped past her toward right field.

"Earl," she called out as he strolled away. He looked over his shoulder. "My sister said to tell you, 'Hello.'"

His eyes shifted.

"Maybe you remember her, Margaret Gordon."

Charlotte reached inside her purse.

"I meet a lot of people. I ain't too good with names."

She strode to him. No longer protected by the terracotta frame, the corners of the St. Thomas photo were crinkled. "St. Petersburg, last week. She met you at a little hole in the wall called Down the Hatch Pub." She flipped the picture and held it in his face. "Remember her?"

"Sorry," he shook his head. His confidence cracked, he muttered, "With a face like hers, I hope I'd remember her, but in the Hatch ya never know."

"Why not?"

"Late at night, on the road, Down the Hatch is the kind of place you try to forget."

"Torch!" the coach bellowed.

"Coming. Listen, I don't want to offend no one. Tell Margaret I say, 'Howdy.' And let my pea brain memory be our secret." He winked. "Maybe I'll see you around, Charlotte."

He pivoted and began a pigeon-toed jaunt to the outfield before she could prolong the uncomfortable conversation.

Earl Traynor was not the cocky he-man she had expected. Witty, appreciative and outwardly kind, he was more than a simpleton with a strong arm. He'd been open to conversation until she uttered, "Down the Hatch." Instant elusiveness.

Chapter Six

The Mets led the Braves one to nothing after five innings. A tight September pennant race and a one-run game—exciting stuff for baseball enthusiasts. The Braves crowd chanted, chopped like tomahawks, and booed the umps.

Charlotte slumped on a folding chair in the photographer pit with Liz. She yawned. Even the electric environment and field level panorama failed to inspire a passion for grown men playing a game in tight pants.

Liz's work entertained Charlotte early in the game. Wielding three cameras, the photographer monitored a light meter and fiddled with shutter speed and aperture f-stops. Intense and less than chatty, Liz gave an uninterested grunt when Charlotte told her she wanted to go to the press box.

She climbed stairs to the concourse above the field level seats. In the aisle behind home plate, she located the stairwell descending to the clubhouse, then looked up. The same stairs rose to the stadium club level and the press box. She ascended two levels of stairs, stopped on the landing, and opened the press box door. Stadium security greeted her, verified her authorization and waved her in.

A low wall guided her into the media hub. Hot dogs, coffee, nachos, sodas and a beer tap were available for the press, compliments of the Braves, in a cafeteria outfitted with closed circuit television. Telephones rang and game noise filled the hallway beyond the canteen. The press pass provided access, but she didn't belong. She walked ahead, trying to fit in, and veered toward voices, keyboard clatter, and the modem static.

News releases, statistic sheets, and press guides blanketed wall-to-wall desks in the narrow room to her left. A few feet ahead, she entered the main press box. Three tiers of continuous desk space rose from an enormous window opened to a classic home plate view. She took a short breath, climbed two stairs, and searched for Pope.

Journalists, their eyes glued to the game, rattled their keyboards and jawed on phones. The crowd roared, and the press box burst into a between-inning break. A steady stream of men herded past her to plunder the Braves-sponsored amenities.

She scanned faces and noted the average cross-section of people comprising the all-powerful press. Ordinary-looking men and women in casual-to-the-extreme attire—a dynamic appearance seemed inconsequential compared to turning a well-construed, grammatically correct, and intriguing phrase.

"Charlotte. Over here." Pope stood and signaled to her from mid booth, on the front row. The *AJC* reporter's guise, his tie knot tight, slender and handsome, was an anomaly among his peers.

She shuffled between the chair backs and second-tier counter, careful not to trip on telephone lines and extension cords powering laptops of every make and size. Note pads, statistics, press guides, and newspapers obscured counter space between the portable computers. She squeezed around a large man, unwilling to yield his posture for pedestrians, and joined Pope.

"I was beginning to wonder if you were going to make it up here," he said. "Great game, huh?"

"I suppose. Guess I'm not much of a student of the game."

"Good for you." He beamed. "I had a feeling you had substance, you know, unimpressed with money and muscles."

She flashed a quick smile.

"Oh, before I forget." He reached for a leather-bound notepad next to his laptop. "Jeb left a message for you. He wants you to call." He ripped the page from the pad. "Here's the number."

Charlotte looked from side to side. "Is there a phone I can use?"

He slipped a hand inside his blazer and unclipped a digital phone from his belt. "Use this."

"Thanks. Can I go somewhere a little less vibrant?"

"Use the back room." He pointed to the long room behind the press box. "When you finish, I'd like to show off my work."

"I'll look forward to it."

She found a quiet corner and dialed Jeb's home phone number. Gretchen Owens answered. Their baby wailing in the background, she summoned Jeb.

Charlotte nestled the phone between her shoulder and ear and thumbed through a discarded press guide. She found Traynor's profile.

"How is sports writing fantasy camp?" Jeb said.

She folded a corner on the page and closed the guide. "How do you do this every night? Everyone's been nice, especially Pierce and Liz, *AJC*'s photographer, but this would have to get old quick."

"And adding rows of numbers with a ten-key calculator is a thrill a minute," he fired back. "How's it going?"

"I'm overdressed and out of place. I wasn't here thirty minutes before a locker room brawl erupted."

"No shit, who?"

"Traynor attacked your friend."

"Torch yoked Pope. No way!"

"Saw it with my baby blues."

"That's huge. Torch will get a ten-day suspension, minimum. And in the middle of a pennant race. Guess with all the bedlam you didn't get within a mile of Torch."

Reporters filed into the press box and settled in for the bottom of the sixth inning.

"You underestimate me, Jeb. I spent a few minutes with him on the field during pre-game. He acted as if nothing had happened in clubhouse."

"Aren't you fitting right in?"

"Not any more difficult than walking into a client the first time and demanding confidential documents."

"What did he say? Did you ask him about Margaret? Did you tell him about the Hatch? What's he like? Did—"

"Whoa. I think I startled him when I mentioned Down the Hatch and showed him the picture of Margaret. He said he didn't know her. He blamed his lack of memory on the masses he meets. He called the bar the kind of place you try to forget."

"Easier to forget when you're blind drunk. What was he like?"

"Receptive. Accommodating, until I flustered him. I watched him sign autographs for kids. He's...well, I don't know."

"He's what, Charlotte?"

She sighed. "I know I'm here to attach a legitimate air to our beer-induced allegations. I'm dead tired so maybe my intuition is on the blink, but he seems like a nice man."

"Be careful. Remember Margaret fell for Mr. Wonderful before he—"

"I know, I know, but he just wasn't the brute I imagined."

"Would Margaret like him?"

She sorted memories of her sister and the recent encounter with Traynor, then tried to picture the couple together. "Possibly. He's likable. He's good looking, although appearance wasn't a high priority to Margaret. If she met him away from baseball there's a chance she'd be attracted to him. This good old boy stuff would turn her off in an instant." She paused, then conceded, "I see your point."

"Just be careful."

"You sound like my father."

"So your old man and I finally agree on something."

She snickered. She leaned against the table edge and crossed her weary feet. "Did you call to check on me?"

"Yes and no. I spoke with Detective Sanders today."

Charlotte pounced to her feet. "Did they follow up on our call?"

"Yes. He appreciated your message. They questioned the bartender at the Hatch. His story convinced them to contact the Braves this afternoon. He spoke to some underling by the name of…let me check my notes… Smithurst."

"Tad Smithurst."

"Tad, that's it. The call must have caused an uproar, because Sanders said Austin Hendricks himself returned the inquiry. Believe me, Charlotte, the Braves general manager doesn't step in unless he considers the issue explosive."

"And?"

"Sanders said Hendricks was upfront and cooperative. He admitted that Torch busted up the bar, but assured Sanders that his teammates escorted him back to the Vinoy and poured him into the bed."

"Bullshit, Jeb! It's a contrived statement to cover for Traynor. Anything to win!"

"Sorry," Jeb said.

"They need to keep digging."

"Hendricks insisted they had witnesses to corroborate Traynor's whereabouts."

"Of course, and I'll bet Hendricks signs their paychecks."

"Sanders told me there is no evidence to tie Torch to the scene. He told me it was a dead end unless more solid evidence is uncovered."

"Dead end! Damn it, they don't know her. It's not a coincidence. Margaret didn't frequent bars like the Hatch. Nice guy or not, Traynor has to be the connection. I'm not giving up that easy. They want solid, I'll claw until I hit stone."

"Don't get reckless, Charlotte."

Charlotte weaved through the electronic maze and dodged hefty writers in spinning chairs. Pope wheeled an empty chair between himself and *The New York Times* beat writer. She plopped on the seat, her face wrenched in an unsettled scowl, pulled unruly hair off her shoulders, and bunched it with an elastic scrunchy.

"Bad news?" Pope said.

"No." Charlotte breathed deep. She seethed at what she deemed lame police work and strived to regain surface composure. "It's been a long day and I'm sinking." She flashed a sincere smile. "Thanks for asking."

"Can you muster enough energy to behold sports journalism genius in the making?" He wiggled his thick eyebrows.

"Sure."

"Then scoot into my office, relax, and let me share my guaranteed formula for success."

Charlotte rolled closer to him. The fifteen-inch color Dell screen was brilliant. "The *AJC* issues nice laptops."

"Ha. That's a good one. Not a chance. *AJC* provides us with recycled dinosaurs, available when the execs upgrade. I'll admit it's a steep personal expense, but if I want to do top-notch work, I need the fastest, most reliable equipment on the market, not some three-year-old model reconditioned by a know-it-all vocation school graduate from the information technology department."

The screen engrossed her.

"Ready for my humble spiel?"

"Ready."

"Doze off if you get bored. No snoring, please." He grinned, watched a play on the field, and continued. "Sports writing is a game. Unlike baseball, to win you must beat the clock—the deadline. The *AJC* deadline for first edition is eleven forty-five, Eastern Time. Subsequent deadlines result in less exposure and fewer readers. Not exactly desired results for my pretentious goal of household admiration.

"The simple secret to winning is to finish the story before the last out. Now, if I could predict the outcome of every game I cover I'd have a permanent residence in Vegas. Nantucket. Santa Fe. Malibu. You get my drift. Since I can't pick the score, the next best scenario is to insert as little of the puzzle, the score and late heroics, as possible.

"I'll show you." His finger hovered over the touch pad. A document named "0915game.doc" popped on the screen. "Every game is a book. Each inning advances the plot. Every night there is different protagonist, antagonist, and victim. A mystery to be solved, the story proceeds. This file is merely factual game highlights. The trick is to create thrills beyond the trivial line score, something that distinguishes each game from the other one hundred sixty-one."

Another file, "0915perez.doc," filled the screen.

"Like tonight. One zip, Mets through eight. Twelve strikeouts, the Mets' starter, Omar Perez, is the hook in this version. Of course, if the Braves get to him late," he called up another file, "0915bpen.doc," "bullpen heroics kept the score close so the Braves could come from behind."

"You forecast various endings," Charlotte said.

"Exactly. Barring extra innings or a huge ninth-inning rally, most nights I hack a version of the game that approximates the conclusion. Blend the animated story into the game file with a little electronic cut and paste, insert a couple of post-game quotes and I'm transmitting copy twenty minutes after the last pitch. No magic, just time management, plot recognition, and a bit of creativity."

The New York writer stared into right field with binoculars. "Hey Pope, your boy Torch is warming up. That's the third time he's been up tonight."

"Robinson won't use him unless the Braves get a lead. Maybe Perez will hold 'em and we won't have to suffer through another Bic-boy flame-out."

The New Yorker laughed.

"Can I ask you something, Pierce?" Charlotte said. "You really don't like Traynor, do you?"

"Nothing personal." He touched his bandaged chin and winced. "Until tonight anyway."

"Everyone except you claims that Traynor is one of the best closers in baseball. I talked to him before the game. He was polite and cordial."

"He's a bum! Thirty-eight saves. With the Braves' offense and number one defense in the league, a fourteen-year-old Pony Leaguer could have saved twenty-five or thirty of them. The rest of them he was plain lucky, or for some unknown, unrepeatable reason he actually pitched well. Most nights he strolls out there with the bases empty, then gets his jollies from filling the bases with opposing runners. A Major League stopper dominates, finishes a game routinely without the 'oh-no-we're-gonna lose' dramatics. One, two, three—game over."

"We'll take him," the New York journalist commented.

"*Lion King* tickets and a Stage Deli pastrami on rye and he's yours," Pope replied.

The crowd erupted. Abbot dashed toward second base. Frank Houseman's sizzling line drive rattled the left field foul pole, for a game-winning, bottom-of-the-ninth, two-run homer.

"Bullpen heroics?" Charlotte asked.

"And a quick paragraph on Houseman's homer. Then it's down to the locker room for earth-shattering quotes. Want to come along?"

The media mob outside the clubhouse waited out the ten-minute post-game cool-down period. Charlotte thought she could lift her feet and not fall, the crowd was packed so tight.

At ten twenty-seven, Pope was collected over an hour before deadline. "A one-liner from the middle relievers, Rojas and Kline, a quote from Houseman, and some philosophic rhetoric from Robinson and this story is ink. Where did you park?" he asked Charlotte.

"First lot north of the Plaza, toward the Capitol."

"I'm in the press lot." He motioned over his shoulder with a thumb. "The streets get a little lonely by the time we finish up. I'll drop you at your car."

"Thanks, but I'll be fine."

"Now, how I will I explain my rudeness to Jeb if some street urchin accosts you? I insist. In fact, I'm heading out to meet some *AJC* folks for a burger and a brew. New conversation would be a welcomed relief." The clubhouse door opened and the mob constricted to fit through. "Liz will be there."

She hadn't eaten since morning. "Well, I am kind of hungry."

"Then it's settled." A burly cameraman pushed them forward. "After quotes, I'll finish in the press box. If we get separated, meet me up there in fifteen minutes."

Elated chatter, strobe flashes, and blinding television lights electrified the locker room, exhilarated by the come from behind victory and pennant fever. Charlotte stood back from the frenzy. Arrogant TV personalities groveled for recognition from the players. Pope wormed his way through the media horde, ducked a swinging light crane, and disappeared into a pack of journalists jabbing microphones into Frank Houseman's face.

Reporters raced from player to player, jockeyed for position, and threw a subtle hip or shoulder like dollar bills rained into the room. Athletes' words lined the journalists' billfolds. Her casual surveillance shifted to the back of the clubhouse when Traynor emerged.

He wore jeans, sandals and a tank top. He headed for his locker, unnoticed. Weightlifter's arms and chest muscles looked as if they were chiseled in stone. Scar tissue on his left shoulder suggested a nasty session with a surgeon's scalpel. Traynor dressed in private beyond the crowd hounding the game heroes.

Charlotte skirted a pod of eager reporters, shooting questions at Frank Houseman. She approached Traynor.

"Damn, Butch," Traynor fussed at Crowder, tying Reeboks in front of the next locker. "If you wanna use my cologne, put it back where it belongs."

Crowder shrugged. "I put it back on the shelf."

Traynor palmed the black Drakkar bottle and slid the cologne between the deodorant and the Advil bottle. "It belongs here, damn it."

"Hello, again," Charlotte said.

"Do you like my hat?" Traynor saw her and said, "Sorry, I didn't mean to be a smart-ass."

"Recent reading?" Charlotte asked with a smirk. "I haven't heard *Go Dog Go* recited since I was five. I gave up Dr. Seuss when I learned to read."

"I deserve that." He smiled.

She looked over his shoulder and pretended to notice what she'd seen earlier. "You sure keep your locker straight."

"Mama always told me, 'Cleanliness is next to godliness.'"

Listening in, Crowder said, "Anal retentive, if you ask me."

"That's Butch," Traynor nodded at Crowder. "It's Charlotte, right?"

"Charlotte Gordon. Nice to meet you, Butch. Big game, huh?"

"Another day another dollar," Traynor replied. "I spent most of the game dry-humping so I didn't see much of it."

"Dry-humping?" Charlotte asked.

"Like doing it with your clothes on." Crowder sniggered.

"Cut out the raunchy crap, Butch," Traynor chided him.

"It's a locker room, and I'll talk raunchy locker roomese any damn time I please."

Traynor looked at her. "Don't listen to him. No one else does."

"So what's 'dry-humping'?"

"Phone rings in the bullpen. Pitcher is in trouble. You start tossing. Another guy gets on base, so you turn up the heat, like you'll need your best stuff any minute. Robby goes to the mound, but the starter talks him out of the hook. Double play. He pitches out of the jam, and you sit. Next inning, ring ring. They called my number three times tonight, pitched nearly two innings in the pen and I get credit for notta. Only my aching arm knows how hard I worked tonight."

"Quit your bitching," Crowder snipped. "I was on the receiving end of every throw—how do you think my knees feel?"

Reporters encircled the Braves' manager across the room. Robinson fielded questions like routine ground balls. He glanced through the microphones and cameras and saw the woman at Traynor's locker.

Traynor had told him the woman mentioned the night his star reliever wrecked the Hatch in St. Pete. Hendricks scolded him about the inquiries from the Tampa police less than an hour after Traynor reported the conversation. Spring training, game strategy, and September pennant races—what a great game, but Robinson hated babysitting grown men. Keep 'em sober for the games and keep 'em out of jail when he failed to keep them sober. Whether she was snooping or not, he didn't want to find out.

Concentrating on his ticket to post-season saves and the woman, he didn't hear the question. "I'm sorry, what did you say?"

A radio guy jammed a microphone inches from his nose. "Three weeks to go and a three-game lead, do you think the Mets are falling apart?"

Cornered animals fight with reckless abandon, kill or be killed, so Robinson always answered with diplomacy regarding an opponent. "The Mets aren't through. Too much talent. Too much pitching. Geez, did you see Perez tonight? House doesn't lose that ball in the ninth it's a one-game lead and we're playing for first place tomorrow. No, we're in for a fight." He pried a path in the congregation. "That's it for now, folks."

He rambled through the clubhouse, smiled to well-wishers, and flinched at the congratulatory slaps on the back. He eased up to Traynor's conversation.

"Torch," Robinson began. "We yanked you around like a yo-yo tonight. How's the shoulder?"

"Little tight, Robby." He looked at Charlotte. "This is Charlotte Gordon." Nodding at his manager, he said, "Joe Robinson, our manager."

"A pleasure, Miss Gordon." Robinson beamed and extended a hand. "Who are you with?"

"I'm a freelance, hoping to sell the secrets of your success to the women's market."

"It's nice to have you with us, but I'm going to have to shut down this interview." Robinson turned to Traynor. "Come on, Torch, I want Doc to ice down that shoulder."

"Right, Robby. Catch ya later," he told Charlotte.

"What about my knees?" Crowder complained.

"Catcher's only as good as his knees," Robinson answered. "If yours are gone, we'll keep one of the rookies on the playoff roster."

"It's a miracle," Crowder blurted out. "I'm healed!"

"Nice to meet you," Robinson said to Charlotte as he escorted Traynor.

Walking toward the trainer's office, Robinson asked, "Is she the one asking about St. Pete?"

Traynor looked over his shoulder. "That's her, Robby. Not bad, huh?"

Chapter Seven

The stadium emptied in a hurry. Cleanup crews shuffled through the corridors of the massive structure by the time Pope transmitted his story. "Cold beer" calls and the rumble of simultaneous conversations had quieted, replaced by Pope's and Charlotte's footsteps clicking across concrete.

He guided her down the stairs, exited the stadium, and headed left. They descended a gentle hill on the sidewalk, shadowed by the stadium's south side. A small crowd milled outside a guarded chain link fence toward Hank Aaron Drive. Headlights swept the gathering. The crowd parted for a Lexus SUV and reformed before the exhaust dissipated.

"Who are all those people?" Charlotte asked.

"Groupies await the idols of their worship." Pope looked downhill at the fans bunched around the players' parking lot. "Faithful admirers hoping for an autograph, a smile, or a glimpse of their favorite ballplayer."

He touched her elbow and pointed to his right. "My car is over there."

A twelve-foot fence enclosed the media lot across Bill Lucas Drive from the players' entrance. He held her arm. They stepped down from the curb and crossed the street. To their right, thick foliage formed a dense, black curtain. Charlotte kept pace with Pope as he hastened for the pedestrian gate.

"House! House! House!" She turned toward the spirited chant. She assumed Frank Houseman's black BMW crept through the mob. The Beemer sped away and the chant faded.

Pope had walked several feet ahead, unfazed by the commotion. Wind rustled the shrubbery to her right. She glanced up to see the enormous pines sway in the breeze. The limbs were still, every pine needle in place. No wind. No noise.

He lunged from the undergrowth. She jerked to the left. His large hands yanked the strap of her laptop case. The vinyl strap grated down her arm, and tangled around her elbow. He dragged Charlotte toward the dense copse.

She fell. Asphalt pebbles ripped her slacks and lodged in her knees. His urgent strength overmatched Charlotte's attempt to free her arm from the twisted strap. "Let go!" she screamed.

He jerked the bag left and right, trying to shake her off. The knot tightened around her arm. He towed Charlotte over the pavement. She tried to see her attacker. The hood of a grimy sweat suit shadowed his face. He reached in a pocket. The blade snapped and locked. The knife glimmered, reflecting distant streetlight.

"Pierce!" she shrieked.

He kept the strap taut. She lay on her hip, disoriented. Her shoulder felt as if he would tear her arm from its socket. "No! Please!" she yelped as the knifepoint neared.

Her arm whipped with the sawing motion. The strap went slack.

"I can't look. Help me, Pierce!" Her face wrinkled her eyes were closed so tight.

Displaced air whistled above her head, followed by a bone-crunching thud.

Metal clinked on the pavement.

"He's gone, Charlotte."

She peeked. Pope stood over her in a tense athletic stance, grasping an eighteen-inch souvenir bat. She looked at the shrubbery in time to see the mugger stagger into the thicket. He clung to his right arm—his hand dangled.

His eyes fixated on the culprit's escape, Pope asked, "Are you okay?"

She gasped for air and found the courage to look at her arm. Not a scratch. Her laptop case lay in the street, inches from the discarded knife, the vinyl strap frayed where he'd cut through it. "I think so."

He bent, supported her upper arm, and helped her to her feet.

"Thanks," she whispered. "What did you do to him?"

Pope thumped the bat against an open hand like a beat cop's nightstick. "I hope I shattered every bone in the scuzball's wrist. Ever since one of those street urchins lifted my wallet at knifepoint, I keep this ten-dollar equalizer at arm's length. Sorry I didn't get here sooner."

"Can we leave?" She crossed her arms and began to shiver.

Pope retrieved the laptop case, the strap cut loose, by the handle. He wrapped his tender arm around her. "You look like you need a drink."

"No," she gazed at him, "I need to buy you a drink."

"Free drink. A writer's favorite words."

Charlotte guzzled her first beer before the plastic pitcher circled the table. Pope sat beside her in the booth, with Liz and an *AJC* crime writer, Carlton Cox, across the table.

The head-on collision with Atlanta's dark side left her shaken. Thanks to Pope, she only suffered skinned knees, torn slacks, and a cut-up laptop case. After he whisked her away, he shuttled her to the rental car. She tailgated, inches from his bumper along Peachtree Street and North Avenue, en route to Manuel's Tavern.

Dark hardwood paneling and sturdy furniture appointed the tavern frequented by loyal local journalists and politicians. Snappy service and a savory grille menu, the regular clientele heralded Manuel's Tavern as the absolute neighborhood watering hole.

Cox puffed the nub of his cigarette. A tuft of his unkempt graying hair fell across his forehead. A permanent frown resided beneath a drinker's ruddy complexion. As smoke escaped, in a crusty voice he asked, "You tell her Manuel's rules, Pope?"

"Not yet."

"This place is crammed with writers, and some that claim to be." He nodded at Pope. "Never say anything in here you wouldn't want to read, quoted out of context, in tomorrow's paper."

"And never offer to pay for anything," Liz added.

"Damn leeches," Cox continued. "Every mooch in here will be your best friend and they'll still misquote you." His eyes flicked to Pope. "So you knocked the pigsticker out of this John Henry's hand with a toy bat?"

Pope's head bobbed as he sipped beer.

"Would've loved to see that!" Cox jiggled his fingers like quotation marks. "*AJC* Writer Takes a Swing at Street Crime."

They laughed.

Charlotte inhaled. The beer eased gravel-like tension knots buried in her shoulders. "How long have you been with *The Atlanta Journal-Constitution*, Mr. Cox?"

"Who's he?" Cox chugged beer. "Twenty-nine years."

"He's seen it all—from convicted Atlanta child murderer Wayne Williams to Mark Barton, the day-trader that shot up those Internet brokers," Liz said.

"While Pope here chases baseball championships, I write about the title Hot-lanta doesn't brag about in those tourist pamphlets." He refilled his glass and held up the empty pitcher. "Kind of like the Braves, Atlanta's always in the hunt. After the Braves dynasty is long forgotten, however, Atlanta will remain in contention for America's murder capital."

"At least you've got job security," Liz teased him.

"If my liver doesn't give out first."

The bartender hollered from across the room, "Carlton, you've got a call!"

"Who is it?" Cox yelled back.

"Chuck Stennett. Says he's with *The Charlotte Observer*."

"Tell him I'm not here."

"I did. He doesn't believe me."

"Son-of-a-bitch wants to bet on the Falcons-Panthers game next weekend. I wouldn't bet against Chuck even if Vince Lombardi's angel swooped down from the pearly gates to coach the Falcons." He raised his voice again, "Tell him I passed out. He'll believe that!"

"Obviously, you don't foresee a downturn in Atlanta crime." A topic other than baseball enthused Charlotte. "Why the pessimism?"

"I prefer professional cynicism. And..." Cox tilted his head. "What are you snooping for? Are you going to join the nationwide fad to rip my fair city? Yankees love to expound on the horrors of Atlanta, yet, they can't build houses fast enough in the suburbs to house the southern exodus. Leave shredding Atlanta to the resident ridicule."

"Give her a break, Carlton," Liz said. "She's not here to write an exposé on the Atlanta we've all come to know and fear."

"Yeah, yeah. What was the question?" Cox asked Charlotte.

"Why the gloomy outlook?"

"It's not top secret. Ghetto crime. Unsuspecting victims wandering where they don't belong. Increased immigration with ensuing ethnic poverty. Hate crimes with Southern spice. We've got a little of all these vicious critters doing the backstroke in a pot of boiling tempers. Wrong place, wrong time—*bang*, you're dead. Pessimism? Nah, I'd say pragmatic realization."

Charlotte grinned and tipped her glass to him. Through his tetchy outer shell, she sensed wisdom, expertise. Could he be a possible source to help her delve further into Margaret's murder? She leaned forward. "Just out of curiosity, do you ever get so consumed with a story that reporting becomes secondary to solving the crime?"

For the first time since they'd met, Cox's blurry eyes stopped shifting, and concentrated on Charlotte's face. "It's happened," he answered evasively. Side to side, his eyes went into rapid motion. "Enough shop, more beer!" Again, he raised the empty pitcher.

The waitress distributed cheeseburgers, fries, and baskets of golden onion rings. Charlotte's hunger pangs had diminished. Draft beer and street mugging, a new diet guaranteed to lessen the appetite. She nibbled on an onion ring while she watched grease drip from Cox's mouth. Deep red cheeks flexed as he gobbled his burger. The hint of high blood pressure, heavy drinking and smoking, Cox was a walking advertisement for coronary disaster.

"How long will you be in Atlanta?" Pope cut a home fry in three sections, stabbed one with a fork and dipped it in ketchup.

Immersed in the journalist portrayal, she hadn't thought about her calendar. The San Angelo audit began Monday morning, in thirty-two hours. The key to her sister's death loomed in Atlanta—she could feel it. She knew she would never resume the hunt if she returned to Texas. "No deadlines for me. My schedule is open-ended. However, if additional brawls and street assaults are anticipated... Well, I'm not sure I can handle much more excitement."

"Southern hospitality, ma'am," Pope overemphasized a Southern drawl. "Just trying to juice up your article. Got your adrenaline going, didn't it?"

"Adrenaline? And I thought I was just scared to death."

Pope grinned. "Regardless, I hope you plan to stay for a while."

"Braves go on the road after the game tomorrow," Liz said.

"Yep. Three game series in St. Louis, then back home on Thursday. Hey, why don't you come along?" Pope asked Charlotte.

"I don't know," Charlotte replied. Another city, airplane ticket, and hotel bill on her wild goose chase—wasted dollars and cents tugged at the accountant's soul. But if the Braves were in St. Louis, so were the answers. "I'll think about it."

"Plane takes off at eight tomorrow night. Come along, I'll show you St. Louis."

"Your fangs are showing, Pierce," Liz jibed.

"I'll think it over." Charlotte smiled and yawned. She glanced at her watch. "I really need some sleep. I'd better go check in."

"Where are you staying?" Liz asked.

"An Embassy Suites, north on I-75."

"If you didn't guarantee the room, you could crash at my place," Liz offered. "It's not the Ritz, but there's plenty of room and the daily rate is a bargain."

"I wouldn't want to be a bother."

"No bother. My apartment is only a few blocks from here. I insist, Charlotte."

"Well." Charlotte paused. "Sure, that'd be nice."

"Not another one of those," Cox slurred his disapproval.

Liz winked at Charlotte, threw her arms around Cox's neck and planted a wet kiss on his cheek. "Another one of those whats?"

"Agh." He wiped the moisture from his face. "Cut the crap, Liz." Cox looked at Charlotte. "If you're not a funny girl, lock your bedroom door, lady."

One o'clock in the morning and too many beers, again, Charlotte was thankful for the proximity of Liz's apartment. She would have to cope with the anguish from Margaret's death soon. However, until the right time to say goodbye arrived, when her obsession with the question *Why?* relented, drinking best numbed the impending pain. Her head swimming in a carbonated Michelob cloud, she had closed one eye to focus on the Jeep Wrangler taillights. She followed the wavering red beacons through tree-darkened side streets, until they turned onto the cracked concrete driveway of a large brick home. She parked at the foot of a wooden stairway rising to a garage apartment.

At first glance, Liz's apartment stimulated the familiar aura of Margaret's home. Not the decor or furniture—a welcoming simplicity, absent of pretentious trappings. High contrast black and white enlargements complemented action-packed color glossies on the walls of her living room. The red light atop a doorframe hinted Liz had converted the walk-in closet into a darkroom. A Gateway computer hogged the top of a walnut veneer dinette table in the cramped kitchen.

"It's not the lap of luxury, but I call this home. I'm not here much, so buying possessions I never see seems wasteful." Liz pointed at the hallway. "You'll bunk in the first room on the left. We'll have to share the bath. It's between the bedrooms."

Charlotte set down her suitcase and laptop. "It's perfect."

Liz deposited her camera bag in the darkroom, and wandered toward the kitchen. "Beer? Wine? I think there's even vodka in the freezer."

"No more." Charlotte rolled her eyes. "I had trouble figuring out which Jeep to follow."

Liz laughed.

"I'm serious!"

"Sorry, there are no locks on the bedrooms."

"They really think you're a lesbian."

"Sure they do. Did you see Carlton grimace when I kissed him? It's easy to convince men that I'm a girl's girl, because it gives their egos an excuse for my lack of interest."

"Do you date at all?"

"Not necessary." She touched a frame on the wall. A dark-tanned and sun-blond hunk beamed as he tightened the noose around an alligator's snout. "This is Paul. He's with the National Parks Service. He's currently assigned to Everglades National Park."

"That's a long way from Atlanta."

"We both have things to accomplish before we settle into anything more permanent. We see each other whenever we can. Paul's great. It's comfortable, no pressure, no expectations, and, for now, all I need."

"Good for you."

Liz opened the refrigerator, grabbed a beer, and twisted off the bottle cap. "No ring. Is there a guy counting the moments until you return?"

"I exchanged mine for a breath of self-worth and a plane ticket."

"Divorced?"

"I prefer 'escaped.'"

"Have you sworn off the three-legged sex?"

"No, nothing like that. There's James," she answered with an air of uncertainty. She hadn't seen James Houston in a month, and hadn't thought of him much until she uttered his name. "He's in Dallas. Who knows where we'll end up."

"Dallas? That's a long way from Tampa. Of course, your eyes didn't exactly flicker at the sound of his name."

"Didn't I mention that I live in Dallas? I grew up in Tampa. I was there due to a death in the family," Charlotte scrambled to cover the slip. "And you're right, I guess James and I are far from the ideal relationship."

"Not that you're interested, but you sure captured Pierce's attention. Did you see the little horns under those gorgeous ebony locks?"

Charlotte's cheeks felt flushed. "He was very kind to me. If I was interested—"

"Single and unattached as far as I know." Liz took a long sip of beer and tossed the half-empty bottle in the trash. "Time for beddy bye. Make yourself at home, Charlotte."

"Would you mind if I boot my laptop and go online? I haven't checked e-mail for a few days."

"There's a phone jack next to the computer, and one over there," Liz waved at the phone by the couch. "Want to ride to the game together tomorrow…today? We'll grab a greasy breakfast at Waffle House on the way."

"Sure. I'll look forward to it." Charlotte paused. "Today would have been tough without your help. Thanks."

"Don't forget the rungs on the ladder to fame. Good night."

Liz staggered down the hall and disappeared into her bedroom.

Charlotte uncoiled a phone cord and connected it to her laptop modem. She wiggled free the cord from Liz's computer and jammed in her connector. The IBM's hard drive whined when she pressed the power button. She fought her heavy eyelids for consciousness while the computer booted.

She would not be in Texas on Monday and felt obligated to notify Payne,

Wyman & Bradford not to expect her. The spontaneous disobedience would likely delay her partner aspirations. For the first time since she joined the firm, her sterile career toppled from its reign as priority champion. An emotionally wrecked manager wouldn't be worth a damn anyway and would only hinder the initial stages of the audit. They'd understand. And if they didn't they'd get over it.

Point and click. Modem static buzzed, and seconds later, she reviewed a list of eighty-seven e-mails. Eighty-seven e-mails from associates begging for her attention even though they knew her only sister had been killed. Eighty-seven e-mails and not one from a personal acquaintance outside the PW&B organization structure. She squinted and studied the business subjects while her agitated subconscious scolded her for subjecting herself to a life that revolved around debits, credits, and bean counters—like herself. She was safe and secure surrounded by cloned peers, indulged in her field of expertise, and, from her intoxicated vantage, boring as vanilla ice milk.

James sent five of the messages. "How are you;" "Miss you;" "Horny;" "Where are you;" "San Angelo"—heavens forbid the waste of billable hours on one lousy phone call when an efficient e-mail would suffice. The bastard could have offered to come to Tampa with her. She fumed and calmed. She wouldn't have allowed him to attend Margaret's funeral if he had asked.

She typed out a nasty-gram to James. She bit her lip and deleted the scalding message. Guilty of what she moments earlier accused him of, she refused to succumb to the electronic vortex sucking the world into sanitized, non-personalized communication. She disconnected from the Internet, turned off the computer, and walked toward the telephone.

Unsure what she'd say, she used a calling card to charge the call and punched James's number.

"Hello," his groggy voice answered.

"James. It's me, Charlotte."

"Charlotte," his tone sharpened. "Where are you? Did you get my messages?"

"Thanks for the messages. I'm in Atlanta."

"Atlanta!"

Charlotte heard a giggle in the background. "Is someone there?"

"Uh, no. It's the television. It's the television."

Repeated words, a nervous habit Charlotte had happened upon when James lied. She heard him whisper and the playful laugh stopped.

"Oh, what's on?"

"Some late-night talk show. Late-night talk show. What are you doing in Atlanta?"

Unwilling to admit weakness, yet unable to find another answer, she said, "Coping with Margaret's death has been dreadful. I'm trying to chase down some loose ends." She sniffled.

"You sound drunk."

"I am. And you sound like you're screwing someone. Who is it? Recently divorced Debbie Wallace, or did you go after one of the rookies, maybe the coed from Arkansas?" She'd seen him flirting with the new hire. "You know, bottle blond, big tits…Leslie?"

James was silent.

"Sorry, James. What you do, and who you do it with, is none of my business."

"Will you be in San Angelo?" his voice deepened, resuming practiced professionalism.

"No." She yawned.

"I need you in San Angelo. I'm counting on you, Charlotte."

"That's why I called. I won't be there."

"And just when do you intend to return?"

"I'm not sure."

"Listen, it's apparent your sister's death has you a little whacked out. The best thing for you is to get on with your life."

Curled on the couch, Charlotte batted her eyes as her head bobbed.

"Payne, Wyman & Bradford depends on the reliability of its people. So get your shit together, and jump back in the trenches where you belong. A couple of days back on the job and you'll be good as new. I'll expect you in San Angelo first thing Monday morning. Don't disappoint me, Charlotte."

"Boring as vanilla ice milk," she mumbled and closed her eyes.

"What? What did you say? Charlotte. Charlotte, are you there?"

She dropped the portable phone to the carpet.

Chapter Eight

Autumn touched the brisk Sunday morning like a swimmer's toe testing pool water. Nearby, Charlotte heard church bells chime, muted by the Atlanta skyline. Hustle and bustle slumbered beyond the city's perimeter while corridors of high-rise steel and glass shadowed tranquil downtown thoroughfares. Occasional pedestrians ambled along the sidewalks, in no hurry and not in a frantic tizzy like the weekday surge of business types soldered to their flip phones.

Liz steered through the back roads to the Turner Field. The dark green Wrangler with tan leather interior fit Liz's outdoor, rough and tumble persona. Cool air rushed through the Jeep, its top down, and the classic rock station blared Toto's "Africa" from dash-mounted speakers. Their idle conversation yielded to indulgence of rare quietude.

Charlotte crossed her arms and leaned back to enjoy the sun's warmth. She had slept hard, only interrupted by the portable phone beeping. She didn't remember dozing off or ending the call with James. *Fiddly-dee*, she'd worry about that tomorrow—in Margaret Mitchell's backyard, Charlotte adapted Scarlett O'Hara's tenacious procrastination. Optimism refreshed her outlook after a good night's rest and a waffle sopped in maple syrup. Call it dodging her problem or simply a new day, thrust into alien surroundings among strangers bred therapeutic escapism.

Liz turned into the media lot two hours before the one o'clock game time and showed the *AJC* parking pass to the attendant. Charlotte cast a wary glimpse into the thorny copse across the street.

"Looking for the ogre's lair?" Liz flashed an understanding smile. "Don't worry, they're vampires. If they come out before dark," the Jeep swerved when she threw up her arms, "*poof*, the derelicts vaporize."

The women climbed down from the Jeep. Charlotte rolled up the sleeves of the khaki shirt she wore over a sleeveless turtleneck sweater. An overdressed attention magnet the day before, outfitted in faded jeans and scuffed lace-up boots, today she would blend-in with the casual-at-all-cost journalist corps. She fidgeted with her belt, then grabbed her computer case from the backseat.

"Wait for me." Charlotte tossed another look at the bushes.

Liz stopped and turned. "You're really spooked?"

"I'll be fine as soon as I buy one of those bone breakers Pierce carries around."

Charlotte accompanied Liz to the press gate with one eye affixed to the shrubby block. At the top of the stairs, a security guard checked credentials.

"Morning, Wendell." Liz waved her pass.

"Beautiful day for stomping Mets, Miss Liz." He smiled. Wendell held up a hand as he studied Charlotte's face. "And you are?"

"Charlotte Gordon."

His finger scrolled down a printout until he found her name. He motioned her forward. "Enjoy the game," he said without a trace of sincerity.

She whispered to Liz, "How do you do that?"

"Think about it. It's actually sad commentary on my life. A budding artist, whose fame is measured in recognition by a ballpark security guard."

"Miss Gordon," Tad Smithurst called from behind them.

"I thought the Spanish omelet made me queasy." Liz pressed her hands against her tummy when she heard his voice. "Thank goodness it wasn't the food."

"Morning, ladies," Smithurst greeted them with a smirk. "Miss Gordon, Mr. Hendricks wants to meet you."

"Why would he want to see me?"

"What can it hurt?" Liz jumped in. "I've been lugging my gear around here for years and what do I have to show for it… I'm on first-name basis with a gate guard. On your second day, the general manager sends his flunky to personally escort you to the ivory tower. Must be the clothes." She glanced down at her own shorts and hiking boots. "What's next, Ted himself? Go for it, Charlotte. I'll catch up with you after you hobnob with the execs."

"Mr. Hendricks is a busy man." Smithurst took a nervous glance at his watch. "He doesn't like to be kept waiting. Come with me."

She parted from Liz and followed Smithurst up the stairwell to the club level. Air-conditioning cooled the elite club level, closed off from the common seats and lined with full bars and high-end concessions for the Braves' favored patrons. He walked through the empty corridors, determined and silent, checking over his shoulder as if she was a boat trailer. Smithurst had been a brash flirt the night before. Today he exhibited an almost jittery, all-business manner. They passed private box entrances—Coca Cola,

Georgia Pacific, and other Atlanta corporate heavy hitters engraved on the doors.

He made an abrupt stop, rapped his knuckles on the door, and entered. Tentatively, Charlotte trailed him into Austin Hendricks's office. The general manager barked into the phone and waved them in.

A stylish tie was threaded through the collar of his starched white dress shirt. Hendricks's well-groomed dark hair grayed at the temples. His trim physique suggested dedication to an exercise regimen. The view of Turner Field through the glass wall behind him looked like a live mural painted in exquisite detail. Braves' action photos and pictures of Hendricks glad-handing with dignitaries covered the inside walls.

He pointed to a leather chair in front of his desk as he ended the phone call. Moving toward the chair, Charlotte glanced back at Smithurst, stationed at the door like an armed sentry.

"Miss Gordon, I'm Austin Hendricks." He gave her a firm handshake and a captivating smile.

"It's a pleasure to meet you." The brains behind the Braves, Hendricks had sustained Atlanta's winning tradition instituted in the nineties by John Schuerholz. Charlotte's experience with CEOs shielded her from intimidation by the shrewd and impressive man. "I'll admit I was somewhat surprised by the invitation."

"Please sit. Can I get you anything? Coffee, water, soda? Don't ask for Pepsi—Coke is king in Atlanta."

"No, thank you." Charlotte sat. "I had a late breakfast on the drive over."

"On behalf of the Braves, I would like to offer our sincere apologies for the danger that descended upon you last night. Needless to say some of our less than desirable neighbors prey upon the success of our organization. We've been negotiating to purchase or clear that lot for a couple of years. I've notified our chief of security, and I assure you additional resources will be deployed immediately to ensure the safety of the media. I hope you will forgive our momentary lapse and that you endured the incident without extensive suffering."

"That's very kind. Except for an elevated fear of scraggly shrubs I'm fine. How did you found out?"

"I bumped into Pierce Pope this morning. He offered journalistic amnesia in return for a new bat and a personal apology."

"Well, thank you for your concern, Mr. Hendricks." Charlotte edged forward in the chair. "I know you're busy. I won't take any more of your time."

"Charlotte Gordon." He twisted the tip of his chin. "In my business I find it advantageous to peruse periodicals, sports related and outside the field, on an ongoing basis. I must have missed your name."

"I freelance," she blurted out. "I'm relatively new and thought a woman's slant on the best organization in baseball might be the break I need."

Hendricks balanced reading glasses on the bridge of his nose and consulted a leather-bound journal. Removing the glasses, he said, "Relatively new, as in never published."

She swallowed, trying to remain calm, and buy time. "Yes. Uh, every writer has to start somewhere."

"True, true." He leaned back in his chair. "Help me here, Miss Gordon. Why would an audit manager with a Big Four accounting firm forfeit a legitimate shot at partner with Payne, Wyman & Bradford to starve as a freelance reporter?"

Charlotte didn't answer.

"Instead of meddling in the private affairs of strangers, you should leave crime investigating to law enforcement professionals, Miss Gordon." His forehead wrinkled. "Do you think because baseball is a game everyone associated with the business is stupid?"

She shook her head.

"Of course not. Thanks to your amateur detective efforts, the Tampa police are investigating Earl Traynor's possible involvement in the murder of a Margaret Gordon. Your sister, I presume?"

"That's right."

"Hours after this disturbing call, Joe Robinson, you met our manager, tells me a woman by the name of Gordon is asking questions about Torch's last trip to Tampa. I don't believe in coincidence—two Gordons, two Tampa stories, one day—no coincidence. I called Detective Sanders again. He informed me the victim's sister is an accountant in Dallas. After that it didn't take us long to track you. I assume you know PW&B represents Time Warner."

"One of our largest accounts," Charlotte said.

"Did you know Time Warner owns the Braves?"

Charlotte blinked.

"Now, what are you doing here?"

The mask ripped from her face, she refused to cower. She cleared her throat. "I also question coincidence, Mr. Hendricks. Your precious pitcher parked on a barstool next to my sister, in a seedy bar she wouldn't be caught dead in. She leaves, Torch wrecks the bar, and hours later some brute murders my sister. Earl Traynor is the last known person to speak with my sister. I need to know what he knows. I need to know if he killed Margaret."

"Traynor was inebriated. His teammates hauled him back to the Vinoy and put him to bed. Women chase ball players. So many women they can't remember names or faces. Even if he wasn't so drunk, I doubt if Torch would have remembered a woman he met at Down the Hatch. He didn't kill your sister. He doesn't even remember busting up the bar."

"Then maybe," Charlotte leaned forward, "he doesn't remember beating Margaret to death either."

"This is going nowhere, Miss Gordon. I refuse to deliberate the fine points of a murder investigation with a self-appointed sleuth."

"You can't stop me. I won't stop until I find out what happened that night."

"As you please, but not as a guest of the Atlanta Braves." Hendricks held out his hand. "Your credentials."

Charlotte snapped the string around her neck and slung the pass across the desktop.

"Tad, how the hell did she get these?" Charlotte's press pass dangled from Hendricks's fingers.

"Pierce Pope arranged the clearance."

"He didn't...doesn't know. No one knows."

"Real life charades can be dangerous and harmful, Miss Gordon. You're welcome to stay for the game. Tad will arrange a courtesy ticket." He aimed a harsh stare at Charlotte. "We're in a pennant race. My job is to keep this team focused on baseball and baseball only. Undue interference will not be tolerated. If I haven't made myself clear, I'll reiterate.... Stay away from my players!"

Smithurst escorted Charlotte to a choice seat. She squirmed in her seat, fifteen rows behind home plate. The sky was packed with lazy cotton ball clouds while tornadoes of uncertainty spun within. A humiliated fool and an enraged stubborn skeptic seesawed, up and down—her emotion clashed with her logical instinct for control. The question *How could I be so naïve to think I could pass for a professional reporter?* plagued her, while an even calm countered, *If I'm so dreadfully wrong, then why does Austin Hendricks consider a nobody 'self-appointed sleuth' a threat?*

She glared at the Mets taking batting practice. Her mind churned and deliberated an answer to, *What now?* Crater, pack up and disappear into a safe house of ledgers and income statements? She could be in San Angelo by morning and resume the public accountant's life as if Atlanta was a dream-induced illusion. Surrender is easy, and becomes easier, a habit, with each occurrence. Give up now, then what would stop her from avoiding confrontation, shying away every time life veered from the expected? Debate over. She would not leave Atlanta without answers.

Earl Traynor. How would she approach him, cajole him to divulge the exchange with Margaret, now that her credentials were revoked? The press pass gone from her neckline, Charlotte became another groupie separated from the superstars by chain link fences, pipe rails, and security drones.

She snatched the *AJC* sports page, rolled up and extruding from her computer case. She needed to cool down before she could come up with a plan fueled by more common sense and less outrage. She opened the newspaper.

The headline drew her attention. She spied Pierce Pope's byline and began to read. She knew the game outcome, and hated the propensity to recreate every moment of every sporting event. She read out of curiosity and found herself entranced. Pope's game recap flowed like a paperback thriller. Good guys, bad guys, victims, a white-knuckle plot, and climactic resolution scribed in eloquent passages she couldn't put down. How could he waste such literary talent on the sports page?

She folded the paper and laid it on her case. The same outer pocket held the press guide she had lifted from the press box. The tussle with the mugger had dog-eared the page corners. She removed the guide, and flipped to Traynor's profile.

Charlotte scanned the data: Number thirty-seven, Earl 'Torch' Traynor, Height: Six two, Weight: 215, Bats: Left, Throws: Right. She studied his portrait. A strong jaw, and a sincere smile, he was handsome. Again, she tried to imagine Traynor with Margaret. A second photo, in black and white, showed Traynor at twelve years old. He wore an all-star uniform with ROME sewn on the jersey. She stared at the photo. The youthful face, the same smile, yet the picture bothered her.

WILSON, she read the manufacturer's label off the fielder's mitt on his right hand. Not an avid sports fan, she even knew right-handers wore their gloves on the left hand. She checked the data for confirmation: Throws: Right. The correct orientation of ROME across his chest erased the premonition that the photo had been printed backwards. Was the all-star another child? No, the smile belonged to Traynor. Was he ambidextrous and relied on his stronger arm to neutralize Major League hitters?

She blinked and peered harder. Bats: Left. He must have left-handed tendencies if he hit from that side of the plate. She skimmed the brief biography for other hidden treasures, looking for pictures within the picture. Hometown: Rome, Georgia. Resides: Atlanta, Georgia.

Her excited eyes swung to the field. She leaned forward and examined players and reporters milling about the batting cage. When she saw him, she snatched the computer case, stood upright, and bolted down the aisle, her eyes glued to Pope. She weaved through fans, carrying cardboard trays crammed with sodas, hotdogs and frothy beers, worked her way to the field, and attached to the autograph hounds bunched against the rail.

"Pierce." He didn't hear her. "Pierce Pope!"

He rolled his head left, unaccustomed to sideline pages. He smiled when he saw Charlotte wave, excused himself from a New York player, and walked across the on-deck circle toward her.

"Good morning," he said, smiling. "Come on down to the field and we can socialize with the wealthy future criminals club." Instinctively, he checked her press credentials. "Where's your pass?"

"Uh, I…it's in my bag. How far away is Rome, Georgia?"

"Hour and a half, two hours north on I-75. Why?"

"I've got to go, Pierce," Charlotte spoke fast. "Tell Liz—if you see her, that is—I took a cab and I'll be back tonight."

She turned.

"What about St. Louis, Charlotte?" he asked as she started to rush away.

She stopped. "St. Louis? I'm sorry, I almost forgot." Hendricks had ousted her after a few menacing questions. She could only imagine how the general manager might retaliate if she showed up on a road trip. "You're very kind to offer. Can I get a rain check?"

"I hope it wasn't something I did." He stuck out a pouting lip. "Will you be here until Thursday?"

"I've decided to do some local background." She looked down at him from the rail. "Unless my calendar changes, I don't think I'm going anywhere before then."

He reached into a coat pocket and handed her a business card. "You can always reach my cell phone. If my luck holds out and if you're interested let's go to dinner Thursday night."

Their eyes connected and lingered. She touched his face. "You've been wonderful to me. I'll look forward to dinner, Thursday."

She removed her hand, reluctantly, and backed away from the rail.

"Call that number Thursday afternoon. Now, why did you say you're going to Rome?"

"Background."

"Ha," Pope laughed. "Sure, sure, she'll let me buy her dinner, but she won't trust me with a story idea. A gifted journalist."

Chapter Nine

She glanced at the odometer. A taxi had driven her to Liz's apartment, then she cranked up the rented Malibu and sped over seventy miles north of Atlanta. Relying on a gas station map, she had exited the interstate north of Cartersville, found US 41 and the turnoff to the US 411 link to Rome. She set the cruise control two miles over the speed limit, leery of the backwoods sheriff deputies depicted by Hollywood, lurking behind a road sign to entrap her and haul her off to a one-cell brownstone jailhouse. The peaceful four-lane highway guided her over rolling hills, lake-speckled terrain, and through hardwood trees on the verge of igniting the Coosa Valley in autumn hues.

The information from the press guide consumed her thoughts during the drive to Traynor's hometown. Charlotte cruised through the streets of Rome lacking a specific purpose. Now that she had arrived in Rome, spellbound with the twelve-year-old all-star's photograph, she realized she had no idea of what to look for or where in the world to begin the search.

She scanned the horizon, noticed Floyd Medical Center to her left, and waited for the traffic signal to turn green. She was parched and saddle sore. She saw a Hardee's ahead on the left and decided the fast-food chain would be a convenient rest stop before she pursued whatever she hoped to find in Rome.

She spurted through a gap in traffic, parked the rental car, and shut off the engine. She stepped on the asphalt and stretched her tight shoulders. North of Atlanta, a brisk breeze chilled the bright afternoon. Charlotte rolled down her sleeves, buttoned her shirt at the cuffs, and walked to the door.

Hot grease odor clung to the acoustical ceiling. Fries spattered in the deep-fry. A teenage boy mopped the counter area during the lull between the lunch and supper rush. She tiptoed across the wet tile floor, leaned against the stainless steel counter, and inspected the menu board.

A second teenager stepped to the counter. The baggy uniform swallowed the boy's scrawny frame. "Can I help ya, ma'am?"

She hadn't eaten since breakfast. She resisted a twinge of hunger, begging for fries, with self-assurances she'd eat a decent meal on the return trip. "Medium Diet Coke."

"Nice day, ain't it?" He scooped ice. "Kind'a cool, but fall's sneaking up, ain't it?"

"Beautiful day," Charlotte gave a polite reply.

He grinned. Cup against the dispenser, syrup mixed with carbonated water. Charlotte sensed his desire to please and decided to pry as he fit the plastic lid over the cup lip, "Rome is not a very big town, is it?"

"Bigger than most places around here. Ya know, blink when ya drive through 'em ya miss 'em." He stared at the register and punched a button. "We got over thirty thousand folks in Rome," he announced. "Dollar twenty-seven."

She dug through her wallet for exact change. "Thirty thousand. It's a larger community than I expected." She handed him a dollar bill and change and looked at him. "Guess I'm out of luck. The population is so large I'll never bump into anyone who knows him."

"I know lots of folks here. Who you looking for, ma'am?"

"Earl Traynor."

"You talking 'bout Torch?"

She acted surprised, raised her eyebrows, and said, "Well, yes."

"Shootfire, everyone around here knows Torch. 'Bout the most famous person ever to come out of Rome—all of Floyd County for that matter."

"Do you know…Torch?"

"Yes, ma'am. Not real good, and I ain't claiming he'd recollect my name, but he'd nod and smile polite-like if he saw me on the street. I even played ball the same place he did. Of course, my Dizzy Dean Baseball days was a few years after his."

"Could you direct me to the ball field?"

"Down that road." When Charlotte turned left, he continued, "See them lights? That's Riverview Park. All ya do is follow them tracks." He aimed his arm to his right. Railroad tracks, elevated on a steep earth embankment, wound into downtown Rome. "'Bout midway between here and the bridge over the Coosa River there's a tunnel cut under the tracks. All there is to it."

"Thanks," she read the nameplate pinned to his wrinkled shirt, "Jason."

"You're welcome, ma'am."

"Will anyone be there? Maybe someone who would remember when Torch played there."

"Always someone there. They pretty much play ball year round, 'cept the footballers." He glanced at a family of four entering the door. "Look for

Coach Al. Albert Haggard. Coach's been there forever, even coached Torch." The family approached the counter. "I'd better tend to these customers. Nice talkin' with ya, ma'am."

"You've been a great help, Jason." Charlotte thanked him again and departed.

Moments later she steered through the tunnel and entered Riverview Park. A football field and a multi-field baseball complex stretched out in a valley from the railroad embankment to the Coosa River. Charlotte parked the car, sipped her drink, and climbed out grasping the press guide.

Delighted screams and laughter were everywhere. Whistles blew and coaches hollered on the football field. Games were in process on three of the baseball diamonds. Charlotte soaked in the surroundings as she walked toward the concession stand at the center of the complex. A metal bat pinged to her left, prompting an excited roar from the aluminum bleachers. A boy, twelve, maybe thirteen, beamed and trotted around the bases.

Too many people. She needed help to find Albert Haggard. A bearded man raked clay at first base on the smaller empty field. Charlotte opened the gate behind the first base dugout and walked onto the field.

"Excuse me," she said to the man. He combed the base path in fluid strokes and ignored the intrusion.

Charlotte neared the baseline. His head down, he mumbled, "Stay off the clay, just raked it."

"Are you Albert Haggard?"

He pulled the rake in. His jeans rode below his waist, weighted down by a protruding beer belly. "Nope, name's Chet Suggs."

"Is Mr. Haggard here?"

"Could be. Who's asking?"

Charlotte shook her head, aggravated with the conversation, and turned away.

His jaw buried in a gray-black beard, an older version of Suggs limped from the dugout. "Howdy, ma'am." He broke out in a broad smile. His light eyes twinkled beneath a red mesh cap embroidered with ROME ALL STARS.

"That's Albert," Suggs grumbled.

"That's right, Albert Haggard. What can I do for ya, ma'am?"

"Is he always so cheerful?" Charlotte snipped, throwing a look over her shoulder.

"Don't mind Chet. Feed him and keep up his distemper shots and he won't bite. Didn't catch your name."

"Charlotte Gordon." She offered a hand. Calluses ridged Haggard's large hand. "I drove up from Atlanta today. I was told you might be able to help me with some background on Earl Traynor."

Suggs stopped raking and rested his chin on the rake handle.

Haggard removed his hat and wiped his bald head with a handkerchief. "Torch know you're here?"

"No, sir."

He studied Charlotte. "You're no policewoman. Must be a reporter."

"Yes, sir. I'm a freelance journalist doing an article on the Braves." She held up the press guide. "When I read Earl was from a nearby community, I couldn't resist the temptation to research a Major Leaguer's upbringing."

Suggs spit. Tobacco juice sprayed Charlotte's boots.

"Enough!" Haggard warned Suggs. "Sorry, ma'am. Chet gets a tad protective of Torch's privacy." He squatted, pulled a red bandana from his back pocket, and wiped the tobacco juice. "Least I can do is answer your questions. Done it before. No scandals or nothing. Fine boy with a helluva lot of talent. Come on, we'll sit in the dugout. Give my old knee a rest."

They crossed the grass, entered the dugout, and sat. A layer of fine clay covered the concrete floors. The odor of sweat and a hint of urine lingered inside the stuffy concrete block structure. Suggs leaned his rake against the chain-link fence outside the dugout, close enough to listen in, and stared away as if he didn't care.

"You goin' to record me?"

"Not today. Just background. I have a memory for detail," she made an excuse for the lack of an obvious prop.

"Ready when you are," Haggard said.

"How long have you known Earl?"

"Since he was six. Tee-ball. He was just another good ball player 'til he started kid pitch. That's when we knew he was special. Never seen a nine-year-old throw the pill like that. Don't expect I ever will again."

Charlotte opened the press guide to Traynor's profile. "Torch is the best closer in baseball—right handed—yet in this picture when he was twelve, he's wearing a lefthander's glove."

"You noticed that, huh? Said he was special, didn't I?"

"So the picture isn't a hoax or a misprint? It's authentic?"

"'Fraid so. You see, when Torch started playing ball he was a southpaw. Sure he horsed around throwing and hitting opposite-handed like all kids do, and he had some ability right-handed, but like I said, he was a lefty. Those boys had quite a run—Dizzy Dean state champs when they was nine, ten, eleven, twelve and fourteen. They won the World Series in Hattiesburg, Mississippi, when they were twelve and fourteen. Right, Chet?"

Suggs grunted.

"Chet caught Torch from the time they were nine 'til they graduated from high school."

"There's a gap. What happened when they were thirteen?"

"Exactly where I was headin'. Up 'til the time Torch was twelve he threw nothing but smoke. Sixty, sixty-five miles an hour as an eleven-year-old. Touched seventy-five when he was twelve. Twelve, that was the year he dabbled with that dang curveball. I'd call for a change-up and he'd throw the curve. Fine curveball, but no kid under fifteen should do that to his growth plates.

"Anywho, there we are in Mississippi playing these corn-fed Oklahoma gorillas in the World Series finals. Torch's arm was tired and those boys were swatting his fastball. He took it upon himself to go to the curve. Pitch after pitch, he mowed 'em down with his bender. I threatened to take him out, but he convinced me one game couldn't hurt. Most driven kid I ever coached, I didn't have the heart to take away his shot at the championship.

"As it turns out, I should have. With a two-run lead in the sixth, his shoulder popped. Scariest thing I ever saw." Haggard's hands trembled slightly as he recited the memory. "He collapsed. Looked like a sack of feed heaped up on the mound, screaming like a stuck pig. And it was all my fault for listening to a kid. There I was with my heart in my throat and he says to me from the ambulance gurney, 'My bad, Coach. Two outs to go. Warm up Johnny Gray, Coach. They'll never touch his change up.' Through his tears he grinned, looked at Johnny and told him to finish what they'd begun."

Haggard inhaled and started again. "We won it. Torch went under the knife the next week. Ligaments and tendons ripped everywhere. The cutter said he'd done all he could, and Torch could play ball, but he'd never pitch again.

"The following year Torch never signed up, and without him we bowed out of the tournament in the first round. We thought he'd thrown in the towel, and no one could blame him.

"Well, it was the week after Christmas and I happened by to check on the fields since we hold tryouts the middle of January. I parked my truck and noticed a boy pitching to an adult on the thirteen-fourteen field. My eyes not being as good as most folks, I wasn't familiar with the motion. Must be a new kid I figured. Man, was he bringing it.... *Pop*, the mitt cracked with each pitch.

"The closer I got to the field I had this feeling I knew the kid. His presence. The windup. Although he threw with his right, the fluid pitching mechanics were a sight for sore eyes—it was Torch throwing right-handed to his daddy. I nearly busted a gut I ran so hard. All he could say was, 'I did it, Coach.' I cried like a dang fool. We all thought he'd become a recluse moping around, while he was home with his daddy learning to pitch with the other paw. We won it all the next year. Bet no other kid ever won the last game of the World Series with both arms."

"That's quite a story, Mr. Haggard."

"Dangest thing I've ever seen, and I expect I ever will."

"Does the intensity you described explain Torch's explosive mound presence, or has his volatility escalated over the years?"

Suggs spit through the chain link fence.

"If ya want me to declare Torch is crazy or dangerous, you're barking up the wrong tree, missy. Sure he's intense, confident, cocky. You don't make it to the show without fire in your belly."

"Don't you worry about him when he stomps around, ranting and raving?"

"Part of the game, ma'am. As long as he leaves it on the field ain't nothing wrong with being hot-headed."

"What if he didn't leave it on the field? Was he ever violent as a child?"

"Nope," Haggard replied. "Well, I guess he had a scrap or two like all boys, but he was a down-deep good kid."

"Wouldn't you consider attacking Pierce Pope in the locker room Saturday an inexcusable extension of his hair-trigger temper?"

"Asshole was begging for an ass-kicking," Suggs lashed out.

"I reckon Chet ain't far from wrong. That *Constitution* writer has been clawing at Torch all year. My guess is that it mounted up 'til Torch couldn't take any more. Not sure I wouldn't have done the same thing."

Suggs barked through the fence, "I would've cracked his scrawny fingers so he couldn't type no more of that shit!"

"Game time in an hour." Haggard stood and eased toward the fence. "Wouldn't want the boys to be disappointed with the infield, now would we, Chet?"

Suggs glared at Charlotte. He snatched the rake and stomped back to first base.

Haggard returned to the bench. "Folks around here don't take kindly to dragging a local hero through the mud. He may only be a baseball player in the city, but Torch Traynor is a legend in Rome."

Charlotte shifted and crossed her legs. "It's not my intent to defame Earl," she softened her tone. "I'm just trying to gain insight into what makes a player of his stature tick."

"You gotta understand, Torch is one of my favorite people, and we've stayed friends all these years. All that fame, all that money, and he comes home to his old friends like nothing's changed."

"It's admirable that he hasn't forgotten his roots. Can you tell me about his home life?"

"Ain't many secrets in Rome. Especially a few years ago, when the city weren't quite this big. Torch's parents, gone to their maker now, bless their souls, were saints. Earl Senior and his mama, Dottie. Earl worked for the county all his life. Dottie stayed at home with Torch and taught near every child in Rome the books of the Bible in Sunday school. They didn't have much, but they didn't want for much either. Took care of their things—kept their place spick and span. Fine people. Fact is, I'd say Torch resembles the best of both of'em. His Daddy's physical strength and his Mama's thirst for perfection."

"Are you implying that Earl is a perfectionist?"

"Yep, just like his Mama. The boy drove us nuts arranging the bats and equipment in the dugout between innings." The memory brought a fond grin. "He hasn't changed a bit either. Everyone thinks he takes forever between pitches because of game pressure except those of us that know him. Watch him. He won't throw a dang pitch until every crease in his uniform is exactly how he wants it. He's like an old hen, primping his clothes like he's off to Wednesday night supper at the Baptist church."

Chapter Ten

Endless darkness shrouded roadside greenery by the time Charlotte left Rome. She felt alone and apprehensive driving on the dark, barren highway. She regretted the post sunset departure.

She had strolled with Albert Haggard to the game in process and found herself enthralled. Even after Haggard slipped away to attend to a hotdog bun shortage, Charlotte watched the twelve-year-olds play. Hunger pangs and a nagging voice that told her to return to Atlanta couldn't break the surprising trance. Professional baseball bored her. These players, twelve-year-old boys, however, held her interest despite the errors, mental lapses, and lack of execution. Their boyish enthusiasm, desire to win, and youthful thirst for fun fascinated Charlotte.

She ate a cheese burrito dinner at the Rio Bravo Cantina, still amazed that she had stayed at Riverview Park until the final out. No glitter, no fanfare, and nothing at risk except the outcome of the contest, the Rome boys sparked a mild interest in baseball as a children's game rather than a testament to chiseled media idols.

Earl Traynor had soared to legendary status from these same simple Bible belt roots. Coach Albert Haggard described a driven boy, competitive to a fault. Personality traits not often associated with murderers. One peculiar detail hounded her amid his glowing testimonial to Traynor's character. She overlooked the boy's tough heroics and dwelled on the child phenom's affinity for dugout cleaning chores between innings—odd behavior for a boy, or any male. Everybody has strange habits. She couldn't dismiss the link to Margaret's alphabetized CDs, no matter how hard she tried to denounce any correlation between cleanliness and a penchant to kill.

The front bumper pierced low fog. A haze swirled off a roadside pond and clouded the highway. The headlights reflected off the dense mist, and the lane dividers vanished beneath the blurry blanket. Charlotte clutched the steering wheel and let up on the accelerator. The white sheet of light intensified ahead of her. She braked and squinted, blinded by the reflection.

She shielded her eyes with a forearm across her brow, suddenly disorientated, struggling to see the road. Illuminated rays beamed underneath her arm from the side mirror. High beams lit up the inside of Charlotte's car.

Where the hell did you come from? The vehicle kept coming toward her. Could it see her? "Nooo!" she screamed and scrunched her neck, braced for a rear-end collision.

The truck swerved left and missed the back fender of Charlotte's rental car. The Malibu shuddered as the large pickup thundered past, separated by inches. It zoomed ahead in the left lane, slowed, and veered right. The truck straddled the centerline, coasted between lanes, and decelerated to a crawl.

The blockade kept her from passing. Charlotte drove closer. She honked and attempted to pass on the right. The truck sped up and cut her off. She slammed on the brakes, spun the wheel to the left, and stomped the gas pedal.

Again, the truck intercepted her course, and swerved from lane to lane as it slowed down. The truck was forcing her to stop, hidden by the thick fog, somewhere between Rome and Cartersville.

"Details," Charlotte whispered. "The police will want details." She noted smoke-tinted windows and chrome mag wheels on the maroon truck. "Ford F-250. License...damn, cardboard and duct tape."

She swung right, the Ford swung right. She wiggled left. The pickup mirrored the maneuver. *Barney Fife, Bubba, Joe Bob, where are you?* Now, she prayed for a chance encounter with a bumpkin deputy.

The pickup angled across both lanes and stopped.

Stopping wasn't an option. Charlotte gunned the engine and darted right. She leaned left, sensing the edge of the road shoulder. She surged ahead.

The Ford barreled forward and overtook her. If a truck can look angry, this one did, aggressive now, resolute to run Charlotte off the road.

She faked left, jerked the wheel, and accelerated right. The pickup went for the fake, but glided right back into her path. Charlotte plowed to the right, determined to outflank the Ford.

The wheels dropped off the shoulder. The rental car spun from the asphalt and ripped a circle in the soft turf. The seatbelt held Charlotte tight. She tromped on the brake. The car stopped and the engine idled. Charlotte gazed forward, dizzy from the carnival ride.

She looked right. Two white taillights. The truck was backing up.

Charlotte pressed the gas pedal. The car lurched forward, then rolled back. The tires burrowed a slippery groove in the soft terrain. Mud battered the inside of the wheel well as she rocked the car, desperate to free the stuck tires.

The truck stopped on the shoulder.

She pulled the emergency flashers. The horn blared when she pressed the panic button on the remote key. Who would hear?

The dome light lit up inside the truck. She spotted the silhouette of a large man wearing a billed hat as he climbed down from the cab. He froze. The driver jumped into his truck. The interior light went out, the truck lunged forward, and rubber squealed. The Ford truck fishtailed and sped away.

Charlotte glanced left. Large headlights approached, like halos gleaming through the distant fog.

Airbrakes squeaked. The eighteen-wheeler screeched to a stop on the shoulder. Gasping for air, she tried to catch her breath. The truck driver jumped down from his rig and ran toward her.

He waited. One traffic signal south of the 441 and US 41 intersection the white Malibu, spattered with red mud, headed for Atlanta. Less than an hour after he'd run the bitch off the road, he cranked the Ford engine and eased onto US 41 behind her.

He'd been too aggressive. The bitch pissed him off thinking she could outrun him. Who the hell did she think she was? He cooled his jets on the side of the road and decided the semi had come along at a good time.

One more violent crime in Atlanta would be just another ghetto killing. He'd follow her back to Atlanta and take care of her when the time was right. "I'll teach ya to mess with Torch, bitch," Chet Suggs mumbled, his eyes tracking Charlotte's taillights.

Chapter Eleven

Late-morning sunshine streaked through leaky blinds and striped the walls. A lawn mower engine roared, emitting gasoline fumes mixed with the smell of fresh-cut grass. Fresh-brewed coffee? Sensory overload besieged Charlotte. She reached for her travel clock. Eleven thirteen. She swung her bare feet to the floor and rubbed her eyes as consciousness dawned.

She trudged into the hallway, her wrinkled nightshirt clinging to her thighs. She hadn't intended to sleep so late, but her instincts demanded total shutdown to recover from the long night. Liz's small apartment was still. She squeezed between the counter and a kitchen chair and gave silent thanks to Liz for the awaiting coffeepot. She poured a cup, yawned, and scratched her pillow-tangled hair.

The front door sprung open. Charlotte spun and sloshed coffee on her hand

"Morning, sleepyhead." Moisture spotted the Nike tank top, sagging over Liz's sports bra and tight running shorts. Her hair was pulled through the back of a khaki cap. Her face, shadowed by the cap, glistened after a morning run. "I was about to give you up for dead."

"Long night," Charlotte said, her first words raspy.

"Not that it's any of my business, but I was beginning to worry. You disappeared from the game and zoomed off to north Georgia alone, without so much as a 'Ta-ta.' If you went off on an exciting adventure without me, I'm going to be hurt."

"Sorry, Liz. I couldn't find you. Did Pierce give you my message?"

"He did." Liz splashed coffee in a fresh cup. "But I can't imagine in my wildest dreams anything that could tempt anyone to stay in Rome until the wee hours of the morning?"

"Traynor is from Rome. I went up there to snoop around, try to add a few superstar childhood memories to my story. I started watching a ball game and didn't leave until it was over."

"Come on, Charlotte, do you really take me for dimwit?" Liz curled a loose lock of hair around a finger. "Not a blond strand in this mane. I haven't known you long, but I can't imagine a baseball game, especially in Rome, Georgia, captivating you."

Charlotte sat at the dinette table. "It's true. Twelve-year-old Dizzy Dean baseball. I swear!"

"Twelve-year-old boys played until midnight on a Sunday."

"I didn't say that. Afterwards I ate dinner, and then there was this altercation on the way back."

"I noticed your car." Liz pulled a chair from under the table. The metal legs screeched the floor. "Looks like Georgia clay spin art." She eased onto the chair. "Car trouble?"

"More like pickup truck trouble. Ever seen *Duel*?" She referred to Steven Spielberg's made-for-television movie starring Dennis Weaver as a businessman engaged in a to-the-death road battle with an evil, revenge-stricken trucker. Charlotte inhaled. "I'm not sure how I infuriated him so." The encounter flashbacked before she looked up at Liz. "I was driving through this…this fog thick as, you know, like when an airliner comes down into the clouds. I couldn't see two feet beyond the front of the car. Out of nowhere this pickup appears, zooms by and starts playing tag at fifty miles an hour. Road rage, I guess. I don't know what I did. Anyway, when I tried to pass him, he ran me off the road. I spun out."

Liz leaned forward. "Thus the mud mural on your car. Were you stuck?"

"Wheels spinning, muck flying everywhere, and he starts backing down the shoulder. Thank God for the eighteen-wheeled angel emerging from the fog. He was out of his pickup, coming toward me. The trucker scared him off."

A concerned crinkle raised above Liz's nose. "Are you okay?"

"A little shaky. Frightened by the what-ifs, but otherwise I'm fine."

Steam spiraled off an oil-black coffee pool and drew Liz's gaze. She uttered, "I'm glad you weren't hurt, Charlotte." The crinkle now an intense scowl, she bit her lip to corral a forming sentence. Her questioning eyes rolled to Charlotte.

"What?" Charlotte straightened her back. Her shoulders tightened. "What is it?"

"I was about to ask you the same question."

"I don't understand, Liz."

"You appear out of nowhere like some kind of freelance princess. Obviously wet behind your journalistic ears, your naïveté was cute, refreshing. All of us have to learn, most of us have mentors, so I didn't mind helping. In fact, it was fun, because I like you, Charlotte. New friends are fun. How long did you think the charade could go on? Do you really believe journalists are so dense, that sports reporting is such a brainless occupation, that Miss-I'm-gonna-make-six-figures-when-I-make-partner-bean-counter can sashay in and pose as a pro?"

Charlotte's hung her head. "I'm sorry. I didn't mean any harm. I just ..." She sniffled. "Never mind."

"The Braves yank credentials arranged by the *Constitution*. Chasing a fictitious background story, death passes before your eyes. The deception is so thick I'm not even sure who I'm talking to, and all you can say is, 'Never mind'?"

The chair slid across the floor when Liz stood.

"Liz, I'm sorry!" Charlotte wiped a tear from her cheek. "You've all been so kind. I didn't want to lie to you...Pierce, Carlton. My mind is so jumbled that my judgment may be on the fritz. I couldn't come up with a better way to get near him." Charlotte rose and stepped toward the hallway. "I'll pack my things."

"Who's him?"

Charlotte stopped, turned and looked at Liz through her misty eyes. "I embarrassed your newspaper. I betrayed your confidence. I've caused you enough aggravation without dragging you into the middle of my problems."

"Never do that to a journalist." The bite in Liz's voice waned. She shifted to the right and continued, "*Desperate woman poses as writer in pursuit of mysterious man*. Leaving me hanging is worse than lying to me."

"It's not your problem."

"You're in danger, aren't you?"

"The pickup was only a coincidence...I think."

Liz walked toward her. "What's going on, Charlotte? Come on, you owe me that much. At least tell me who *he* is?"

Charlotte folded her arms. "How did you find out?"

"I tell you, you tell me."

"I don't know, Liz."

"I go first. Among his exhausting, loathsome, despicable, and appalling characteristics, Tad Smithurst is a blabbermouth. He took great joy in leaking that you were an impostor."

"Sorry, again."

"Who is *he*?"

"I'm not sure I should do this," Charlotte hesitated.

"Good sense hasn't stopped you up to now. Why ruin a streak of bad choices?"

Charlotte sighed. "Earl Traynor."

"Torch?" Liz cackled. "What are you? One of those stalking fans?"

"I…I think Traynor murdered my sister."

Charlotte's arms dropped. Her chest heaved. Salty droplets moistened her nightshirt. Liz rushed to her, and wrapped her long arms around her. Charlotte sobbed into her shoulder.

When the tears ebbed, the whole story followed—Margaret's brutal death, her immaculate home, the matchbook collection, the bartender's account of her sister's encounter with Torch Traynor, and Jeb Owens's beer-rinsed scheme to approach the ace reliever. Charlotte shared her misery, relaxed on the couch and sipped coffee.

"You need to go to the police."

"The Tampa police think I'm a grieving basket case. She was killed in their jurisdiction, and they think I'm sticking my nose in where it doesn't belong. Now do you honestly believe the Atlanta police will buy the theory of the victim's wacko sister, meanwhile jeopardizing the Braves' World Series campaign? There's no hard evidence. It's all intuition, circumstantial, but it fits. I know it was Traynor."

"You have a point. APD wouldn't touch it with a bomb robot unless the evidence smacked 'em in the gut. Maybe informal cooperation would be a better approach."

"Do you have APD contacts?"

"A patrolman here and there, but even if I was kissing cousins with the Chief himself it wouldn't do any good. For once it's not an Atlanta crime."

"Another dead end, I suppose," Charlotte replied, deflated.

"The resource I had in mind is outside the law enforcement community. Instead of fretting about jurisdiction, he'll embrace the challenge, savor the chase, and with any luck give you guidance. If there is any substance, breaking a story of this magnitude could be the highlight of his career."

"Carlton Cox?"

"Yep. He's seen it all. He's been watching cops chase murderers since… Well, I think he was doing the crime beat during Jeff Davis's administration."

"Would Carlton be interested?"

"Interested!" Liz howled. "He'll be giddy with the opportunity to slam the cell door on a celebrity of Traynor's status. Charlotte, don't forget who brung ya to the dance. I want photo exclusives."

Chapter Twelve

Charlotte nursed her glass of Chardonnay. She squinted at Manuel's front entrance through smoke streamers swirling in the yellow light. Sitting among a subdued Monday night crowd, vacant booths and lonesome barstools, she looked for Cox. "Where is he?"

"He'd never pass up a night cap at Manuel's," Liz assured her. "It's a stretch to say he's a man of his word, but drinking here is sacred to Carlton."

The door opened. A wrinkled shadow, topped with a rebellious mop, shuffled to the bar. Without ordering, he accepted a Budweiser from the bartender, guzzled from the longneck, and eyed the Manuel's clientele.

Charlotte waved to Cox. He lowered the beer and walked toward their booth.

"Hey, Carlton," the bartender called from behind. "That Stennett guy from North Carolina called again. He wants you to call him."

"Cory, if he calls again, tell him I'm in the john puking. He'll believe that."

He stood at the end of their booth.

"Hey big fella." Liz puckered her lips.

Cox cringed and plopped down next to Charlotte. He stared up at the television airing an *Andy Griffith Show* rerun above the bar. "Braves win?"

"Aren't we friendly tonight?" Liz said.

"Did they win?"

"Rain delay," Charlotte answered.

Cox stretched his arm, squinted, and looked at his watch. He burst into raucous laughter.

"What? What is it?" Charlotte's eyes spun to Liz.

"It's, it's," Cox tried to catch his breath, "it's eleven thirty-three. Twelve minutes to deadline. Can't you just see preppy Pierce Pope plotting prose now?" He chuckled until a throaty smoker's cough gagged him.

Liz grinned.

"What's so funny?" Charlotte asked.

"Sweat beads on his lip. The double Windsor knot unraveled from the blue Oxford collar." Cox lit a Marlboro. "When the deadline hour strikes the literary prince transforms into an illiterate peasant."

On the television, the Busch Stadium groundskeepers rolled the tarp from the infield.

"Inside joke, Charlotte. Pierce doesn't handle deadline pressure well," Liz added.

Cox howled again.

"I don't understand. I watched him work Saturday night. He's prepared, organized, and efficient," Charlotte said. "No one can stop time."

"Time disintegrates his masterpiece." Cox sipped his beer. "Listen I don't mean to bash Pierce. He acts so prim and proper, it's damn near impossible not to laugh when he falters."

"I've read his articles. He's a wonderful writer."

"Hell, yeah," Cox replied. "He turns a phrase like Pat Conroy. But no matter what he claims, Pierce is no journalist. All that rhetoric about plot, twists, and ballplayers as characters... A baseball game ain't a novel. As soon as the ball game leaves his outline, he implodes. Sure there are times when you can brush up a story's syntax, find just the right word, but real reporters write a sound synopsis of a breaking story and transmit fast. It's all about speed. React, rearrange and remit. Home runs, elections, or murder, journalists write news, not bestsellers."

Charlotte clenched her jaw. She traced the rim of her glass with a drop of white wine and turned away.

"Don't take it so personal. Pierce isn't a bad guy, and I'm a cynical sumbitch." Cox shifted his beady gaze to Liz. "I could berate Pierce all night. That's plain ugly fun, not urgent as you mentioned when you arranged this party. What's up?"

"We were beginning to wonder if you'd show up," Liz said.

"Some John Henry blew away a shopkeeper on Auburn Avenue. Sixty-two-year-old oriental." Cox chewed the cigarette filter. Smoke escaped as he spoke. "Got away with one hundred and twenty-seven dollars. Metro section, page three."

"That's awful," Charlotte returned to the conversation.

Cox shrugged his shoulders. "Hey, I didn't pull the trigger."

"Are you so callused, so tragedy hardened that you've forgotten common decency, respect?"

"Behave, Carlton," Liz insisted.

"Yeah, yeah. Thought I was out for a beer with friends, not an inquisition.

What's so important that we couldn't talk on the phone?"

"Forget it." Charlotte glared at Liz. "I'll deal with this myself. And I'll pay for his damn beer! I'm ready to go."

"He can help, Charlotte."

"Sorry, I'm an ass." Cox calmed. "Will one of you tell me what this all about?"

Commotion on the television distracted Charlotte. The Braves jogged over the soggy infield to their positions. She looked at her watch. The game had run beyond deadline. From the corner caption, she noted the Braves led four to two in the bottom of the ninth. "Who's pitching?"

Liz and Cox turned to the television.

"Tino Orez pitched the first eight innings," he answered.

Gazing at the television, Charlotte muttered, "Torch Traynor murdered my sister."

"What?" Cox smashed his cigarette in a plastic ashtray. "Glad I didn't have a mouth full of suds, I would have sprayed all over Liz. Tell me more."

Her eyes rolled from the screen to Cox. She began in stoic syllables, "The Braves traveled to Tampa last week. The last person to see her alive was a bartender at Down the Hatch Pub, a ballplayer's refuge in St. Petersburg. Traynor talked to her, she used the phone, she left, and he ripped the bar to shreds. Two hours later, she was beaten to death in her house."

"Beat with a blunt object?" Inquisitiveness emerged through his sarcastic crust. "No suspects? I remember reading about it online. I don't see the connection to Traynor."

"Tell him the rest, Charlotte."

She closed her eyes, grasped the painful memories, and continued, "Margaret never married. The night she died she left me a message. She was so happy. She said she had met the love of her life and she might move away with him. Traynor was seen with her in a rancid bar that she would never set foot in."

"A chance encounter and no physical evidence tying him to the scene. I don't mean to pop your bubble, but there's not much to go on."

"Let her finish."

"I'll shut up," Cox said.

"As much as I love…loved Margaret, her passion for life lacked organization and awareness of petty issues, like housecleaning. She never cleaned unless absolutely necessary. When I went to her house to pack her belongings, the house had been scrubbed, dusted, vacuumed and rearranged."

"Rearranged?" he asked.

"CDs alphabetized. Books in descending order. Stacks of periodicals in chronological order."

"How does it tie to Traynor?"

"The police think I'm just a dizzy grieving sister. Whoever killed Margaret cleaned her house after he beat her. You should see Traynor's locker. A Major League all-star," she pointed to the TV and saw Traynor stroll to the mound. Eyes glued to the television, she continued, "with hygiene products lined up neater than Publix shelves. Country music arranged in alphabetical order."

"I'll play the devil's advocate," Cox jumped in. "Coincidence."

"Sunday I drove to Rome, Traynor's hometown. I spoke with his Little League coach, Albert Haggard. He said Traynor has been a perfectionist all his life. The kid straightened the equipment in the dugout between innings. Look at him. He can't throw a damn baseball unless his uniform is perfect."

Torch wiped sweat from his brow, tugged at his belt, and smoothed a wrinkle from his thigh. He toed the rubber and checked runners at second and third.

At the bar, a bottle slammed on the counter. Fans watching the game erupted, vocalizing their disgust as a looping line drive dropped into left field and pushed the tying run across home plate. Traynor lip-synced a lengthy string of four-letter expletives, slammed his glove against his thigh, and kicked the rosin bag off the pitcher's mound.

"If one coincidence is a single point, then with each additional coincidence a line forms. A line right at him." Charlotte pointed at a close-up of Traynor. "Vicinity, opportunity, explosive temper, and a quirky clean fetish you'll have to admit is peculiar for a Major Leaguer."

Loud cheers erupted when Traynor picked off the Cardinals' runner from first base, advancing the game to the tenth inning.

"I agree. Bundled coincidences can form concrete leads. I got to tell you, I'm not convinced Traynor's involved. I'm more interested in your sister's house. You're sure the killer cleaned house after he murdered her?"

"Absolutely! He bathed her, dressed her in night clothes, and tucked her in." Charlotte doused the distasteful blurb in a long swig of Chardonnay.

"Maybe he wanted to remove evidence," Liz said.

Cox rubbed his gray cheek stubble. "Wanted to or had to?"

The Braves' second baseman, Billy Lester, rounded first base after a seeing-eye grounder rolled into right field.

"What are you suggesting, Carlton?" Liz asked.

Her eyes fixed on the television, Charlotte blurted out, "Why is he batting?"

Traynor walked to the plate, ripped a practice swing, and looked down the third base line for signals.

"If they pinch-hit, he can't pitch the tenth," Cox assessed the game situation. "He only threw one pitch last inning. He'll bunt Lester to second and hope they take a lead."

"Who cares about the damn Braves?" Liz peered at Cox. "What's with this *want to had to* windiness?"

"Obsessive-compulsive disorder."

"Like excessive hand washing?" Charlotte asked.

"Yes, but intensified. Persistent fears, concerns, obsessions involuntarily combated by compulsive behavior. 'My hands are dirty, I must clean them.' Relentless impulses repeat until compulsive rituals provide temporary relief from the anxiety. Lists, counting, checking—anything to ward off the unwanted ideas welled up in the mind. Then the cycle restarts. Whether an obsessive-compulsive would turn to violence as a compulsive reaction, I don't know. But I'd wager housecleaning with a corpse looking on and lethal injection a squad car away borders on severe OCD. I'm saying maybe the killer couldn't allow himself to leave until he fulfilled a compulsion for cleanliness or perfection."

"Now I get it," Liz said. "You were drummed out of the medical profession for being drunk and obnoxious, Dr. Cox. When did you become such an expert on OCD?"

He glared at Liz. "When you write about crime as long as I have, occasionally you learn why people do the atrocious things they do."

"Carlton, do you think Traynor could have OCD?" Charlotte asked.

"It's possible, but I'm no expert. I do know a shrink at Emory who is. I'll call him in the morning. Maybe he'll meet with us."

"Call me at Liz's. Thanks Carlton."

Cox raised his beer bottle until the bartender noticed. "I presume the reporter bit is crock of shit."

"I apologize for lying to you."

"I knew there was something I liked about you. I don't like journalists. Too much like me."

She smiled.

"With the playoffs looming and the pestilent Mets breathing down the Braves' stuffy necks, who else knows your mission in life is to incarcerate the Braves stopper?"

Charlotte watched Traynor bat.

"Hendricks revoked her press pass after the Tampa police inquired about Traynor," Liz responded.

"Tad knows," Charlotte added.

"Smithurst," Liz said. "Hendricks's big-mouthed assistant."

Traynor faked a bunt, straightened, and swung. The bat head connected with an inside curve. He pulled the ball down the right field line. The soaring line drive sneaked inside the foul pole for a two-run go-ahead homer.

Manuel's Tavern burst into triumphant bedlam.

Chapter Thirteen

He stood behind Megan and watched her slide the key card through the electronic lock. A tiny light blinked red. The lock denied access. She jammed the plastic key in the slot and shoved it up and down with futile vigor.

"Hate…these…things…"

"Turn it over." His gentle hand rotated her wrist and reversed the magnetic strip. Together, they guided the key.

"Oops." She giggled. The green light flashed. She twisted the handle and leaned her shoulder against the door.

She clutched his hand and towed him behind her. She spun into him beyond room four twenty-two's entrance. Supple breasts flooded the shallow cartilage valleys connecting his ribs. Her chilled hands circled his wrists and steered his open palms to her firm buttocks. He fumbled for her zipper, lowered the wool suit skirt, and fondled her silky backside. She moaned and thrust her hips forward, ramming his spine into the handle. The door slammed. The metal doorjamb rattled, reverberating down the Marriott hallway like rolling thunder.

He closed his eyes and let her moist lips engulf his mouth. Her warm breath and bourbon-soaked tongue intoxicated his animated taste buds. Suffocating in the slobbery kiss, he did not realize she probed below his waist until she kneaded his arousal with cool fingers.

"I want you." Megan licked moisture from the corner of her mouth.

He kissed her neck. Her head rolled as she sighed. He sampled her cleavage, smothered in skin-heated perfume. He wiggled the plastic buttons through tight holes in her white blouse.

Sexual energy, a concentrated blast of adrenaline, stalled the demons' rally like a fire-hose discharged upon rebellion. Thwart the little bastards with total immersion in this woman. Megan. Ignore the inward chants for vengeance. A looping single and another blown save—a stupid baseball game, not a command for the executioner's blade. Drown swelling intolerance with her willingness, give her his physical all, then pass out spent in carnal bliss. When he awoke, they'd be gone, bored to a dull edge with the beastly opportunity bypassed. Come daylight the Cardinals versus the Braves would again only be a ballgame.

Her blouse parted, he teethed on her fleshy mounds. His wandering tongue touched a salty blend of cosmetic fragrance and the vat of Wild Turkey she'd consumed. They'd met at the Marriott bar an hour before last call, exchanged telling glances, and cajoled in a dark corner booth. Meg…he toiled to recall her name…Megan Rivers. A contract agent with Southwestern Bell, in St. Louis for the week from…San Antonio. Early thirties, divorced, and a low-light, early-morning bombshell, she derailed his incessant brain barrage imploring habitual hostility.

Pulsing desire fueled impatience with the stubborn blouse. Megan hastened the disrobing ritual, her manicured fingertips undoing the final three buttons. Her blouse opened, like a stage curtain drawn for the next act, revealing her flat tummy and navel.

He unhooked the front-fastened brassiere and nibbled on her right breast. Megan's breasts bounced from the lingerie. He massaged her right breast and craned to tongue the opposite nipple. He shuddered and pushed away, his eyes flickering with astonishment.

"You found my pet. I should have warned you. It's just a tattoo. Makes me unforgettable, huh?"

The coiled rattler, forked tongue extended and perched above her nipple, glared at him. I BITE BACK was engraved near the tip of her bosom beneath the twisted contour of the snake's tail.

"Cute, isn't he?" Megan tugged at the elastic band of his boxers and slid her hand inside. "My covert statement on equality. I wanted a snake, too. Your python is standard equipment."

He blinked in rapid groupings of three. He clenched his fists to fight the trembling. A tattoo artist's needle marred simmering seduction. A cold-blooded reptile slithered across his lustful fixation. The demons, beaten into retreat by the woman's alluring hex, adopted a snake-eyed flag as their emblem, the battle cry for an at-all-cost counterattack. Rattlesnakes belonged coiled inside a Florida palmetto or sunning atop Texas rock canyons—not on Megan's tit. He closed his eyes and filled his lungs with controlled breaths.

Her cool, caring hand touched his cheek. "What's wrong? Are you sick? Let Megan take care of you."

She guided his face to her breasts and stroked his hair. Where he longed to indulge seconds earlier, now, nestled in her soft cleavage, the ugly mark that scarred Megan's enticing curves besieged his consciousness. The demons' war cries impaired his sexual drive. His stiff anticipation went limp, distracted by the relentless noise of the demons' pending onslaught.

Legions of glory-bound troopers surrounded him, demonstrating their brutal strength before they unleashed ruthless punishment. He'd rather endure the assault of a thousand gouging bayonets. Dust clouds billowed, darkening his view of the horizon beyond. Fight them and die slow, institutionalized, strapped to a state-funded bed, in a medicated comatose. Surrender, feed them, and send them away like conquering heroes with the spoils. Fight them another day, on favorable terrain when victory was more than a fleeting prayer.

"It's late. Road trips are exhausting. Guess I'm a little woozy." He withdrew from her pillowed chest. He applied circular pressure to his temples. "A bath might help."

"Cool water," Megan slipped the blouse and bra from her shoulders, "hot bodies." She eased her fingers inside the waist of her silk panties and wiggled her hips. Her underwear fell to her ankles. She leaned against the wall and flicked her discarded panties into the closet with her toe. She kissed him, backed away, and sauntered toward the bathroom, bare-assed in two-inch heels. "I'll start the water. If you keep me waiting too long, I'll have to begin without you."

The pipes groaned as water rushed to the tub. Frozen in the doorway, he yearned to be outside the door, outside the hotel, back in Atlanta, anywhere removed from Megan and her damn rattlesnake. His forehead throbbed, pounding like a wrecking ball smashing condemned brick walls. If he ran, they ran with him, stowaways boring into the lining of his skull with tiny sledgehammers and chisels. The sound of running water compounded the excruciating pressure.

He unbuttoned his shirt and stepped forward. He smoothed wear wrinkles and hung the shirt on a courtesy hanger.

The water stopped.

"Your bath awaits," Megan beckoned him.

His loafers clicked on the bathroom tile. Tunnel vision. A telescope-like view seeking Megan, censured by demon central, opened in the hazy blanket. There...submerged to her chest. Her rattler frolicked in calm bath water surf.

"You can't bathe or have your way with me in your trousers."

He surveyed the small bathroom—the toilet inches from the tub, the vanity an arm's length from the commode, and a towel rack, loose above the water closet. He stepped out on his shoes. Toe to toe he positioned the loafers beneath the vanity. He removed his trousers and boxers, folded each, and piled the clothing in the furthest corner of the vanity counter.

Megan gazed at his crotch. "He looks so sad. Come here, baby, I'll get his attention."

In black socks, he ambled toward her. Water beads streaked over her bare curves. Megan rose to her knees, grabbed him, and squeezed her breasts around his shaft. She gyrated her breasts, his manhood trapped in the luscious vise, allowing the snake to snap at him.

An anchor had squirmed free from drywall. The end of the chrome-plated towel bar dangled by only a thread or two. He gripped the square bar.

"Almost ready," she responded to the hardening sensation lodged between her breasts.

He yanked the bar from the wall. Screws and plastic anchors pinged on the floor. He cocked the rod above his head and sliced downward through a puff of drywall powder. The blow mangled the scalp above her left ear.

Blood sprayed the shower wall. Megan wavered, dazed, but didn't fall, kneeling as if she begged for mercy. Drunk and maimed, she raised her left arm in defense.

Whoosh, like a PGA three-wood, the bar whistled. As if an axe splintered brittle hardwood, her bone cracked, fractured above the elbow. Megan's crippled arm splashed in the reddening pool.

His lethal strokes pulverized her bobbing head. He hammered until she toppled. Her head slammed against the faucet, bounced, and tumbled into the water.

He'd forgotten to breathe. He gulped air, his chest heaving. His vision cleared. The acute head pain subsided. Megan's blood spotted his naked torso. He checked his clothes, grateful they were beyond the range of the red specs of death.

He steadied a knee in a thick, warm floor puddle. He rolled her by the ankles on her back. Her battered head thumped the tub bottom. He shoved her face beneath the water. Air boils rippled as the blood-dyed water flooded her lungs.

The rattlesnake watched Megan swallow the water from its desolate flesh island in an ocean of death.

"Go outside, son," his mother pleaded. "Play with the other boys."

"My room isn't straight, Mama. Cleanliness is next to godliness, right, Mama?"

"You work so hard, my darling. It's a beautiful day, please go outside and play with your friends."

"Ain't got no friends. They just want to wrestle in the dirt. Filthy pigs all of 'em. And it's gonna rain, Mama, the man on the television said so. My clothes will be caked with mud and grass stains. You shouldn't have to clean up after me. I'll just stay in and sort my baseball cards."

The conversation hounded him now that the demons slept off the savage binge. Motionless on Megan's hotel bed, he visited childhood. Mama knew. She begged him to interact with others, forget his chores, and have fun. He never did. He had wanted to please her. Shun the rigid structure order demanded. When he strayed, the compelling thirst for perfection tethered him to disciplined determination like a rabid pit bull chained to a clothesline pole. He strived to be the best and only resorted to a psychotic tantrum when events beyond his immediate control went awry.

He stroked Megan's wet hair, her head on the pillow beside him. The tantrums restored sanity, giving him another chance to sidestep the consequences of unpredictable mistakes, or better yet, eliminate the imperfection in entirety.

He glanced at the clock beside the bed. It was after four. Time to go, leave Megan to be discovered by a Marriott maid. He swung his feet to the floor and stood.

Proper cleaning supplies were not available. He had improvised with complimentary shampoo, bar soap and hotel towels. As hard as he had scrubbed, he failed to wash away the pinkish sheen from the bathroom floor and tub. He had folded and piled the blood-soaked towels in the corner.

He showered, cleansing her blood from him, after he washed Megan and enshrouded her in bed sheets. He had been wise to undress, avoiding blood stains on his clothing, noticeable and near impossible to get out of fabric, although he'd heard dabbing hydrogen peroxide on the brownish spots might work.

Megan's wool suit hung in the closet. He had even ironed her blouse and hand-washed her panties. Her room was acceptable to receive visitors.

He wiped all the surfaces to smear fingerprints he could have left. The towel bar was different. Even one print on the murder weapon was too risky. He shoved the chrome rod down a trouser leg and walked toward the door. He would dispose of it far from the realm of suspicion.

Chapter Fourteen

"I've got to stop drinking." Cox's cough resonated over the phone receiver.

"You ought to stop smoking, too." Charlotte shifted the phone to her left hand. A disheveled *Atlanta Journal-Constitution*, Liz's computer, and Charlotte's laptop were heaped on the dinette table like clearance merchandise in a thrift store.

"They're going to prove beer causes cancer someday, then I'd have to learn to smoke all over again." He paused. "Like I was saying, I drank too much last night. My head's throbbing like a paving breaker, my mouth feels like the bottom of a pigeon cage, and I'm hallucinating."

"Hallucinating?"

"Yeah. Engrained in the brain cells I didn't nuke, I woke up with the premonition that Torch Traynor murdered your sister. Crazy, huh?"

"I wish I were delirious, Carlton. When I step back, I find it hard to believe Margaret is gone, and even harder to accept that an Atlanta Brave killed her."

"Damn. I was afraid you'd confirm my drunken recollection. The bright side is that I can continue my tireless liver abuse research."

Charlotte pressed the power button on the laptop. "Did you arrange a meeting with your psychiatrist friend?"

"Kenneth Daniels. Meet us at the Varsity at eleven thirty."

"The Varsity?"

"You've never been to the V?"

"No."

"Corner of North Avenue and Spring Street. Liz will give you directions."

She snatched a pencil off the kitchen counter and scribbled the street names across the top of the sports page.

He chuckled. "What did I tell you about Pope? Did you see his article?"

She opened the sports section. "I looked earlier. This edition carried a short AP version."

"Exactly. The rain delay and that base hit busted his outline, and his plot blew up. He missed deadline in all editions."

"I'm sure there's more to it," she said.

Liz entered from the hallway, brushing her wet hair.

"Yeah, yeah. And I'm spearheading a movement to reinstate prohibition."

"Okay, okay, Carlton. Your opinion is clear."

"See you at eleven thirty, Charlotte. Be prompt."

"I'll be there," she said, and she turned off the phone.

"Carlton reveling in Pierce's shortcomings?" Liz asked.

Charlotte watched the laptop boot. "Does he really dislike Pierce so much?"

"No. He approaches cynicism as if it were an art form. Carlton doesn't like anyone or anything."

Charlotte grinned. "Mind if I check my e-mail?"

"My connection is your connection." While the modem whined an annoying electronic concert, Liz asked, "Are you meeting with Carlton's OCD expert?"

"At the Varsity. He said that you'd tell me how to get there." She read her notes. "North and Spring."

"Less than fifteen minutes. You know the way to Manuel's. The Varsity is five minutes west on North Avenue."

Liz scooted out a chair, sat at the table, and perused the newspaper.

Eighteen messages waited for Charlotte in her electronic inbox. She scrolled down the bold subjects of the unopened e-mails and assessed the recurring theme—"Where's C. Gordon," "Absent Audit Manager," "San Angelo PROBLEM." She told James that the San Angelo audit would have to begin without her. Midway down the screaming messages, she opened one.

To: Charlotte.Gordon@PWB.net
From: James.Houston@PWB.net
Subject: Coming to Atlanta
Sent: Monday, September 17, 6:44 PM

Charlotte,
I arrive Atlanta Tuesday, 9/18, 7:35 PM, Delta #1465. Meet me at airport. Bring your laptop...transporting software upgrade.
- James

She gazed at the screen, motionless. What were the words between the concise sentences? *I'm sorry. I miss you. Kiss and make up*. Or was James Houston, the managing partner, flying to Atlanta to convince a billable resource to re-engage her sensibility and take charge in San Angelo as she had committed? Charlotte's mind scrambled through interpretative iterations, her fingertips frozen to the keyboard.

"Something interesting?" Liz eyed Charlotte around the back page of the Living section.

"Huh?"

"Earth to Charlotte." Liz folded the newspaper. "You look like you just read your own obituary."

Charlotte licked her lips. "James wants to meet me at the airport tonight."

"I'd better change your sheets." Liz hit her forehead with the palm of a hand. "Where's my sensitivity? Is this rendezvous a good thing?"

"I'm not sure. I haven't seen him since the middle of August. With my thoughts elsewhere, I haven't thought much about James lately."

"Maybe he misses you. Relationships are two sided. Just because you've been tackling insurmountable obstacles, interfering with whom and what you were, doesn't mean James has lost his perspective."

"Should I go?"

"I would. Can't hurt to hear what he says."

"I suppose you're right. He is the boss."

"You're sleeping with your boss?"

"Not for a while, but yes."

"Sex is one thing, but your job is another. You have to go."

"Maybe seeing James will give me a jolt of reality. Tear me away from my obsession with Margaret's murder."

"Sweep you up in his arms, and fly you away—"

"To romantic San Angelo, Texas. It's not Aruba."

They laughed.

"Am I in too deep, Liz? Should I give up chasing Traynor and resume a life of discrediting the financial worth of my clients?"

"Who am I to say?" Liz shrugged her shoulders. "If it was me I'd go see James tonight. You're smart. Let your instincts take over."

"My father says that my instincts are my biggest problem. A couple of beers, a conversation with a bartender and I'm on the next flight to Atlanta without a shred of concern for a career I've driven all over Texas to establish. Here I am. Great instincts, huh?"

"Stop beating yourself up, Charlotte. It can't hurt to see him. Take it from there." Liz nodded at the photo of Traynor hitting the home run. "Any earth-shattering quotes from Torch?"

"It's an Associated Press article. No quotes. Only a quick game story."

"Deadline affects the national press, too. Check out the *St. Louis Post-Dispatch* online."

Charlotte readied her fingers on the keyboard. "Do you know the Web address?"

"No need. Go to ajr dot newslink dot org." Liz looked over Charlotte's shoulder. The American Journalism Review Web site filled the screen. "Click on Newspapers," her eyes followed Charlotte's site navigation, "By state," she paused, "Missouri, *Post-Dispatch* and presto you're in St. Louis."

"Slick," Charlotte admired the virtual newsstand. Absorbing the *stltoday.com* layout, she spotted the sports tab and scooted the cursor across the online newspaper.

"Look!" Liz shook Charlotte's shoulder.

"What? What is it?"

"There." Liz's fingernail tapped the screen beneath the *Breaking News* heading. She read, "San Antonio businesswoman found murdered at Marriott. Open it, Charlotte."

"Why…oh." Charlotte pointed and punched the headline. She drummed her fingers waiting for the article to open. "Do you think Traynor killed her?"

"I guess so. No way. I don't know."

The women hunched over the laptop. The article emerged. They read the brief account of the murder in silence. Southwestern Bell co-workers became worried and called the hotel when Megan Rivers missed a high-level breakfast meeting. A hotel employee found her dead in her room minutes past eight o'clock. Withholding most details, a St. Louis police source indicated from the nature of the head wounds and defense wounds on Ms. Rivers's left arm it appeared the killer bludgeoned the victim with a blunt object.

"He did it, Liz." Charlotte stared at the electronic article.

"It could be anyone. Right? What makes you so sure?"

"Look at my arms. Goose bumps. I'm tingling all over." She turned her head to Liz. "Traynor killed this woman just like he killed Margaret."

"Female intuition doesn't hold up in court. Celebrities beat forensics, physical evidence, even DNA. What links Margaret to," Liz glanced down at the screen, "this Megan Rivers?"

"I'm not sure." Charlotte clicked the 'Back' icon, which returned the screen to the *Post-Dispatch* home page. She surfed and entered the sports page. Underneath a photo of Traynor's home run swing, the headline proclaimed, *TORCH BURNS CARDS*. "That's it! The game. It has to be."

"The game has to be what?"

"The bartender in St. Pete told Jeb and me that Traynor pitched awful the night Margaret died. His pitching is the catalyst. He freaks when he performs poorly."

"Let me get this straight. You're saying when Torch blows a save he vents by pounding on some unsuspecting soul."

"Yes. It ties with the obsessive-compulsive theory Carlton explained last night. Obsessed with perfection, if his plan hits a pothole, he soothes the obsession with compulsive action, in this case violence."

"So every time Torch flounders on the mound, he kills."

"Maybe. Maybe only if the opportunity knocks."

"This is crazy. Torch is good, but even the best falter periodically. Earned runs, wins, strikeouts, and murders per inning. I don't buy it, Charlotte. A serial killer fleeing the scene of the crime on the Braves' charter jet. Think how many others—" She paused. "Surely someone would know."

"Traynor was in Tampa and St. Louis. He blew both games and two women died. Similar circumstances, similar outcomes. It's possible there are other victims and no one would ever dream of linking the Braves' schedule to unsolved murders."

"And it's possible our imaginations have transformed a ballplayer into Ted Bundy's evil twin," Liz said. "This is so insane I almost believe it."

"Is there a way to cross-reference Traynor's bad appearances with murders in the city he pitched badly?"

"Sure. The Internet might work, but it can be tough to search for old news on most city paper sites." Liz smiled. "Carlton has sources nationwide. Ask him at lunch. He'll help, or choke with belittling laughter."

"Lunch!" Charlotte glanced at the clock in the lower corner of the screen. "Eleven eleven. I need to go. Go to Manuel's, turn right, and continue on North Avenue?"

"Red and white everywhere. The Varsity is impossible to miss."

She hurried through the shutdown sequence, disconnected cords, and slipped the laptop into the carrying case. Charlotte grabbed her purse, hurried to the door, and turned the knob.

"See you later, Liz." She sprung to the landing. Charlotte poked her head in before the door closed. "The Jeep is behind my rental. Would you mind moving it for me?"

Liz reached for keys on the kitchen counter, paused, and picked up her khaki cap. She tossed the keys to Charlotte. "Take it. I'm not going anywhere this afternoon."

"Are you sure?"

Liz smiled as she nodded. "And wear this," she approached Charlotte and handed her the cap, "or you'll look like Medusa by the time you get to the V."

"Here are my keys, if you need them. Thanks, Liz. See you later this afternoon."

"Feed that delusion, girl." Liz laughed.

Charlotte rushed out and swung the door closed. The stubborn bolt hit the brass striker, refused to slide, and left the unlocked door ajar.

Chet Suggs, parked half a block from the garage apartment, scrunched low in his pickup seat when the Jeep backed down the driveway. With her hair pulled through the back of the khaki cap, the driver braked, shifted into drive, and sped away.

He had followed the nosy bitch here Sunday night. He returned last night, but she clung to the tall woman like a calf to its mama. Suggs figured maybe the women would split up during the day, so he called in sick, cussed at the yuppies commuting to Atlanta down I-75, and bumped against the curb a few minutes past nine.

After a thermos of coffee and half a pouch of Redman, the Jeep drove off, leaving the rental car and the snooping bitch alone. About time too, his kidneys were close to popping. He'd held his bladder longer, perched in a deer stand waiting for a buck to roam into the crosshairs.

No one messed with Torch. In the middle of a pennant race, his old buddy had to deal with enough shit without some cunt slinging crap all over the media about him being a psycho. He owed Torch. Friendship, trust, and cash to live on whenever Suggs drank away his paycheck. Hell, Torch even bluffed their high school coach into believing he pitched better with ole Chet catching him. If she wanted psycho, he'd show her psycho.

He spit chewing tobacco into a Styrofoam cup. Brown juice dripped from his beard. Find an oak to pee behind, and then he'd shut the bitch up for good.

Chapter Fifteen

Red, white, yellow, and stainless steel art deco spanned two city blocks. Only a blind drunk could miss the Varsity. The world's largest drive-in, complete with double deck parking, overlooked Atlanta's 75/85 connector. Charlotte turned right, coasted through the curb service area, and accelerated up a concrete incline to the raised lot.

She entered through a sturdy glass door. Early lunch-goers milled around the vast fast-food restaurant moments before eleven thirty like ants marching crumbs to the queen. She studied the faces, searching for Cox in the upper seating area. No wonder he wanted to meet early, she would never locate him in a noon crowd.

Charlotte descended a short stairway and failed to spot him in a television sitting room to the left. "What d'ya have?" rang out like a machinegun spewing rhetorical bullets from the slew of cashiers stationed along the endless stainless steel counter. Customers bunched at the registers and placed orders to employees in red paper hats.

An arm waved above the hungry heads. Her eyes, drawn to the motion, tracked the man's arm swinging like a grandfather clock pendulum. Cox's rumpled gray mop comforted her in the sea of alien mayhem. A recognizing smile arose as she stepped toward him.

"Come on," Cox turned her to the counter, "let's get in line before a bus load of school kids show up or the BellSouth folks overrun the place." He shoved Charlotte ahead and snapped his head to the left. "Charlotte, this is Kenneth Daniels. Kenneth, Charlotte Gordon."

"Nice to meet you." Daniels attempted to offer his hand but couldn't reach Charlotte over Cox's advance on the counter. "Now you know what it is like to swim amid a shark frenzy."

Charlotte leaned her head to see him around Cox. Daniels, clean-shaven with rimless bifocals, was lean beneath his tweed jacket, pale denim shirt, and earthy tie. "Thanks for meeting with us."

"Doc Daniels will do almost anything for a Varsity chili slaw dog," Cox said. "Especially if I'm paying."

"We all have our Achilles' heel. And Carlton kicks mine once a month just for laughs. I had to postpone an appointment for this escapade. You might be paying, but this hour cost me a hell of a lot more than it will you. Of course, the indigestion provides a lasting memory of your company."

"What d'ya have, Charlotte?" Cox imitated the cashiers.

"What's good?"

"Chili dogs, fries, rings, even glorified steaks if you want to get fancy." Cox pointed at the food on the tray in front of them. "Fried pies, too, peach or apple."

Charlotte, swept up in the chaos, sneaked a look at the menu. "Do you ever eat vegetables, fish, salad, anything that's not fried?"

"Why? I'm betting my lungs and liver will give out long before my heart. There's salad on the menu. Never tried it. The V cooks with peanut oil if it makes you feel healthier."

"What d'ya have?" the cashier said to Cox.

"Doc will have two chili slaw dogs, rings and a small frosted orange." Daniels nodded as Cox ordered. "Charlotte?"

"Diet Coke."

"Suit yourself." He turned to the cashier. "And three chilidogs, fries, fried peach pie, and two Diet Cokes. Calories don't count if you wash the meal down with diet soda. Oh, don't forget the chopped onions."

The cashier piled food on a plastic tray, Cox paid, and they meandered through the swelling line to the closest television room. Charlotte sat on a plastic chair that wobbled when she leaned left. Cox hoisted the industrial-sized condiment dispenser and squirted a pond of ketchup. He sprinkled a layer of raw onions on the chilidogs. She craved sushi and sipped her drink.

"I understand you have some questions about obsessive-compulsive neurosis." Daniels bit an onion ring and wiped his mouth.

"Yes. Carlton suggested your expertise might be helpful. How do you spot it, treat it? How severe can it become?"

Doughy chilidog clung to Cox's teeth and tongue. "She thinks an obsessive-compulsive murdered her sister."

"Carlton!"

"If you waltz around the question we'll be here until dinner." Cox swallowed a large bite and hit his chest. "Doc, could an obsessive-compulsive kill to alleviate the obsession?"

"Compulsive violence? Rare, but not unheard of. Maybe you could enlighten me with the background?"

Charlotte's nails gouged Cox's forearm. "You've said enough. I'll tell him." She collected her thoughts while she fiddled with the straw. "A week ago last Friday, my sister was beaten to death in her home in Tampa. No signs of forced entry or robbery. Margaret, my sister, was a kind soul with horrible homemaking skills. Dust, piles, unorganized, she never bothered with cleaning house.

"After her funeral, I offered to help pack her possessions." Charlotte's eyes rolled up to Daniels. "How can I explain this? You know, when you go somewhere you've been on hundreds of occasions, but you feel like you've never been there before. It was eerie. I'd been to Margaret's house countless times. Then I realized the difference—the floors sparkled, vacuum marks on the carpet, not a speck of dust. The Tampa police think I'm an idiot, but I swear her killer thoroughly cleaned before he fled. I shared this with Carlton last night, and he said these actions resembled obsessive-compulsive behavior. Could Margaret's death be OCD related?"

Daniels propped his elbows on the table, interlocked his fingers, and rested his chin on his hands, engrossed with the topic. "Certainly a criminal's tendency would be to put as much distance as possible between himself and the victim. I imagine attempts to efface physical evidence are typical. If I'm not prying, can you elaborate on what you believe the killer altered?"

"Your food's getting cold, Doc," Cox said.

Daniels's eyes never strayed from Charlotte.

"Yes, Kenneth," Charlotte said, ignoring Cox. "The kitchen floor had been mopped. The dishes washed and put away. Newspapers and periodicals stacked in chronological order. The shelves, tables and knickknacks dusted."

"Don't forget the CDs and books," Cox added.

"Right. He alphabetized Margaret's music. The books were rearranged by height. The carpet had been thoroughly vacuumed."

"And where was your sister?" Daniels asked.

"That's the strangest part. The police found her in her bed, bathed, hair washed and combed, in her favorite nightgown...with her head caved in!" No tears trickled through closed eyelashes. She inhaled and opened her eyes. "The bastard bathed her, then scrubbed the blood out of the tub."

"Not that I doubt you, Charlotte, but is it possible your sister straightened her house for a visitor?"

"The cops insist that's what happened," Charlotte's head swung from side to side, "but they don't know her. No, Margaret didn't, wouldn't, and couldn't clean her home like I saw it, even if she wanted to."

Daniels removed his bifocals. "A sibling would know. I believe you." He buffed his eyeglasses with a napkin.

Cox slurped the bottom of his drink. "So what do you think, Doc?"

"Compulsive cleaning with total disregard for the consequences of an illegal act undoubtedly bears a likeness to a ritualistic reaction, to an obsessive thought or fear. From the limited data you relayed, I am relatively convinced this killer exhibits OCD traits."

"I knew it!" Cox slapped his palm on the table and nodded at Charlotte.

"However," Daniels continued, "based on what you've told me, the theory that the murder was an obsession-stimulated compulsion is less credible. Although tidiness and compulsive behavior are not exclusive to OCD and often are attributes for successful, driven individuals, the majority of people suffering from OCD experience similar symptoms such as persistent housecleaning, washing hands repeatedly, hoarding, changing clothes incessantly, constant rearranging of tabletops, furniture, even utensils in the dishwasher. You've described a text book compulsive purging of an involuntary obsession, and yet you've implied two compulsive acts occurred in succession."

Charlotte looked confused, her expression blank, and felt stupid. "So he has OCD or not?"

"Yes, there is a high probability your killer suffers from OCD, but it's less than conclusive that he killed due to the disorder. Can someone with OCD kill? Sure, as can someone with cold or dandruff. The question is, did he kill *because* of OCD?"

"I must be dense, Kenneth." Charlotte sensed the doctor's frustration in communicating the clinically obvious in laymen's terminology. "Please help me understand."

Daniels scooped frosted orange in a plastic spoon and savored the bite.

"Go back a step or two," Cox suggested. "Give us the *OCD for Dummies* version."

"Okay, Carlton. Square one. Obsessive-compulsive neurosis is the inability to resist or stop continuous abnormal thoughts or fears combined with repetitive, involuntary defensive behavior. Long ago it was believed life experiences caused the disorder, but we now are convinced OCD is biological. Coexisting disorders such as depression, organic brain syndrome, and schizophrenia often make the disorder difficult to diagnose and may even contribute to its onset. With me so far?"

"Yes," Charlotte said while Cox crammed the end of a chilidog in his mouth.

"The disorder is comprised of two features: the involuntary invasion of conscious awareness, an obsession with," Daniels paused, "danger, contamination, worry—"

"Imperfection?" Charlotte interrupted.

"Worry about the execution of a project, plan, scenario," the doctor thought aloud. "Sure. Where was I? Oh, part two, compulsion, or the action compelled in response to obsession.

"The compulsive action temporarily relieves the obsessive-compulsive from his or her raging neurosis. I've returned to the barrier in my communication capabilities. Generally, a second compulsive action does not piggy-back—"

"Now, there's medical jargon I can latch on to," Cox said.

"On the first." The doctor turned from Cox to Charlotte. "At your sister's house, if murder served as compulsive response, the killer would have experienced short-lived relief, thus nullifying the necessity to clean house, since he had already expelled the obsession. Clearer?"

The chair shifted when Charlotte crossed her legs. "Yes, thank you. One compulsion to each obsession."

Daniels chewed on a chili slaw dog and nodded.

"But could a compulsion become violent?" Charlotte asked.

Attempting to swallow, he held up a hand. "Yes, I suppose hostility is possible, but highly unusual. However..." Daniels deliberated while he licked teeth beneath his lower lip.

"However, what?" Cox bellowed.

"Well, I suppose an unfulfilled compulsion could create sufficient anxiety such that an obsessive-compulsive might resort to aggression."

"Pent-up anxiety? Compulsion ticking like a time bomb?" Rubbing a thumb on her chin, Charlotte leaned forward. "So if he arrived with stoked-up anxiety he could have killed Margaret to appease a by then substantially suppressed obsession."

"Yes, but that doesn't explain the compulsive housecleaning," Daniels said.

"What if something in her home set him off, smacked him into an immediate relapse?" Cox asked.

"Like Margaret's tousled house," she added.

The doctor rolled his eyes up and bobbed his head. "Back-to-back obsessions. Yes, again it's possible. As one subsides, another thrives. But again, a compulsion severe enough to kill is not common." He ate the last onion ring and shoved his plate away. Daniels stretched his arm and checked his watch. "I have a one o'clock. I really should be going."

"You've been very helpful," Charlotte said. "Can I ask two more questions?"

"If they're quick."

Cox eyed the remaining chili slaw dog on Daniels's plate. "You finished, Doc?"

"That's why he orders me two," Daniels said to Charlotte. "Help yourself, Carlton."

As Cox dragged the plate across the table and shot a stream of mustard atop the slaw, Charlotte said, "Is there a way to detect OCD?"

"I'm afraid diagnosis can be a challenge. First, as I said earlier, compulsive behavior in itself is not abnormal. Nearly all obsessive-compulsives are cognizant of their condition. Unfortunately, due to embarrassment or the inclination of *I can beat this myself*, they often hide the malady and are proficient in cloaking their illness from others. The simple answer to your question is that most treatment of OCD comes as a result of an individual seeking help." He rose from the table and reached inside his coat. "I didn't even say I'm sorry about your sister. I have a sister. I can't even imagine what you must be going through. Here's my card, Charlotte. Call me if I can be of further assistance. I need go."

"Can't be late for a patient with an inferiority complex, Doc?" Cox asked.

"Something like that." Daniels backed from the table.

"Last question," Charlotte hurried her words. "If an obsessive-compulsive squelched an obsession by killing, would he be compelled to kill again to stifle the same or a similar obsession?"

She sensed Cox's gaze and looked at him. He stopped in mid-chew. She enjoyed shocking the ever-alert journalist masked as a rumpled drunken cynic.

"Given a previous hostile compulsion, a low-probability assumption, I mind you, yes, the likelihood of a repeated behavior to an identical stimulus, much like muscle memory, is a highly feasible occurrence. I'm afraid it's human nature to solve parallel problems with the comparable tools." He retrieved car keys from a trouser pocket. "Nice to meet you, Charlotte. Thanks for lunch, Carlton."

They bid Daniels farewell, and he merged into the horde of Varsity patrons.

"What's with the kill again mumbo jumbo?" Cox blurted out before Daniels had even walked out of sight.

"A San Antonio business woman was murdered in St. Louis early this morning. Beat to death at the Marriott. Could bad pitching and murder equal obsession and compulsion?"

Cox yanked a cigarette from his shirt pocket, then glared at the no smoking sign. "Damn. How did you find out?"

"Dumb luck. Liz and I surfed the *Post-Dispatch* Web site for the game story. The story was under the breaking news section." Charlotte paused before she posed her question. "What if he kills after each bad performance?"

She braced for ridicule.

"An OCD serial killer?"

"Liz thought you might consider helping me cross-reference Traynor's blown saves to contemporaneous murders in the cities where he pitched poorly."

"You bet your ass I will." His chair toppled over as he bounced to his feet with energy Charlotte had not witnessed from Cox. "What are you waiting for? We'll use my office, it's only ten minutes away."

Chapter Sixteen

Suggs stood at the garage apartment door, exposed to casual observation, and scanned the yard and street from the stair landing. He tapped on the door, satisfied no one had seen him climb the stairs. His gloved knuckles muffled the knock.

He waited for her to answer, unsure what he'd find and what he'd do inside the apartment. A car engine roared below. He froze. A fire engine red Suburban barreled down the serene street. The hatband of his Rome all-stars cap absorbed sweat trickling from his hairline. He shifted his weight and checked again for onlookers.

He knew she was here, alone. Why the hell didn't she answer? He jiggled the doorknob. The door eased open. Stupid bitch had left it unlocked. He lowered a shoulder, nudged the door, and entered.

Suggs withdrew the tire iron, wedged between his belt and flabby waist, like a cavalry officer unsheathing his saber. He cocked the tire iron lug end up, and hunched his shoulders like a wrestler stalking an opponent, ready to swing at anything that moved. He caught a waft of breakfast coffee and heard a small appliance whir. He listened to a vacuum cleaner or hair-dryer humming down the tiny corridor ahead.

He checked that the living room and kitchen were uninhabited and crept toward the electronic hum. Yellow streams spilled from the hall light into two open doorways.

He stood in the entrance to the first room, his girth blocking the light. Spurts of daylight seeped through mini-blinds and provided enough light to see in the otherwise darkened bedroom. A twin bed, a two-drawer bureau, and a suitcase, a fancy carry-on model with wheels, almost filled the walk-in-closet-sized bedroom. The flap was unzipped and folded clothes were stacked near the luggage like someone was living out of the suitcase. Suggs concluded the reporter bunked in this room.

Erratic splotches of movement disrupted a vertical light beam emerging from the bathroom door. The small appliance purred beyond the illuminated door crack. Two steps into the room, Suggs leaned over the dresser and peeked through the gap.

She sat on the vanity stool, like a picture out of *Playboy*, butt naked, facing a mirror, blow-drying her mid-back length hair while she brushed out knots. Hair bristles whisked the small of her back. The sight of her taut rump unnerved him. His noble plans to protect Torch turned toward more self-gratifying intentions.

He stared, aroused by a glimpse of her breasts. *Playboy* live. When he turned twelve, Suggs had gawked at less revealing photos and his mama whupped him until he blistered. So disturbed by the devil at work in her boy, she vowed to enrich him with classic art at a museum in Atlanta. She dragged him through rooms crammed with oil paintings of fat naked woman, lounging around with each other like a pack of dikes. He had thought the lesson was you were allowed to gape at pictures of naked women you'd never think about touching with a distant cousin's cane fishing pole.

His fantasy girl flicked off the hair dryer. She mussed her hair, separated the shiny mane into three strands, and began to braid.

Suggs swung the door open. "Remember me, bitch!"

The woman jerked left.

He ogled below her neckline.

She leapt off the stool and dove for the door opposite him.

Suggs pounced. Sure-handed, he snatched the wrist of her trailing arm.

Her hand on the knob, she tried to yank her arm free from the powerful grip. He wrenched her arm until the doorknob popped from her fingers, clinging to the only way out.

He wrung her arm, trying to separate it from her shoulder. She twisted toward him, and kicked, her foot aimed for his crotch.

He chopped down. The tire iron split her shin. She crumbled, raised her head, and begged, "Please let me go."

Suggs squinted, alarmed and confused. "You ain't her."

"I'm not who?"

Suggs hoisted her up from the floor. "The reporter cunt, Charlotte what's her name."

"No, I'm not her. I'm Liz. This is my place. I'm sure this must be a mistake." Blood gushed from the deep gash beneath her knee. "Please let me go. I won't tell anyone. I swear to God."

"Shit." Sugg's face twisted in a befuddled gaze. "You switched cars."

"She has my Jeep."

The tire iron slipped from his hand, bounded on the tile, and fractured floor squares. Still holding her wrist with his left hand, he pressed his right on Liz's breast.

Her body shivered. "That's nice. Can we do more?" Liz pleaded in a shaky, fearful tone.

"Hell fire!" Suggs shoved her.

Backside first, Liz shattered the glass shower doors. The tub caught her calves. She tripped, floundering backward. Glass shards shredded the underside of her legs. Her body took flight. Her head slammed the shower tile like a police battering ram.

Her legs, hung on jagged glass and streaked with fresh blood, draped over the tub edge. Liz's body slumped into the tub, her arms, neck, and torso tangled in a contorted glob.

"Shit. It's the other one," Suggs mumbled.

Chapter Seventeen

Charlotte pointed to the *Post-Dispatch* article on Cox's monitor. He clicked the print icon and picked up the phone.

"Ted, this is Carlton Cox at the news desk." Cox stuck an unlit cigarette in his mouth. An *AJC* sportswriter, Ted Benson wrote Braves' sidebars and filled in when Pierce Pope was not available. "I need an assist from sports."

"How can I help, Cox?" Benson replied.

"Statistics on Torch Traynor."

"You freelancing a sports piece? That ought to stand the hair on Pierce's neck. You know the Internet is crammed with stats."

"I'm in a hurry, and I'll bloody my fingers surfing for the detail I need," Cox said.

"All right. I'll give it a shot."

"Blown saves." He pretended to inhale the cigarette and added, "Opponent, when and where."

"The fiasco in St. Louis last night should be fresh on your mind. Give me a couple of minutes. What's your extension?"

"Seventeen twelve." He thanked Benson and hung up.

The Hewlett Packard inkjet printed the report of Megan Rivers's murder. Charlotte retrieved the document and handed it to Cox. He devoured the text, reading like he ate.

"You were lucky to stumble on this tidbit." He laughed, enticing a growling cough. "Ironic, isn't it? If Pope had transmitted by deadline, you wouldn't have logged on to the *Post-Dispatch*."

"I guess not." She crossed her arms and waited for Cox to smile, give a thumbs up, or any sign of confirmation. "Well, is it him?"

"Woman alone. Wee hours of the morning. Blunt-force trauma. Lot of similarity." He clenched the cigarette filter between his teeth and grinned. "Yeah, I think there could be a connection."

Charlotte smiled.

"Instinct's not enough," Cox said. "We need to add facts to this cerebral love fest. We'll start with the surface stuff. Media coverage. I want to build a file with game coverage of each blown save, and the corresponding murder reports. If the time, places, and modus operandi spell out a compelling and plausible scenario, maybe the cops in one of the cities will catch the scent. Once the cops compare and share notes, including the signature evidence they keep close to their chests, like the neat freak bit, then maybe murders will link. I can get *AJC* coverage of the blown saves from Ted. Do you have *The Tampa Tribune* article on your sister's death?"

She shook her head.

"No, I suppose that's not a keepsake to fold in your wallet."

"I'll call Jeb. He writes for *The Tampa Tribune*. He'll send me a copy."

The phone rang.

"Cox," he answered on the first ring. The cigarette tumbled to his lap as he scrambled for a pen. "Right, Philadelphia, got it.... Keep going, Chicago, August twenty-second." He wrote fast as he repeated pieces of Benson's information. "September seventh, and St. Louis. Thanks, Ted. Oh, can you get your hands on a copy of the stories for me?" He listened. "Three o'clock is fine. I owe you a beer."

She peered over Cox's shoulder at the illegible scribble. "I can't read it."

"My own shorthand." He squinted. "Philadelphia, June twelfth. July one, and July fifth in San Fran and, well, this could be interesting, Atlanta. Chicago, August twenty-second. And of course, Tampa and St. Louis, the seventh and seventeenth of September."

Her face somber, Charlotte said, "I feel like a ghoul, Carlton."

"Digging for bodies distasteful? Shake it off. We very well could be chasing your imagination. But if we do trip into an open grave or two, remember we didn't kill them, and if we're damn lucky maybe we can prevent the next murder."

Cox ignored the no smoking poster taped to the wall above his cubicle and lit the gummed cigarette. He pointed at an empty cubicle that mirrored his workstation. "Call your friend. Fax it here." He handed her a business card. "I'll start with the *AJC* stacks, July sixth, then follow up with Philly and the Windy City."

"Dial nine to get out?" Charlotte crossed the aisle.

He flipped pages of a tattered address book. "Yep."

Much like Cox's desk, stacked files and heaped correspondence cluttered the desk. A sun-faded 1999 Hooter's calendar drooped from a jumbo paperclip rigged as a hanger. Thumbtacks pinned children's school photos to a fabric cubicle panel. Charlotte opened her laptop case, found her Day-Timer, and pinched the address tap.

Italian leather enclosed her calendar, address book, and daily journal. She hadn't accessed the Day-Timer in more than a week. Pitiful, her whole life amounted to the contents within the one-inch binder. The time away from work had broken the trance, the addiction to the type 'A' bible she consulted before each breath. She was tempted to fling her once all-consuming existence in the trashcan, cast her former self away with fast-food wrappers and discarded coffee cups. She hesitated in a tense blink, rebuffed the sublime inclination, and scrolled a finger through the 'O' listings. She stopped at Jeb Owens's cell phone and punched the number.

"Hello," a grumpy voice responded.

"Did I wake you?"

"Charlotte!" Jeb perked up. A horn blared. "Shit, I almost gave that Benz a Corolla enema. How's journalism 101?"

"I flunked out."

"I knew you couldn't sustain a lie. I just knew it. How'd they find out?"

"Does it matter?" Charlotte closed the Day-Timer and lowered it to the open laptop case pocket.

"I should have known. You're too dignified to pass as a sleazy hack."

She glanced across the aisle at Cox keyboarding and talking on the phone. She envisioned the pair of writers reveling in an intense session ripping their chosen vocation. "Is bashing yourself a journalistic ritual?"

"Writers carry illusions of grandeur; however, as reporters reality slaps us daily with our inferiority. Where are you?"

"*The Atlanta Journal-Constitution*. They've been very helpful, Jeb...even after I confessed." A twinge of guilt caused a brief pause. So much had happened since Sunday when Pierce departed for St. Louis, she had forgotten to reveal her guise to him. Make a note in her Day-Timer.... No, she could remember on her own. "I'm here with Carlton Cox. He's a crime writer. You won't believe it. We think Traynor killed another woman in St. Louis."

"No way! I watched him go from goat to hero last night. You're pulling my chain, right?"

"Remember the Down the Hatch bartender said Traynor pitched badly the night Margaret died?"

"I was at the game. Whoa! I've seen my share of locker smashing, but you're implying blown save equals murder."

"Unbelievable, isn't it? He might have obsessive-compulsive disorder, OCD. It explains Margaret's immaculate apartment. Pent-up anxiety released a violent explosion. Carlton is helping me research the possibility of other deaths close to Traynor's bad performances. That's why I called. I need a favor."

"Give me an exclusive if you bag Torch?"

"Jeb Owens! Are we negotiating? If there really is a story it's Carlton's. You understand, don't you?"

"Sure, can't blame a guy for trying. You know I'd do anything for you, but the cost of Pampers is killing me."

"Can you dig out the *Tribune* report on Margaret's murder?"

"I'll plow through the stacks pronto. Give me a fax number."

She recited the number on Cox's card. "Send it to Carlton Cox's attention. Thanks, Jeb."

Charlotte hung up and walked up on Cox's conversation.

"Is that all? Thursday, August twenty-third edition, right?" A frown highlighted Cox's scowl as he listened. "Well, thanks anyway, Max."

Charlotte propped on the edge of his desk. "Who was that?"

"Max Sheppard, *Chicago Sun Times*. Rosalyn Metcalf, an old friend at the *Chicago Tribune*, gave me his name." He looked at Charlotte, his cheeks sagging with dejection. "Nothing close in Chicago the day after blown save four in Chicago. A couple of domestic disputes, a robbery shooting, and a carjacking."

She lifted the pad and reviewed the list. "How about Philadelphia?"

"I left a message for Dominque Valenti at the *Inquirer*." Cox nodded his head at the computer monitor. July sixth articles, the titles underlined in blue, filled the screen. "Zilch. I wrote half of them. Two accidental deaths, and a house fire started by a Fourth of July Roman candle. If no murders in the *Constitution* is good news, then why do I feel so shitty?"

"Because I'm grasping at air and you're trying to keep me from facing the harsh truth that I'll never drum up enough proof to accuse Traynor of being anything more than another drunken ballplayer." Charlotte leaned forward and laid a hand on Cox's forearm. "Beneath the banter, the gruff exterior, and the secondhand smoke cloud, you have a good heart. Thanks for trying."

"Now, don't you go around vindicating my soiled reputation. I've invested countless hours and half my liver to become who I am. Colorful. Memorable—"

"Unapproachable, distant, drunk, cranky." Charlotte quipped.

An electronic ring interrupted them.

He thumped the speaker button on the phone. "Cox."

"Carlton, Dom Valenti here. Got your message. What's cooking down *yonder*?"

Cox reduced the speakerphone volume. "Do you have rapid access to the *Inquirer* stacks?"

"All business today, aren't you? Yeah, I can log in from here."

"I'm looking for a metro-Philadelphia murder in the Wednesday, June thirteenth edition."

Keystrokes rattled through the speaker. "You going to cut me in if your story ties to a Philly murder?"

"It's the end of the rainbow, Woodward and Bernstein shit. There's plenty to share if the stars line up."

"You're blowing smoke, Carlton," Valenti said. "Aren't you? There, June one three, right?"

Charlotte swallowed a nervous breath, and shifted closer. A schoolteacher in Tampa and business traveler in St. Louis murdered with the Atlanta Braves in town. Two cities, two women clubbed to death. A third murder would dispel skepticism with bulging probability and proximity. Her heart fluttered like an out-of-work father holding a lotto ticket, his first five numbers flashing on the television, spellbound as the last lottery ball is sucked into the opaque tube. Charlotte wished not for millions, only corroboration.

"Yeah, Dom, the thirteenth," Cox said.

Valenti cleared his throat. "Here we go. Cop shot by motorist. A John Doe, knifed—homeless guy it appears. Lover's spat, gay couple, murder-suicide. Any nibbles?"

"Nowhere close," Cox, disappointed, answered. "Anything else?"

"I know murders are a dime a dozen down there, but three in one day is big news up here, Carlton."

"Maybe a Caucasian, female, thirty to forty?"

"Nope," Valenti replied. "There goes my Pulitzer."

Cox thanked Valenti and hung up. "Strike three, Charlotte."

Clinging to the waning supposition, Charlotte said, "What about San Francisco?"

"It's early out west. I'll call the *Examiner* later." The chair squeaked as he spun. "Bottom of the ninth and we're down by ten, kid. I have an article to write. I'll call you at Liz's after I speak to Benny Latchman in San Fran."

Charlotte lifted the computer case and shuffled toward the exit, grim and defeated.

Chapter Eighteen

Charlotte released the clutch and rolled forward in the pre-rush hour gridlock on North Avenue. A stark blue sky above, a steady autumn breeze whipped through the corporate tower gauntlet. She steered the topless Jeep and basked in brilliant sunshine while the chill speckled her bare arms with goose bumps. She stopped at North and Piedmont, reached behind the passenger seat, nabbed Liz's gray fleece, and wiggled into instant warmth.

Who the hell did she think she was, a Sue Grafton heroine? What in the world made her think she was qualified to solve a murder and expose a deranged serial killer with a hand washing fetish? The time had come to end the charade, quit teasing her obsession with accountability—blame for Margaret's death—and face responsibility.

Time, she checked her watch. Ten 'til three.

She remembered James's e-mail. He landed this evening. Texas, accounting, James—in a modest span of days, her immediate past seemed months ago. She should apologize to James, depart for San Angelo, and resume her work with vigor, a hunger like…like Cox gulping a cheeseburger, chomping balance sheets and income statements, drooling variable margin from the corner of her mouth.

Charlotte coasted into the peaceful neighborhood, thankful to exit throbbing traffic. The line of mature oaks blocked warm rays. She downshifted, turned in the driveway, and parked behind the rental car.

A gust of wind ruffled the tree line. Hickory leaves took flight and drifted to trimmed fescue for a future skirmish with a rake. A burst of sunlight rushed through wavy limbs and basted the cracked concrete drive in blondish strokes. A fine spray of illuminated dots, like gold specs glistening beneath a mountain stream, twinkled from the pavement surrounding the Malibu.

Charlotte unbuckled her seatbelt and climbed down from the Jeep. The breeze subsided, slammed shut the beam's momentary portal, and painted the driveway in bleak shade. She removed her sunglasses, wrapped them on the bill of her cap, and eased toward the luminous particles.

Glass. She squatted and picked up a glass sliver. Thick glass. Tempered glass chunks. She grimaced, certain of the damage she'd discover when she looked left, uncertain if the insurance coverage she selected would pay for broken windows.

She rose from the ground and inspected the Malibu. Shattered remains of the front windshield and left passenger window buried the beige cloth interior under a glassy carpet. A loose shard fell from the rubber windshield seal. Charlotte examined the debris for a ball, a brick, any hint of an accident or deliberate vandalism.

She spun her head to the stairs. Liz must have heard the crash. Her gaze climbed the stairs. The open door surprised Charlotte. "Liz. Are you there?"

Her boots crunched the broken glass. She walked to the wooden staircase, her eyes fixed on the door. She gripped the weathered wooden rail and ran up the stairs.

"Liz," she said, louder this time. "Where are you?"

The door curtain flapped through the top half of the wood door. Door glass glazed the landing like a sheet of crushed ice.

Her heart rate soared to triple digits. Charlotte bounded to the landing and burst into the apartment. A smoldering odor, more like sparking wires than burnt toast, stopped her just inside the door. *That's it.* Liz had opened the door to air out the smoky aroma.

"Liz! This isn't funny."

A thump. Rapid movement to her right. She flinched. A tabby cat scurried from beneath the overturned sofa, darted past Charlotte's feet, and out the door.

She stared at Liz's sofa, wooden peg legs pointing upward from the ragged furniture underside. A couch arm rested atop a pile of splintered wood, once a coffee table. Her eyes scaled the walls, each blink like a camera shutter photographing the destruction.

Liz's picture frames were smashed, shattered on the floor, the photos mangled beyond recognition. She edged forward, her stunned glower sweeping from the small living room to the kitchen area. Minuscule smoke curls spiraled up from severe cracks in the Gateway CPU tower and monitor. Rippled veneer and dinette table parts littered the floor. The refrigerator door was open. Broken beer bottles, crushed condiments, and squashed vegetables coated the linoleum like a landfill layer.

Sudden fear screamed, *Run!* And she would once she was sure Liz was gone. Where? Out on a long run. A burglar cased the apartment, waited until Liz jogged away, and broke in.

"Liz!" Charlotte entered the dark hallway. She flipped the light switch. Nothing. She glanced up. The fractured fixture swayed by a single wire.

An angled shadow blocked the light from Charlotte's bedroom. She drew a deep breath. The upended dresser obstructed the entrance. She shoved the bureau enough to wiggle into the room. The room smelled like a neglected portable potty. Soaked clothes piled next to her luggage formed an island in the urine puddle. She bunched her nose, disgusted by the thought.

She took cautious strides toward the bathroom through toiletries strewn from the dresser top. Near the door, Charlotte studied the vanity, undisturbed except for the blow dryer on the floor. She hadn't noticed the broken tiles before, but she could have overlooked the chipped floor. She swung her head to the right.

"Oh, my God! Liz!"

She spotted a foot inches above the floor. Jagged glass impaled the calf muscle. A brown tributary snaked down the tub side to form a pond of coagulated blood.

Charlotte rushed to the tub, and dropped to her knees. Dried blood matted Liz's tangled hair. Liz's other leg was wrenched behind her knotted body. Pinkish gray tissue oozed from the crushed left side of her head. Although her eyes were open, the witty smile in Liz's eyes had extinguished.

"No, Liz." Charlotte pressed fingers against Liz's throat, gagged, and swallowed the urge to vomit. Liz's bronze skin felt cool. Desperate, she probed Liz's neck for a pulse. "Please, Lord," she prayed for the faintest flicker of life.

A door slammed. A chill raced up Charlotte's spine, through her shoulders. Her fingertips tingled. The floor joists popped and creaked. Panic and die. She spun on her knees searching the bathroom for a defense.

Chapter Nineteen

Charlotte crawled to the vanity. Toilet paper, Comet, sponges, and a plunger—she found nothing in the cabinet to fight with. She slid open the drawer, careful to be quiet. Toothpaste, vitamins, Tampons. She dug deeper. Scissors. She grasped the handles like a dagger.

She clambered from the floor. She pressed her shoulders to the wall between the tub and the door and gasped in short spurts, the terror depleting oxygen as fast as she could replenish it. Jab and run like hell. She raised the closed scissors over her head.

A hefty voice spoke indiscernible words from the hallway. A grumbled whisper answered him from Charlotte's room. Two? If they had returned, they wouldn't expect her to be here. A quick attack, shock them, run, and scream bloody murder all the way. A thin wall separated her from... She glanced at Liz and tightened her grip.

She heard him inhale followed by a click that sounded like child's toy cricket. Two static bursts ensued as if a second cricket replied.

The door from Liz's bedroom burst open. His brown eyes bulging, the policeman dropped to a knee and aimed his semi-automatic weapon at Charlotte. "Drop it, now!"

The scissors whirled and bounced on the tile. "Oh, thank God."

The second policeman jerked Charlotte's left wrist and spun her arm behind her back. "Nobody cuts Calvin Hines! On the floor!" He shoved her forward, and lowered her to the floor face first.

"Shit, Calvin!" The first officer gawked at the tub. "It's a bad one."

Hines wrestled handcuffs onto Charlotte's wrists. He turned to the tub. "Man, the things folks do to one another. Call it in and tell 'em to get homicide here, fast."

Cox flicked the cigarette nub, burned to the filter, to the driveway and bounded toward the stairs.

"Can't go up, there," Officer Hines said. "You know that, Carlton. Homicide and the GBI techies," he referred to the Georgia Bureau of Investigation crime scene investigators, "are tagging and bagging."

"Where is she, Calvin?" Cox frequented crime scenes and recognized the policeman.

Hines pointed at an Atlanta police cruiser.

He spotted Charlotte's profile in backseat. "You couldn't possibly think she is a suspect?"

"Thought so at first. We found her in the bathroom with the victim. Tried to stick me with scissors, she did. She must have thought I was the guy that done that to her friend. Anyway, the Gilberts, the folks that own the house, noticed the broken glass and open door around two thirty and called us."

"She was with me," Cox interrupted.

"That's what she said. The Gilberts watched Miss Gordon arrive. Poor woman tripped over the body before we got here. A bad scene, even for an old-timer like me. She asked us to call you."

Cox stomped toward the police car through an emergency vehicle maze.

Charlotte folded her arms to stay warm. A chill numbed her toes and fingers like her blood refused to circulate.

The sharp tap on the window startled her. She looked up and smiled. Cox's nicotine-stained grin greeted her. She fumbled for the door handle, amazed how much she wanted to see the paunchy grouch. Alone, she sought comfort from a man with the compassion of a boulder. Where was the damn handle?

Cox pulled the door open. "Hotel California, kid. Riders only check out when the driver is ready."

Charlotte leapt from the seat, wrapped her arms around his thick torso, and burrowed her face into his shoulder. "It was awful, Carlton. Hideous. Poor Liz."

Cox draped his arms around her slight frame. "It's okay, kid. Are you hurt?"

She shook her head into his shoulder. She wanted a good cry, but overworked tears vetoed the impulse.

"Do you want to tell me about it, Charlotte?"

She rubbed her nose against plaid shirt wrinkles. The broken windows, the ransacked apartment, Liz's haunting stare, the terror proceeding, and the relief to be cuffed on the floor, she muttered and rambled, never lifting her head from the embrace. When her scary tale ceased she snuggled close to Cox, feeling safe, protected.

Minutes later, she whispered, "Thanks, Carlton."

"For what?"

"You're a good hugger."

"Lots of padding. All the time away from the gym finally paid off. I'm soft as a feather mattress." He reached for conversation. "I brought you a copy of the file, including the fax from your friend in Tampa. It's in the car. Came up empty at the *Examiner* and the *Chronicle* in San Fran. Goose eggs."

She eased away from him. "Wild goose chase. Goose eggs. Appropriate, huh? I'm giving up before this black cloud chasing me hurts someone else."

"Don't you dare blame Liz's death on yourself!"

"I show up, move in, and she dies. I'm sick and tired of coincidences that end in death. Brutal death to people I care about. Bad news comes in sets of three. What's next?"

"That's plain bullshit. Don't start this poor-pitiful-me crap. That's not you, Charlotte. Get this through your pretty head, you're not involved unless by some implausible fluke the same son-of-a-bitch killed your sister and Liz."

"Do you think that's possible?"

"No fricking way. Not from what you've told me." He pulled a cigarette from his shirt pocket. Cox waved the unlit smoke and went on, "This guy wrecked Liz's place. In Tampa, the creep hangs around mopping and dusting like he's the night janitor. If he's OCD, like Doc Daniels said, order is restored temporarily. He's calm. Upstairs," he pointed as a cop came out Liz's door, "he goes ballistic, raging bull in the proverbial china shop, busting everything in his path. If the killer *is* one in the same, he cleans up his toys after he plays."

Cox struck a match and touched the flame to the cigarette. He inhaled the tobacco, alive with orange heat. "Atlanta, middle of the damn day. Tampa and St. Louis, after midnight. Rough and tumble throw Liz's head into the shower wall versus flailing an object with precision strokes. And—"

"Traynor is in St. Louis."

"That's right. If the murders are connected, your prime suspect," Cox looked at his watch, "is shagging fly balls about now."

She rubbed a raw wrist. "My watch came off when they cuffed me. What time is it?"

"Did they hurt you?"

"I can't blame them. Women with sharp objects scare the bravest of men. The time?"

"Five twenty-five."

Charlotte glanced at the crowd. Police held back television cameramen, while GBI and medical examiner personnel cataloged, photographed, and dusted Liz's apartment.

"I'm supposed to meet someone at the airport tonight," she mumbled, overcome by the whirl of activity on the lawn.

"I'll drive you."

Two police cruisers blocked Liz's Jeep. "I hate to inconvenience you, Carlton, but I'll never get out of this parking lot. Should I tell the police I'm leaving?"

"Always found it easier to beg for forgiveness than ask for permission. They'll never let you go and they'll never know you're gone."

"Let's go." Charlotte followed Cox toward the street. "Wait. He wanted me to bring my computer. It's in the Jeep."

Chapter Twenty

Rude, business-at-any-cost travelers plowed toward their next destination. Executives and salespeople barked into cell phones, immune to the airport milieu, juggling their laptops and carry-on bags. The hurried pace, the buzzers, blinkers and bilingual signs could intimidate, frighten the weakhearted or inexperienced. The Hartsfield-Jackson Atlanta International Airport pandemonium exuded a comforting familiarity for Charlotte, visions of herself, under normal circumstances, scrolling through voice mail in a full sprint to a connecting flight.

Airport security allowed only passengers with valid tickets to go from the main terminal to the gates. Connecting with James in the main terminal would be a logistic nightmare. Using her return ticket to Dallas, she checked in on a late flight so she could greet James Houston at his gate. With no intent of flying tonight, she would later rebook the ticket, claiming she'd been delayed, and missed the flight.

She waited at gate seventeen in the 'A' terminal. The gate seats overflowed with passengers, carry-on luggage, and briefcases. Charlotte leaned against a floor-to-ceiling window and admired the horizon ablaze in a burnt orange sunset. The Boeing 767 obeyed the glowing traffic wands and veered toward the terminal. The jet lurched forward and shuddered as the jet engines rumbled. She looked at the inexpensive Timex she purchased in an airport gift shop. Seven thirty-seven, flight 1465 was a mere two minutes late. Luggage, catering, and fuel vehicles wheeled toward the airliner and blurred the tarmac in activity.

James always flew first class, showing off the badge of the privileged. He would be among the first to disembark. She found a compact in her purse and cringed at the haggard likeness that stared back. She folded Liz's cap and shoved it in her handbag. She brushed hat tangles straight and pinched pale hollow cheeks pink.

The gate door opened. Charlotte meandered toward the arriving passengers.

A flight attendant emerged with impatient passengers, yakking into flip phones, on her heels like a pack of starved wolves. Then came James, poised, tall, wrinkle free. How did he do that? He strode forward, polished, elegant, unusual for most men and impossible in a brown suit. He closed his phone and slid it into a rich leather portfolio.

"James." Charlotte waved. "Over here."

She wriggled through the crowd, threw her arms around his neck, and rose up on her toes to kiss his cheek.

He dropped his arms to his side. His shoulder muscles flinched.

"I'm so glad to see you, James. It's been horrible," Charlotte rambled on. "How long will you be in Atlanta? Maybe…"

Charlotte saw the bleach blonde exit the tunnel over James's shoulder. Leslie—she forgot the recent Arkansas graduate's last name—approached them. She wore a gray wool suit, and a burgundy blouse over her huge breasts.

Her eyes glued to the PW&B rookie accountant, Charlotte asked, "Did you check your luggage, James?"

"You remember Leslie Burlington?" He nodded to the blonde.

Leslie extended a hand. "We met in Dallas."

Her arms resting on James's shoulders, Charlotte turned to him. She shunned Leslie's greeting. "What is this, James?"

"No luggage, Charlotte. We have a late dinner with an irate client, and return to Dallas on the redeye. Do you have any idea the revenues Time Warner generates for Payne, Wyman and Bradford?"

Charlotte lowered her arms and shook her head.

"I suppose not." James clenched his lips. "Of course, you must be aware Time Warner owns TBS and the Atlanta Braves."

"I am."

"Then you understand that your unprofessional and accusatory meddling in the affairs of Atlanta Braves' personnel may cost PW&B millions in fees."

Charlotte gasped. "I'm sorry. I didn't realize."

"I'm afraid *sorry* won't suffice, Charlotte. Austin Hendricks has relayed his version of your masquerade to a disturbing level. Unless I can convince Hendricks that your actions were a rogue act, unsanctioned and unbeknownst to our assets, then it is highly probable that Time Warner will enact punitive measures against PW&B. I hate groveling." He swept brunette curls from his forehead. "At a minimum, I'll offer a rate reduction to entice them to stay with us. You can imagine the wasted margin your indiscretion will cause."

"PW&B shouldn't be held accountable for the personal behavior of its employees," Charlotte said.

"Public accounting is integrity. We sell our people by the hour. Clients shop, thump our rinds like a cantaloupe, and if they catch even one rotten whiff, then they run to the competition like an Ebola-enraged primate is in pursuit."

"Let me talk to Hendricks." Charlotte folded her arms. "I'll tell him the misunderstanding is my fault, independent of the firm. It's the least I can do, James."

James turned to Leslie and held open his hand. She lifted a folder from her shoulder bag and gave it to him.

"I'm glad you see it that way, although meeting with Hendricks will not be necessary." He opened the folder and offered Charlotte a single sheet of stationary engraved with the PW&B logo. "We've addressed your regret. A peace offering, before I cave on billing rates."

Speed reading, Charlotte scanned her resignation. "Are you firing me?"

He held out a gold Mont-Blanc pen. "Should you unwisely decline to resign, then involuntary termination will be a necessary alternative."

"I've worked my ass off for you, James." Her upper arms trembled. "I've been in every godforsaken snake pit it Texas and never complained, never whined once. This is the thanks, the support a PW&B partner gives a steady employee that falters…once."

"Your choice. If it was me I'd take the severance package. Three months' pay, COBRA benefits, and," he paused, "well, check with human resources for the details. Of course, you can mount your high horse and go down swinging, meanwhile we'll present a second letter," Leslie held up a similar document, "indicating that PW&B terminated you for conduct contradictory to our professional standard. Probably a more palatable negotiating point with Hendricks. So decide quickly, before I change my mind. Oh, and I'll need your computer and company credit card."

She scribbled her signature. "I have personal files on the laptop."

"Company property, you know that, Charlotte. Don't worry, I'll have someone review your files and send your personal items."

Leslie took the letter and pen. "Good luck," she said, lowered her eyes, and walked away.

Charlotte dug out the PW&B American Express card from her wallet, removed the IBM laptop from the tattered case, and surrendered her company property to James.

"Although this situation has caused agonizing anxiety for me and the firm, I wish you well, Charlotte."

He turned right and began the journey to the underground train.

Charlotte called to him, "What about us?"

"Us!" James spun, his granite expression cracked with agitation. "*Us*, as in two people that care for each other. A man and woman together, sharing life, in the same place, even if only occasionally. We were lust receptacles at most, but we were never *us*. Goodbye."

He stormed away in long strides with Leslie scurrying to keep up.

"Damn you!" Charlotte stomped the carpeted corridor, irritated he had severed their relationship before she dumped him. Rejection hurt, even though she'd rather walk barefoot through scalding crushed glass than spend another thin second with the arrogant ass.

She counted fingers. One, Margaret's murder. Two, Liz's death. Three, she lost her job. James was gone—a blessing broke her string of bad luck.

"Delta Airlines is now boarding Flight 527 to St. Louis through gate A-sixteen." Fuming as passengers brushed past her, Charlotte heard the announcement from the gate across the corridor. St. Louis? She turned and verified the destination on the electronic board behind the gate agents. St. Louis—departure eight twenty-five.

Charlotte had been torn between responsibility and irrational obsession. James Houston had deleted one variable from the delicate life equation. Now that her career was fixed at zero, the obsession with Margaret's death roared, the obvious challenge, the lone problem to decipher. Her PW&B future splattered in mangled flaming debris, Austin Hendricks's leverage to manipulate Charlotte's course sputtered like an untied balloon darting to the ceiling, blowing out hot air. What could he do to her now?

She dodged oncoming pedestrians and drifted to the counter. At five after eight, the first class passengers boarded Flight 527. The gate agent busied herself, tallying tickets as a loud printer spit perforated paper behind her.

Without looking up, the agent asked Charlotte, "Can I help you?"

"Is the flight full?"

"It is. Do you want to go stand-by?"

"How many ahead of me?"

The agent held up two fingers. "You should make it."

"I'll do it."

"Ticket." The agent held out her hand.

Charlotte exchanged her return ticket to Dallas for the St. Louis fare. She found a payphone after she swore her briefcase had been in her possession since birth and no ruthless terrorist had sweet-talked her into delivering a ticking bundle from cousin Osama. She wedged between a red-faced man in a shabby blazer and elegant businesswoman holding one gold hoop earring as she conversed. Charlotte rummaged through her purse contents until she located his business card.

She charged the call to her home phone and closed her eyes, hoping he had coverage in St. Louis, hoping he would answer.

"Pierce Pope."

Charlotte smiled. "Pierce, I'm so glad you answered."

"Charlotte," Pope replied with urgency. "I heard about Liz. Are you all right?"

"Shaky, but I'm fine."

"I can't believe it," Pope said, press box clatter and ball park noise behind his voice. "Ever since my editor called, I've been worried that you were involved. I tried to call that old goat, Cox. Manuel's couldn't even find him. Then I really worried."

She laughed. "He's been with me. I'm not sure I would have survived the afternoon without Carlton. I found her, Pierce."

"Damn." Background noise elevated, followed by jeers from the stadium.

"What happened?"

"Abbott hit one into orbit—a grand slam, four zip Braves. Keep it up Bravos and keep it out of Bic-boy's hands. Sorry, Charlotte. Finding Liz must have been horrible. Is there anything I can do?"

"Well, that's why I called. About your invitation to show me St. Louis, is it too late to accept?"

"Absolutely not," Pope responded without hesitation. "When can you be here?"

"The flight leaves in ten minutes."

"Am I that predictable?"

"No, not at all." Charlotte glanced at the dwindling line of passengers boarding her plane. "I'm coming to St. Louis anyway, and I thought it'd be nice to see you."

"What's going on, Charlotte?"

"I'd rather share this saga face to face."

"Ha," Pope hooted. "Love a good mystery. Let's see, you leave around eight thirty, Eastern. That puts you at Lambert Field before nine thirty, Central. The Metrolink, St. Louis mass transit, isn't bad, but catch a cab. I'm staying at Adam's Mark, about a twenty-minute ride. If Robinson will keep Torch's fumble fingers in the bullpen, I should be there around eleven."

"Where should I meet you?"

"There's a nightclub, opened 'til all hours, AJ's is the name, I think."

"Elevenish, AJ's, got it." Charlotte watched the gate agent searching for last-minute passengers. "Time to go. Bye."

"Looking forward to seeing you, Charlotte."

Charlotte hung up the phone. She dashed for the gate and recalled her father's comments—full speed ahead. How about reckless?

Chapter Twenty-One

The taxi wheeled into the Adam's Mark's entrance at the corner of Fourth and Chestnut.

"Twenty-two fifty, Miss." The ancient hippie flung his gray ponytail over the headrest.

Charlotte peeled out a twenty and eight singles. "The rest is yours." A bellman opened her door. She slid across torn upholstery. "Do you know who won the game tonight?"

"Atlanta spanked us. Caught it on the A and M before you flagged me down at the airport. Eight to one. Don't know who I hate more, the Braves or the damn Yankees."

"Did Traynor pitch?"

"Why waste Torch on the Bad News Bears? The way the Cardinals are slumping, the Redbirds couldn't hit their way out of a wet paper sack. The Braves threw a no-name rookie just up from Richmond to mop up the ninth."

"Thanks." Charlotte stood and said, "Have a good night."

"Right on."

The bellman closed the car door and the taxi pulled away. The Missouri wind chilled Charlotte. Again, she cuddled in the fleece she'd borrowed from Liz's Jeep.

"Evening, ma'am." Another bellman welcomed her to Adam's Mark and opened the brass-framed door.

A speck in the colossal atrium, she roamed over polished tile in scuffed lace-up boots. She craned her neck and admired the mammoth arched windows and exquisite Ludovico de Luigi bronze horses glimmering beneath magnificent chandeliers bolted high above. Fashion sirens scolded Charlotte's jeans-casual attire like she had smashed a car window and triggered an ear-piercing alarm. Her underdressed phobia dwindled when she observed baseball fans, clad in jeans and Cardinals caps, loitering the grand lobby.

She located directions to AJ's Nightclub across the ornate vestibule. It was after eleven. Charlotte wandered toward the deep bass, cymbals, and a shrill voice, crooning in rhythmic pitch.

Charlotte allowed her eyes to adjust inside the night owl haven, a cave of blaring melody, clinking glass, and smoky plumes. She waited for the blindness to ebb and pondered the bar lighting. Illumination, or lack of it, banished reality's harsh glare and bolstered the esteem, escapist solace, drinkers sought from the bottle.

She scanned the sparse Tuesday night crowd looking for Pope. Three couples danced on a rectangle patch of wood squares. Thirsty business people and tourists, slouched in the burgundy and lime-shaded chairs, belittled the dancers. Thirty-one, divorced, and alone as of seven forty-five EST—Charlotte's thoughts leaped to the grim premonition of a middle-aged CPA barhopping for entertainment.

Her eyes combed the men parked on polished brass barstools, their bellies pressing against the heavy oak bar. The bartender, in a black tie and white shirt, reached for a pilsner glass suspended from beveled glass cabinets. He pulled a tall draft beer, drained frothy run over, and delivered it to a brawny customer at the end of the bar.

Confidence? Arrogance? Charlotte bridged the ravine between familiarity and recognition. Traynor! Earl Traynor, knotted up in the corner like a muscle-bound hermit, gulped beer.

Charlotte's pulse rocketed. No sign of Pope, she surged ahead, snubbing the internal frequency issuing a prudent plea to evade an imminent collision. *Here I go again, center ring, climbing into the tiger cage without my chair and whip.*

"Earl Traynor. Imagine finding you here." Charlotte faked a smile. "Great hit last night."

His eyes rolled to her. "I pitched like shit. If I had to hit to eat, I'd be on Peachtree cleaning windshields for nickels."

"Mind if I join you?" She patted the leather stool seat. Did dirty car windows also stimulate the obsessive-compulsive cycle? "That is, if you're not waiting for someone else."

He chugged half his beer and wiped a foam dribble with the back of his hand. "Robby told me to steer clear of you. He said you were trouble with a double 'T.'"

"I won't bite."

Traynor chuckled. "Suit yourself, if you can stand the company. We off the record?"

"Sure." Charlotte held up open palms. "I'm not wired either."

"Want a drink?"

"Merlot, if they have it."

He waved at the bartender and pointed at his glass. "And a Merlot."

He tipped his glass to Charlotte and guzzled the last third of the beer.

"Do you always drink so much?"

"Beer breaks the tension."

The bartender spread napkins and set down their drinks. "Six seventy-five, Mr. Traynor. I can run you a tab."

"Cash." Traynor unfolded a twenty from his money clip.

"Baseball is just a game."

"Just a game, huh?" He smirked. "We're in a white knuckle pennant race, millions at stake, not to mention the owners' egos, player bonuses, contract negotiations, and my arm feels like overboiled collard greens. Games are for fun."

The bartender laid the change on the counter. Traynor fiddled with the money.

"Do something else then. Getting drunk doesn't magically wash away your worries."

"Sure sands the edges smooth. If you ain't conscious you don't worry. Kind of like that *does a falling tree make noise if no one is th*ere shit." He stacked two ones and centered the quarter on Washington's face as a tip. He arranged the ten and remaining dollar bill, faces up, unfolded the wad in the money clip and sorted the bills by denomination.

"We all have to work. Don't take it so seriously."

"Pitching is all I know, lady. It's who I am." He shoved the folded money into his pocket. "Look at me. I'm a North Georgia bumpkin with a ninety-eight-mile-an-hour fastball. I wouldn't know what to do if I wasn't out there staring down some all-star yo-yo that thinks he can touch my heat. I'd end up with grease under my nails," he fanned manicured fingertips, "like my daddy. Torch Traynor is a Major League pitcher. Earl's a nobody."

Distress registered in Traynor's eyes. "What's wrong, Earl?"

"Come close." He dropped his arm around her shoulders. "I ain't gonna bite you either. Tad the weasel Smithurst is walking his beat. He's checking up on Hendricks's toys. If he sees me with you, Robby'll cuss me 'til the Mississippi dries up. Not sure how you got them so worked up. Help a fella?"

His rigid arm trapped her as if a snapped hickory limb had fallen on her. Charlotte wondered if Margaret had nestled in his shoulder and indulged in the pleasing soap-clean and cologne scent. Had this arm struck her sister down? Her eyes roamed to Traynor's face. His eyes flickered, like an unruly child hiding from an irate parent, tracking Smithurst's whereabouts, then looking away. An overgrown child. Beyond his raw manhood, what could have attracted Margaret to him?

"The rodent went back to his hole." Traynor withdrew his arm. "Sorry." Again, he quaffed a healthy portion of his beer.

"You keep swilling beer like that you'll go Jekyll."

"What the hell is 'Jekyll'?"

"You know, gentle country boy transforms into bloodthirsty fiend—Jekyll." Charlotte glowered. "Like the night you ransacked the bar in St. Petersburg!"

Traynor's eyes narrowed to a steely stare. "You ain't gonna let that Hatch ruckus go, are you? You still checking on me for your…sister, right?" He turned away. "Tell her I said, 'Hello.'"

"She's dead!"

His head jerked left. Accosted by Charlotte's hateful glare, he said, "I didn't know. Damn shame… She seemed nice."

"You said you didn't remember her. Meet too many people. Not good with names. Wasn't that it?"

"I was in a Budweiser fog," he mumbled, "but I remember her. A woman like her is hard to forget. Most women I meet, especially at places like the Hatch, want one thing—a kid, fathered by a Major Leaguer, blood kin to a multi-million-dollar payday. She wasn't the least bit interested in all that fame and fortune crap. Funny, you get accustomed to the red carpet treatment, then you cross paths with a grounded woman like Margaret, not some hero-worshipping bimbo, you get pissed. I couldn't believe she brushed off the mighty Torch Traynor like a fleck of lint."

"What did you quarrel about?"

"No quarrel. Takes two to quarrel. She wouldn't give me the time of day."

"Who did she speak to on the phone?"

"Hell if I know. I was buzzing with one thought. I was obsessed with luring her back to the Vinoy."

"Obsessed," she repeated. "Did Margaret meet you at the Vinoy?"

"No." Traynor tugged at his goatee. "She left. Guess I blew a gasket. Busted up the Hatch pretty good from what the fellas told me."

"Angry, whipped up into a rampage. *Obsessed* with Margaret." Charlotte sipped Merlot, and licked her lips. "She said no, so you followed her home… and beat her to death!"

"No! Now, I get it. That's how you got under Hendricks's skin. You've been poking around trying to pin a murder rap on me." He thrust a hand toward Charlotte, shackled her wrist, and squeezed.

"Stop it!" She squirmed to escape the powerful hold. "I'll scream."

"Listen, Charlotte. The Braves don't take kindly to scandal. No matter how good I am, they'd drop me like a rotten Jack-o-Lantern. Traded to Milwaukee and never heard from again."

"You're hurting me. Let go!"

"I didn't kill nobody." He ratcheted his grip, like a human crescent wrench, around her wrist. "Don't fuck with me!"

Charlotte swung her free hand at his face. He caught her fist and sneered.

"Finally found someone you can overpower, Traynor?" Pierce Pope stood between them. "Let her go before I make you page one."

Traynor glared at Charlotte. "Didn't do it!" He released her wrist.

"Come on, Charlotte." Pope urged her to stand with a gentle hand.

"Wait." She yanked her arm from Pope. "Don't underestimate me! Your threats and strong-arm tactics only fortify my desire to show the world what a monster you are. Or in words you'll better comprehend, I've only begun to fuck with you!"

She lifted her briefcase from the floor and sorted through file folders, note pads, and random paperwork. "I know what you're doing. It's all here." She flung a file at Traynor. The accounts of Traynor's blown saves, Margaret's murder, and the recent St. Louis killing spilled on the bar. "Put those in your scrapbook, asshole!"

Chapter Twenty-Two

Charlotte staggered, hate-filled eyes aimed over her shoulder at Traynor. Pope stretched her arm like a tow bar and dragged her away. He plopped her in a booth and scooted in, barricading her fiery belligerence from retaliatory strikes.

"Welcome to St. Louis." Pope smiled. "Why in the hell are you sparring with Zippo the sputtering butane lighter?"

"He killed my sister! I'm not done with him!" Charlotte felt her cheeks burning furious red. "Let me out!"

"When you calm down, I'll consider it."

Charlotte fidgeted with her trembling hands. She glared at Traynor. "Bastard."

Pope reached an arm around her, pulled her close, and rocked side to side. "You're shaking like a six-point-five earthquake."

"I'm so angry, I could spit nails."

"Shh. It's okay."

Pope's voice offered soothing refuge, a scabbard to sheath the hatred-honed sword she yearned to slash at Traynor's gnarled neck. She exhaled and gulped air. Her head collapsed to his shoulder. She closed her eyes. She pinched his blazer lapel. Pope's lean frame absorbed her contempt as if his body, his tender demeanor, sucked venom from a snakebite.

"I came here to tell you," Charlotte whispered. "You were gone. I didn't want you to find out like this."

"About Liz?" He swept tousled hair from her face. "I told you my editor called."

"About me!"

A cheerful waitress laid out napkins. "Can I get you something from the bar?"

"Chardonnay." Pope nodded at the wood-framed advertisement displayed on their table. "Bring us a bottle of Robert Strong."

He lifted her chin. She blinked, studied the shadowed angles on Pope's face, and aligned her eyes with his concerned gaze.

"You, Carlton…Liz." Charlotte paused. "You were all so good to me. Took me in like an abandoned puppy. No questions asked. I'm no writer. I'm a fraud, Pierce. I deceived you, took advantage of the kind welcome, and I feel dreadful."

"Because?"

"Because I lied—"

"No. I understand your remorse, and as far as I'm concerned, you're forgiven. One less journalist is good news. However, I'm curious why you, and I guess Jeb Owens, scripted this elaborate impersonation?"

"Earl Traynor murdered my sister, Margaret."

"Whew. That's quite an accusation. I can think of nothing more satisfying than the image of Torch Traynor etching his initials in a cell wall. Care to share the basis of your pointing finger with an intrigued listener?"

Charlotte watched the waitress pour their wine, twist the bottle into an ice bucket, and wander away. "He was with her the night she died. He even admitted it. Puffed-up ego and bulging bankroll, he hit on Margaret. She refused to relieve his animalistic urge, so he clubbed her to death."

"Where did this happen?"

"Margaret lived in Tampa. The Braves were on the road playing the Devil Rays. He followed her home and murdered her."

Pope sampled his wine. "Are the police involved?"

"The Tampa police think I'm a loon. There's no trace of Traynor in her house, and Hendricks waltzed around their inquiries."

"The silver tongue of success. No trace, and the appearance of chance encounter, call me an idiot, but I don't see the trail to Bic-boy."

"The killer sanitized Margaret's house."

"Criminals hide evidence."

"Mopped floors, dusted shelves, rearranged books, and alphabetized music. He bathed and dressed her, damn it."

"Weird."

"I thought so." Charlotte twirled her wine glass by the stem. "Have you ever noticed Traynor tug at his uniform?"

"Sure. Baseball players are superstitious. Lots of pitchers have nervous habits."

"He's not nervous, Pierce. Until every button is in place, his crease is just right, his cuffs are rolled an equal interval from the knee he can't pitch. Look at his locker. Martha Stewart couldn't arrange it any neater. Everything has to be perfect or he can't perform. Carlton thinks Traynor suffers from severe obsessive-compulsive disorder. Are you familiar with it?"

"I've heard of it."

"Perfection is his obsession. When imperfection rears its ugly head, his compulsion, the temporary cure to his agony, is violence. You've witnessed his explosive temperament." She grazed the wound on Pope's chin with a fingernail. "Poor performance, blow a save, and smash someone's skull."

"The way he's pitching, the death toll could become catastrophic. Hold on. Are you saying there are other victims associated with his bad outings?"

"It's possible," she said. "As recent as this week...in St. Louis."

"A Major League serial killer. Can you make it stick?"

"I thought so. Until earlier today. Carlton and I attempted to cross-reference the blown saves with similar murders in the corresponding cities." Charlotte formed a zero with her finger and thumb. "But I'm not giving up. I'll harass him until prison serenity seems like the more tolerable option."

Near the bar a verbal exchange escalated to inflamed decibels. Shouts contested with the singer's teary ballad. Charlotte craned her neck toward the disturbance.

Tad Smithurst's arms gyrated in large backward loops like a runaway double Ferris wheel off its stanchion. He flailed at air, grasping for balance. The offspring of a stumbling idiot and a Michael Jackson moonwalk, he staggered across the dance floor. His shoulders slammed into a glass memorabilia case and he collapsed to the carpet.

"Stay the hell away from me!" Traynor heaved his glass. Smithurst cowered beneath a shattered glass and beer shower. "You sniveling twit!"

Traynor tossed a wad of cash on the bar. His fiery gaze fixed on Smithurst, he said, "Oughta cover the damages." Traynor's biceps pulsed. He sauntered from the bar and paced before his crippled prey like a panther ready for the kill.

Charlotte slid closer to Pope. "Let me out. He'll kill him."

"What's wrong with killing a snake? Bic-boy could be doing us all a favor."

She shoved Pope's shoulder. "I'm going to help him."

"Not funny, right? Look, Charlotte, every bloodshot eye is hooked on the impromptu wrestling extravaganza. Even drunk businessmen make believable murder witnesses. This episode has run its course. Don't throw gas on smoldering embers."

Clinking glass hushed, the music preempted, Traynor backed away from Smithurst as if he sensed the concentrated bolts of attention aimed at him. He pointed a finger. "What I do and who I talk to is none of your damn business. Got it!"

Smithurst conceded with a timid nod as Traynor stomped out of AJ's. Traynor's departure thawed the fear-frozen nightclub. Instantaneous chatter resumed, and the band cranked up Pat Benatar's "Hit Me With Your Best Shot."

"Drinking all night, fist fights between games, detailing the exploits of cavemen armed with Louisville Sluggers instead of hand-carved clubs, pacifying the whims of these…these media-embellished heroic characters like they're some kind of superhuman action figures." She gulped wine and closed her eyes. "What kind of life is this? How can you stand it? How could anyone lead a normal life, sustain a relationship outside this baseball-is-life bullshit?"

Pope grinned. "I'll admit it's not for everyone, Charlotte. Normal life? I came from a normal life. I grew up in Tarboro, North Carolina. Tobacco country. My father left my mother and me when I was three. I never saw him again. My mother cleaned houses during the day and sewed at night to feed us. She sewed and nagged me about my grades. I hated school, thought it was a waste of good daylight, until Carolina offered me an academic scholarship. She shoved me out of a future as a factory worker or tobacco farmer, away from a *normal life*. I guess ever since then I'm partial to the abnormal. I marvel at the absurdity of Major League Baseball, any professional sport for that matter. Guess it's my destiny to record the lunacy. As for relationships—"

"I'm sorry, Pierce. I've never been good at biting my tongue. Traynor whipped me into a vicious tizzy and I'm taking it out on you."

"As for relationships," Pope continued, "in this *baseball-is-life bullshit*, there are friendships, mentors, villains, and lovers. You savor each moment of each life you touch, for tomorrow they get reassigned, fired, or traded. Yes, relationships exist. Lasting relationships are rare. Call it a tradeoff between security and variety—serenity and infatuation—fulfillment by different means. Better for me. My antics and ego wear thin quickly."

"I doubt that."

"You're too kind, or too drunk. Besides, if I was chained to a desk nine to five with a minivan in the two-car garage and two point three kids, I would never have met…" his eyes rolled to the wine bottle. He tore the label corner and turned to Charlotte, "you."

She clenched her lips to calm a nervous quiver.

"What about you?" A wide smile followed his robust outburst.

"Me?"

"Yes, you. You're not a freelance writer. What are you other than a pain in Torch's overpaid ass?"

"I'm a CPA."

"Talk about absurd—all those years of higher education to count other people's money. Which firm?"

"Independent as of tonight." Charlotte lifted the wine bottle and refilled her glass. "Payne, Wyman and Bradford dismissed me for conduct unbecoming a bean counter. Accusing a client's asset of murder can be detrimental to career aspirations."

"They represent the Braves?"

"Time Warner."

"You should choose your battles more carefully. I always thought David got lucky against Goliath. The giant usually wins. Where's your slingshot?"

"I didn't realize what I was diving into. I went for a stroll in the dark and stepped off a cliff."

"A sneak preview of the future is a luxury most of us don't have." Pope reached for her left hand. He glanced down at her fingers. "How about the rest of your normal life? Why is a beautiful woman like you drinking wine with a low-life reporter miles away from... Where are you from?"

"Dallas. Or I live there. I grew up in Tampa. I went to high school with Jeb. FSU. I married Rocky Randall two weeks after graduation."

"*The Rock*. I remember him. Linebacker, right? He slammed all-American running backs like they were tackling dummies."

"Rocky never stopped slamming. He slammed his beers. He slammed other women. He slammed me. We were divorced two years after graduation. I passed the CPA exam and started with PW&B. I dated my boss...until tonight."

"Rough night."

"Until now."

The waitress appeared. "Last call, folks."

Charlotte shook her head, and Pope declined.

"If you'd like, I'll escort you to your room."

"That'd be nice, Pierce."

"Where are you staying?"

Prodded by jilted retaliation, romance's luring possibilities, or another dose of recklessness, Charlotte pressed her chest against Pope's and kissed him. As they parted, she whispered, "With you?"

A taxi horn blared. A bus roared. Twelve floors below, downtown St. Louis yawned. The commuter concert stirred Charlotte. Modest streams of light squirmed through ruffled curtains and washed the walls, the furniture, and Pope's bare chest in an ocean fog gray. A jackhammer broke distant pavement like a drum cadence celebrating dawn. She rolled her eyes to the alarm clock—seven o'clock on the nose.

She hadn't slept long. It was after two when they ripped back the covers. Hours of ecstasy preceded rest for either. Her sleep-laden eyes studied his peaceful expression, the dark hair fanned across his brow, his gentle, slow breaths. Her breasts were nestled against his ribs, and her head lay upon his firm shoulder. Charlotte wanted to fall back into deep slumber entangled with him but knew the effort would be futile.

Her Chardonnay-coated tongue and knotted hair begged her to loiter beneath a steamy showerhead. She pulled back the sheet with a graceful, guarded motion, lifted his hand perched on her hip, and folded Pope's arm across his chest. He twitched and rolled onto his side. Charlotte crawled out of bed, leaned over her vacant imprint, and wrapped his shoulders with bed linens.

She tiptoed to the bathroom and closed the door with a soft clunk. She started to twist the lock, paused, grinned, and released the deadbolt. She drifted toward the shower, tickled that she almost locked Pope out. What else did she have to hide?

Goose bumps flourished as she crossed the cool tile, barefoot and naked. Charlotte sat on the edge of tub, turned the knobs, and diverted the flow to the shower. She slid the shower curtain and entered the steady warm spray.

She doused her face, immersed in the stream of instant comfort. Soothing water pelted her brow. Charlotte's mind let go, and as often happened, vague and jumbled thoughts unraveled. Her subconscious summarized, categorized, and organized twenty-four hours of personal chaos, agony, and elation.

She rubbed water from her eyes, reached for the complimentary shampoo, and opened the mini-bottle. She massaged the lather, exuding a faint tango essence, into her scalp.

A murder in St. Louis connected to Margaret's death. She had left Liz, vibrant and feisty, to meet with Cox and Kenneth Daniels. Her serial killer theory floundered, uncorroborated by the facts and Cox's contacts. Carlton Cox. She needed to call him. Liz, the picture of health, beaten and broken like a discarded mannequin. Charlotte held back tears as her thoughts dwelled on her lost friend. The cops. The handcuffs. James! The asshole. In a matter of seconds, she'd been fired, sabotaged her career, and been dumped by her lover. The jolt sparked an irrational response. She boarded a St. Louis bound plane and crashed into Pierce's arms. Pierce, her four-leaf clover in a field of woe. This morning Charlotte felt lucky, ready to go on.

The shower curtain fluttered as she rinsed shampoo. Cold air surged over her dripping body. A clunk, a bolt hitting a striker, and the air stream ebbed.

"Pierce, is that you?" She gazed through the moistened current liner. A distorted shadow paraded, growing, noiseless as if the apparition hovered above the tile. Charlotte backed into a shower corner. The soap dish pressed against her back. "Pierce! Answer me."

Pope jerked the curtain open. Two grommets ripped from the curtain rings. His blank expression inspected Charlotte, coiled against the tile shower wall.

"What are you doing?" Charlotte splashed his face. "You scared me."

Water dripped from his lip as a smile broke his stone appearance.

She extended her soapy hand. "Join me?"

He clutched her hand and stepped over the tub wall. They embraced beneath the hot waterfall.

Chapter Twenty-Three

Charlotte lounged on the hotel bed, wearing only Pope's white button-down shirt, and read the *Post-Dispatch*, inattentive, her smile fastened to fresh memories. She had spent the day sightseeing, clutching Pope's hand like a smitten teenager. She saw Illinois sprawl forever from the peak of the Gateway Arch, six hundred feet above the historic riverfront. She had toured the Mississippi, wrapped in Pope's arms on the top deck of a paddlewheel riverboat, imagining Derringer-toting gamblers and dancehall girls in net stockings.

Pope left for Busch Stadium an hour ago, and she already missed him. She realized, after spending a day alone with the handsome and witty journalist, his balance, his well-rounded presence, attracted her. Their conversations wandered through concert halls, stage lights, gourmet cuisine, and the rise and fall of dot com stocks. They'd been together since the intimate sunrise shower, and not once had he uttered a single word about sports—an astounding feat for any man and paramount for a professional sportswriter.

He offered to take her with him to the game. Her spirits mending, if only for the moment, she could imagine nothing worse than facing Traynor, the Braves, and baseball fanatics tonight. She glanced at the bedside clock. Here she was, alone in St. Louis, with Pope gone for at least another five hours. What to do?

She flung the newspaper to the floor. Maybe an in-room movie would help span the time. She bent to pick up the remote control and spotted the headline on the bottom of page one—*SOUTHWESTERN BELL EMPLOYEE MURDERED.*

She lifted the paper to check the date. Wednesday, September 19. "Hmm. Must be a follow-up."

The article on Megan Rivers's death shook loose thoughts Charlotte had managed to mothball for the day. She meandered through the catacombs that led her to St. Louis. *Let it go, Charlotte*, she scolded herself. *Get on with your life*. A specter engulfed in blue cigarette smoke guarded the imaginary entrance to a cavern from her immediate past. She needed to call Cox.

She lowered her feet to the floor, walked to the dresser, and dug through her briefcase until she found Cox's card. She sat at the desk and dialed his cell phone number.

Cox answered on the third ring.

"Hi, Carlton."

"Charlotte! Where the hell have you been? I've been looking everywhere for you. Even called your pal in Tampa, what's his name?"

"Jeb."

"Yeah, yeah. Where are you?"

"St. Louis."

"What the hell? I swear you're a damn lightning rod if I've ever seen one. You just can't stay away from Traynor, can you?"

"Stop, Carlton. I was calling to thank you for helping me Monday. I wanted you to know I'm surrendering my amateur detective badge and reentering my life, boring and safe as it may be."

"The hell you are!"

"I refuse to chase any more shadows, Carlton."

"I'm not sure what's eating at you. Did you read the *Post-Dispatch* today?"

"I glanced at it."

"Was there an article about the Rivers murder?"

"Yes. I saw the story a few minutes ago. Old news, isn't it?"

"Paper news. When you stumbled over her death, the story was breaking news. Electronic news."

Charlotte fidgeted with a rough fingernail. "So."

"Charlotte! Pull your head out of whatever hole you stuck it in and tune in. I couldn't sleep last night, so I flipped through the file we compiled. It didn't hit me until I read *The Tampa Tribune* account of your sister's death. I finished scanning it and happened to notice the date—September ninth."

"That's right. They found her the eighth."

"And the *Tribune* reported it, in print, the next day. You read about the Rivers murder—"

"The same day," Charlotte said. "We looked for the wrong dates. The victims would be found the next day, but the newspaper wouldn't print it until two days after Traynor blew the save."

"At-a-girl! I spent most of today retracing our steps."

"What?" The chair toppled over as she sprang to her feet. "What did you find, Carlton?"

Cox coughed. "Philadelphia. Torch bombed, June twelfth. Dom Valenti verified the June fourteenth *Inquirer* reported a flight attendant was beaten to death in her room. Atlanta, July fifth, Torch rocked. July seventh *AJC* reported a Cobb County schoolteacher was murdered in her townhouse off Moores Mill. She was last seen on her way to the High Museum Matisse exhibit. I left for vacation on the sixth or I would have remembered, damn it. Hell, I would have written it."

"What about Chicago? San Francisco?"

"Zero so far, but I still got feelers out."

Disappointed, Charlotte replied, "Oh."

"Oh? Is that all you can say? Traynor blew six saves. Four out of six times an attractive woman, thirty to forty years old, alone, is found bludgeoned in the same city. I meet with Atlanta homicide tonight. Once I pitch this story, I guarantee you they'll be on the horn with the other cities by morning comparing notes. If one hair, one fiber, one link from the scenes lines up, Traynor will be behind bars before the weekend."

"I can't believe it, Carlton."

"You did it! A scrawny CPA did what the whole National League has been foaming at the mouth to do all year—you clobbered Torch Traynor." He paused. Charlotte detected a click in the background. She imagined the orange cigarette tip and his first puff of smoke. "This is exciting stuff, but remember with the plausibility of your accusations comes the reality that Traynor kills…often. I'll give it to the cops tonight. There's no need to harass Traynor further. Stay away from him, okay?"

"If I never see him again it will be too soon. Let me know how the police respond."

"Sure. Where are you staying?"

"Adam's Mark, room twelve oh four," Charlotte answered. "Thanks, Carlton."

Chapter Twenty-Four

The ring wailed like a screaming siren, alerting sleeping citizens that a killer tornado gouged a devastating path toward them. Charlotte squinted as Pope reached for the telephone. He fumbled the receiver, cussed, and held the phone to his ear.

"Hello," he growled. Pope shifted and listened. "It's my room, who did you expect to find at this unholy hour?"

Pope held his hand over the mouthpiece and turned to Charlotte. "It's for you. Sounds like Cox."

She brushed her breasts on his chest, leaned over him, and lifted the phone. "Carlton?"

"You could have told me," Cox spoke in a hushed voice. "Doesn't make a hell of difference to me."

Charlotte yawned and swept the hair from her face. "Told you what? And you already woke everyone here, so there's no need to whisper."

"When are you coming back to Atlanta?"

She delayed her reply, unaccustomed to an open calendar, exploring her memory for an appointment that didn't exist. "I don't know."

"The Braves finish in St. Louis today, right?"

"I think so," she said.

"Ask lover-boy. He ought to know, it's his job."

"Pierce." She touched his shoulder. "Is today the last game of the St. Louis series?"

His head buried in the pillow, Pope said, "One o'clock game, then they charter back to Atlanta tonight."

"Did you hear that, Carlton?"

"Yeah. You need to fly back this afternoon. That is, if you want to watch APD haul Traynor off for questioning."

Charlotte sat upright and kicked her heels. The bed shook. Her movement tightened the phone cord and jerked the telephone from the bedside table. "What time? Where? Tell me every gory, delicious detail."

"Guess I've got your attention now, sleeping beauty. I was with Atlanta homicide until…hell, I don't know what time it was, but Manuel's was closed. Had to settle for home frig Budweisers—"

"Carlton! What about the cops?"

He chuckled. "I started with Roger Chawk, the detective assigned to the Sheri Cowens case. She's the teacher murdered here in July. He treated me like a crackpot at first. I explained how we linked Traynor's bad performances to murders in other cities. I corroborated the dates with the newspaper clippings in our file, but he shrugged it off as an uncanny coincidence. He told me our theory was pure speculation and said that I should leave profiling serial killers to the FBI."

"The Tampa police gave me a similar reception," Charlotte said.

"Right, and you didn't even have the file. Anyway, I was going down the crapper at warp speed, so I threw the trump card. I asked him if the Cowens scene was peculiar. He perks up a little and asks, 'How so?' I asked him, 'Was your killer handy with a mop and sponge?' I thought his damn eyes would shoot out of the sockets. He tears through the file with renewed vigor. I relayed what you said about Margaret's house, how the murderer bathed and dressed her.

"Chawk had TPD on the phone in minutes, paged a Detective Sanders, and they started comparing horror stories. Eavesdropping like any reporter worth his pay, I find out the killer dolled up the Cowens woman and scrubbed her townhouse, too.

"He hangs up, leaves his desk and brings in his lieutenant. I recite the whole story again, and before I know it we're in the lieutenant's office huddled around a speakerphone yakking at Philadelphia and St. Louis. Both hotel rooms sparkled, the blood mopped up, and the women's possessions arranged with meticulous care. Apparently, he even packed the flight attendant's carry-on bag for her."

"How did the others die?" Charlotte asked.

"Blunt-force trauma. Multiple blows from a blunt object. I'm sure their forensic troops will be busy sharing morbid tidbits today."

Charlotte was silent.

"You there, Charlotte?"

"I'm here." She paused. "It's real, isn't it?"

"As of this morning, your hypothesis is a full-scale multi-state serial killer investigation. APD will nab Traynor as soon as the Braves touch down at Hartsfield. I have two complimentary front row seats. Want to go?"

"I'd swim through a school of great white sharks to see the look on Traynor's face. Yes, I'll be there. Will you pick me up at the airport?"

Chapter Twenty-Five

St. Louis homicide detective Karen Fuller flashed her credentials to Busch Stadium security at one forty-five, followed by her partner Mack Bedell. They meandered through tunnels beneath an afternoon crowd, escorted to the visiting team's locker room by a security guard.

A small man paced outside the locker room doors. He extended his hand and said, "Detectives. I'm Tad Smithurst, Atlanta Braves, Special Assistant to the General Manager."

"Detective Karen Fuller." She shook Smithurst's hand and smiled. "This is Detective Bedell."

The barrel-chested detective's large hand squeezed Smithurst's dainty fingers.

"How..." Smithurst stammered. "How can I help you?"

"We need to speak with," Bedell checked a small note pad, "Earl Traynor."

Smithurst's eyes cut to his watch. "It's the middle of the game. You will have to wait until afterward."

"Mr. Smithurst." Fuller glared at him. "We ask only as a courtesy. You can discreetly comply with our request and we ask Mr. Traynor a few questions in the privacy of the Braves' locker room, or we call for backup and haul him to the city jail, handcuffed in the back of a patrol car. Your choice, sir."

"No cars. No handcuffs." Smithurst waved his hands. "Traynor won't pitch until late in the game, if at all. I suppose a brief interview could be arranged."

"If he's not here in ten minutes, we send in the uniforms," Bedell said.

"Wait inside." Smithurst opened the locker room. "Don't do anything too hasty. I'll get him. Make yourself comfortable."

He held the door for the detectives and then scampered down the corridor, his wingtips clacking.

"We scared him shitless, Karen."

Her eyes scanned the locker room until she spotted Traynor's name written on a piece of athletic tape. "I doubt we'll have the same effect on Traynor."

She wandered to Traynor's locker and noted the clothes and personal items arranged with obvious care. She eyed the locker next to Traynor's for comparison. Shoes and towels cluttered the floor, hygiene products scattered on the top shelf in random fashion. *Crowder*, she read the name in silence.

"Mack," she said to her partner. "You're a man."

"About time you noticed."

"Is it me or is this locker particularly tidy for one of your macho brethren?"

Bedell stood behind her. "Some guys are more finicky with their stuff. Most guys are slobs though, like that one." He pointed to Crowder's locker. "I don't know. I'll be honest, accusing a guy of murder because he keeps his locker orderly is a long shot."

Fuller grabbed the Advil bottle from Traynor's top shelf.

"What are you doing, Karen?"

She tipped over Traynor's toothpaste and cologne, then scooted the Advil to the far side of the shelf. "I want to see if it's true."

"That OCD crap Atlanta mentioned last night?"

"You saw the bathroom floor at the Marriott, Mack." Fuller sat on the bench in front of the locker. "The killer beat her beyond recognition, then he mopped the floor like a Saturday morning chore. I can't explain it, but it sure is worth exploring, one way or another."

The double doors burst open. Traynor's cleats grated against the carpeted concrete floors. Smithurst followed the pitcher toward the detectives.

"I'm Earl Traynor. Tad says you want to talk to me. Make it quick, Robby doesn't like us ducking into the locker room during the game."

"Mr. Traynor, I'm Detective Fuller, St. Louis homicide." She nodded to Bedell. "This is my partner, Detective Bedell."

Traynor walked around her, disturbed by his locker, and snatched the Advil from the shelf. "Damn it, Tad, you gotta tell Butch to stay out of my shit." He realigned the items on the shelf and turned to the detectives. "So what's up?"

She watched Traynor restore order to the disheveled shelf and fired a told-you-so look at her partner. "Just a few routine questions."

"Do I need a lawyer?"

"This isn't an interrogation. Preliminary questions only; however, if you'd rather have an attorney present, it is your right."

"Maybe you should wait for a lawyer, Torch," Smithurst said.

Traynor glared at Smithurst. "I ain't got nothing to hide." He sat down in front of Crowder's locker and crossed his legs. "I'm all yours."

Fuller cocked her head and leaned toward him. "Do you know Megan Rivers?"

"No."

"Where were you Monday night, and early Tuesday morning?"

"Maybe you'll recall that I hit a home run to beat the Cardinals Monday night."

"Congratulations, Mr. Traynor. And how did you celebrate?"

"No parties when my pitching stinks. I drank a few beers and turned in."

"Where?"

"The hotel bar."

"Which hotel?"

"We always stay at Adam's Mark."

Bedell took notes as Fuller continued asking questions. "Adam's Mark has several bars. Which one did you choose?"

"The disco. Not much different than any other hotel bar. I can't remember the name."

"AJ's?"

"That's it," Traynor answered.

"Maybe you have a credit card receipt?"

"For a few beers? I pay cash."

"Were you with teammates or anyone that can verify your whereabouts?"

"The boys caught a cab to the titty bars in East St. Louis." He grinned. "I like to be alone when I fuck up."

"Call me naïve, but I thought game-winning homers were moments to celebrate." Fuller wasn't fazed by the sudden vulgarity.

"They pay me to pitch."

"Is there anyone who would remember you at AJ's? A bartender? Another patron? A woman?"

"I don't know. Maybe a bartender."

"And what time did you…turn in?"

"I left the bar around one."

"When you travel, who is your roommate?"

Traynor howled. "You've been watching too many baseball movies, lady. I bunk alone. It's in my contract."

"So no one can confirm what time you…*turned in*?"

"I drank alone. I stumbled to my room alone. And I slept…alone."

Fuller shifted on the bench and crossed her legs. "Is it possible you met

Megan Rivers at AJ's?"

"Never heard the name."

"Maybe you met her at the Marriott?" Bedell handed Fuller a manila envelope. She opened the flap, withdrew Megan Rivers's photo, and showed it to Traynor. "Does her picture jostle your memory? Pretty, wasn't she?"

"Was?"

"Megan Rivers was murdered early Tuesday morning?"

The bridge above Traynor's nose bunched. "Charlotte Gordon put you up to this, didn't she?"

"I don't know a Charlotte Gordon."

"Yeah, right," Traynor huffed. "I don't know any Megan Rivers. And I sure as hell didn't kill her. And you can tell that bitch I didn't kill her damn sister either!"

The locker room door crashed open.

"What the hell is going on here?" Austin Hendricks roared. "Tad, explain!"

"Uh, Mr. Hendricks, sir. The police had some questions for Torch, sir."

"You idiot! Without an attorney?"

"Torch didn't want one, sir," Smithurst said.

"And you just went along while the cops grill one of our ballplayers?" Hendricks looked at Fuller. "Do you have a warrant, Detective?"

"No, sir."

"Interview over!" He thrust a finger toward the door. "Torch, I don't pay you to chitchat in the locker room. There's a ballgame going on and we're in the middle of a pennant race. Back to the bullpen, now!"

Traynor stood and departed.

"Traynor's name has been mentioned in a St. Louis murder investigation, Mr. Hendricks," Fuller said.

"Then arrest him, but don't sneak in here and expect me to let you coerce a confession in the middle of a ball game. Now, get out!"

Fuller rose from the bench. "We'll be back, I assure you."

"You'd better have a warrant or I'll have you thrown out on your cute little ass."

"Enough!" Bedell stomped forward.

Fuller's fingernails dug into Bedell's arm. "No harm, Mack. Don't do something you'll regret." She slapped her rear end and smiled. "All the step classes, and miles of jogging. I'm thrilled someone noticed."

Hendricks's eyes shot at Smithurst. "Upstairs now, you moron."

"You can bet your ass they'll be back!" Hendricks hissed. "Get Torch out of here, now."

Pinned against a corridor wall, Smithurst could smell hot dog and onions on Hendricks's breath. "Where should I take him, sir?"

"Away from here. The airport. Meet us at the charter. I can't have my stopper detained on some drummed-up charges with two weeks left in the season. We fly him out of here and stall until the post season is over."

"What about the game today, sir?"

"We'll just have to outscore them. And if we lose because Torch isn't here to close, then it's your ass, Tad!"

Chapter Twenty-Six

Rain pellets bombarded the golf umbrella in a vociferous patter. Charlotte edged closer to Cox to avoid the runoff that encircled them. Her boots and blue jeans cuffs were soaked. Left of them, two Atlanta policemen lit up like a Disney night parade in fluorescent raingear, leaned against the squad car parked outside Terminal E and chatted with homicide detectives under flimsy folding umbrellas.

Charlotte glanced at the dark telescopic gate structure. Her eyes strayed to backlit windows, fogged with condensation, and the dry terminal beyond. "Why trudge through this monsoon, when the airport is designed to shield travelers, especially VIPs like the Braves?"

"Ballplayers don't mix with mortals." Cox's eyes cut to a large bus idling near the terminal. "The bus shuttles them to their vehicles at the stadium. That way they don't have to face a single fan that might have the audacity to beg for precious autographs."

Cox fingered his shirt pocket for a cigarette and lowered his empty hand. His outlandish, ornery persona had stiffened into an all-business, speak only when spoken to, and aloof severity. Was this Carlton Cox, the reporter, so attentive, so enthralled with the scoop his journalistic instincts shut out all distractions? She doubted it.

"Well, this marks the first time I've seen you obey a no smoking sign," Charlotte said.

"Nicotine shakes beats getting charred in a jet fuel fireball," he mumbled as he watched the runway.

"What's wrong, Carlton?"

"Nothing."

"Are you upset that I was with Pierce?"

"I don't give a shit who you sleep with." He turned to her, unfamiliar concern deep seated in his bloodshot eyes.

"Carlton," Charlotte squeezed his arm, "I'm sure you won't understand, but Pierce was there when I needed him. My whole life, my hopes and dreams, have unraveled in one week. People I care for, love, gone forever… some by choice. I needed to he held, swept away from the anguish barraging me with relentless cruelty. Pierce helped me, made me feel good about myself, just as you have. I won't apologize for a few moments of selfish pleasure. Where he and I go from here, I'll admit I'm uncertain. But I will say if I have I hurt you in any way, I assure you it was unintentional, and I offer sincere regret."

"Sure could use a smoke." Cox licked his lips and sighed. "You deserve better than Pope."

"A man like you."

"Hell no!" Cox laughed. "Is that what you think? If I was ten years younger, better looking, with a real job, maybe."

"I could do worse."

"You deserve better than Pope or any journalist. Good reporters are married to their jobs. Gone all the damn time. Drink too much. The phone rings and you're out the door again. Ask my ex-wives. On the flip side, who wants to be hitched to a bad reporter or, come to think of it, a bad anything?"

Charlotte rose on her toes and kissed Cox's ruddy cheek.

"What the hell was that for?"

"My father told me when God closes a door, he always opens another. I'm thankful you were on the other side when that door opened. Thanks for caring."

"There." Cox pointed to a Delta jet crossing a runway intersection, its nosecone aimed at the greeting party. "Coming our way."

The police stirred as the airliner approached. Smiles dissolved. A patrolman straightened and hitched his gun belt.

"Ain't it fun, Charlotte?"

"I'm nervous."

"No need. Ballplayers, and I guess it goes for anyone else aboard an airplane, aren't armed. These guys," he nodded toward the police, now engrossed in serious tactical discussion, "will protect us."

"No, I'm worried I'm wrong."

"Stop doubting yourself. If you were so wrong the cops wouldn't be here standing in the rain."

The Boeing 737 rolled through the steady downpour, across the damp tarmac, and veered toward Terminal E. The brakes squealed two hundred feet short of the gate. The engines shut down. A convoy of baggage carts, catering trucks, refueling tankers, and the charter bus converged on the Delta charter jet.

Traynor's eyes opened, his head on the pillow. Five in-flight beers had knocked him out.

"Man, I'm glad we already played." Frank Houseman pressed his nose against a window. "We would've spent all night sitting through rain delays." Houseman looked over his headrest at Traynor. "Why you so tired, Torch? Whittled my bat down to a toothpick driving in runs so you didn't have to work a lick. I'm talking to Robby, when we score twelve, the hitters ought to get a cut of your payday."

"Shut up, House." Traynor smiled at the all-star.

A flight attendant opened the forward cabin door. Players stretched, yawned and gathered their carry-on bags.

Houseman turned, captivated by the activity surrounding the charter arrival, ducked under the overhead compartment, and announced, "One of you boys must be late on child support. Cops waiting for us and I don't see no baseballs for y'all superstars to scribble on."

Traynor's pulse shot up like the go ahead run led off third in the bottom of the ninth. He peered through the sheet of rain and examined each member of ground crew. Two men unloaded suitcases and team gear onto luggage carts. The tanker driver extracted a fuel hose. He found the police car beyond the airplane's perimeter. Cars—he noted the unmarked sedan. Two cops in uniform, two suits, and maybe two more behind them. After the locker room interrogation and an afternoon of dodging the St. Louis police, he knew the cops waited for none other than Torch Traynor.

A line of his teammates descended the stairs and scurried past the cops toward the bus under a canopy of Delta umbrellas. The police studied each Brave and detained none. Traynor looked over his shoulder at the back of the cabin, hoping to find a rear exit. The 737 wasn't a movie theater.

Stragglers bumped Traynor's row. Pierce Pope sidestepped into the empty row behind Traynor. Whenever the charter wasn't full the Braves seized the pubic relations opportunity and offered the Atlanta press complimentary passage. Beer and wine flowed like a frat party and the Braves pampered the players with gourmet catering. Pope always accepted the invitation.

"Where were you today?" Pope asked.

"Bullpen corner. Almost took a nap," Traynor answered. "We won twelve to three, if you didn't notice. Nothing for me to do out there."

"I heard different."

"Don't believe everything you hear, Pope."

"Twenty bucks is a lot of cash to a stadium rent-a-cop. I understand you punched the clock a little early today."

Tad Smithurst appeared from the back of cabin like a theater usher picking up popcorn cups after the credits. "Move along. Leave him alone, Pope."

Traynor's eyes never strayed from Pope. "Mind your own business, dipshit."

Smithurst flinched and blinked.

"Me and Pope are talking," Traynor added. "Now, haul ass before I finish what I started Tuesday night."

"Time to disembark, Torch."

"I'll get off when I damn well please."

Traynor feigned a jab at him. Smithurst stumbled and banged his lower back against a seatback.

"We leave in five minutes with or without you," Smithurst declared before he stormed away.

Smiling, Traynor whispered, "Weasel."

"Are you continuing on to Delta's next destination?" Pope asked.

"I ain't in a hurry."

Pope nodded to the window. "She's out there, Torch."

Air rushed from the tail of the plane. A drink cart rattled when the flight attendant rolled it from its compartment.

"Who you talking about?" Traynor responded.

"You know damn well who I'm referring to."

Traynor stared through the window. A gust of wind lifted the golf umbrella. Charlotte Gordon wore the same gray fleece, and her hair was pulled back tight. She watched his teammates transfer to the bus.

"What the hell is she doing here?"

"In her eyes, you're a cold-blooded murderer. She tells a convincing story, Torch."

"It's bullshit!"

"True or not, from the crowd of admirers eagerly anticipating the arrival of the great Torch Traynor, I'd say you can plan on an extended visit with APD tonight." Pope rubbed his chin. "Of course, there may be another option."

"Another option?"

"Say you miraculously slipped away from this ambush. Hire a competent attorney. Tell your version on your own terms, not theirs."

"The Braves will take care of all that."

"Sure, they'll protect you through the post season. Then what? You know better than me, baseball is business. You're on your own after the last pitch. And depending on the outcome, or should I say verdict, then Hendricks will dictate your future. A big enough scandal and you're off to Milwaukee regardless. Small market, empty seats, petty endorsements, puny salaries—the rookie proving grounds and has been bone yard. Get away, Torch."

"How? There's only one way out."

Pope opened the palm of his hand and swung his arm toward the galley.

"The catering truck?"

"Slip the driver some cash. Tell him it's a joke. Stowaway and get the hell out of here."

Traynor stuffed his phone and CD player in a leather flight bag. He bolted from his seat and shuffled down the aisle. He stopped and looked at Pope. "You've been blistering me all season. Why help me now?"

"Pure greed. The playoffs would be a sincere letdown without your pitching inadequacies to dissect and condemn. You'd deprive the public of my best stuff. The Braves might actually win. Such a waste of cynicism." Pope pulled a card from a coat pocket. "Here. Call me if I can help, Bic-boy. The cell phone is always with me."

Chapter Twenty-Seven

Empty seats and a surprising stillness were visible through the jet's cabin windows. Charlotte noticed animated chatter among the police.

"Pierce," Charlotte called out. "Is Traynor still on the plane?"

Pope ambled down the metal stairs. He exchanged glances with the police and stopped in front of Charlotte and Cox. "No 'Hello, how are you?' No kiss on the cheek?"

Charlotte cocked her hands on her hips and fired an ugly glare in return.

"Guess not. He was in his seat when I walked by him. Stage fright. Houseman spotted APD before the engines shut down. The rest of the team is on the bus. Even Traynor is smart enough to know the cops are waiting for him." He nodded to Cox. "Exciting stuff, isn't it, Carlton?"

Cox said, "The cops are going on board."

Charlotte watched a patrolman duck inside the APD cruiser, reappear with a shotgun, and pump a shell into the chamber. He joined a detective, holding his handgun in a safety position, and they stalked toward the open airliner. The second uniform barked into the radio on his shoulder while the other detective scanned the tarmac for suspicious movement.

Traynor crouched behind a row of drink carts inside the catering truck, anxious for the hydraulic lift to return the elevated van to the chassis. He heard voices from within the fuselage. Male, gruff, angry. He recognized the flight attendant's sweet tone, protesting their presence.

Cornered again, Traynor searched for an escape route. He grabbed a yellow rain slicker off a hook near the roll-up door. He donned the Nike golf cap in his bag, put on the slicker, looped his neck and an arm through his flight bag strap, and drew the hood tight around his face.

Rain doused the walkway between the rectangular van doorframe and the curved 737 fuselage. Traynor rushed from behind the carts, stood on the loading platform, and jumped up. His fingers grasped the top edge of the van.

He secured his grip and pulled up enough to swing his feet through the crevice. He stood in an awkward stance, one foot on the jet and the other in a corrugated ridge on the side of the van.

Traynor lowered himself, hand over hand, one foot at a time, down the van side, like a mountain climber on a steep slope without the safety ropes. His right foot slipped. His leg dangled. His fingers ached, clinging to the slick ridges. He pulled in the leg, found a foothold, and breathed hard.

Three feet from the bottom of the container, he lowered a foot and probed for the van bracing. If his faint recollection of catering trucks alongside airliners was accurate, the legs formed an 'X' and moved up and down like scissors.

Traynor kicked a metal beam. He shimmied down corrugated ridges, hung from the container bottom, swung backward and flung his legs over the metal support brace. He wrapped his legs around the beam, grabbed at cables and bolts, and crawled across the underside of the container. He climbed down the bracing with ease and leaped to the wet concrete from the truck bed.

The ground crew tended to the 737. Traynor trained his eyes on the remaining cops. He blended in with mechanics and luggage handlers, clad in identical rain gear, and drifted toward the luggage carts. The key to the luggage tractor hung from the ignition. Traynor tossed his bag on the tractor floor. He reached behind the tractor and separated the trailer hitch from the first luggage cart.

A luggage tractor, driven by a ground crew member in a yellow slicker, in the country's busiest airport—what a disguise. On board the jet, he imagined the search, the cops opening overheads, bathrooms, and storage bins. Traynor cranked the engine, stepped on the accelerator, and sped across the tarmac.

He drove into sheets of rain, exposed without a windshield. Droplets stung his face. The catering truck driver would tell the cops he thought it was a joke, and probably forget to mention the fifty-dollar bill Traynor gave him to hide in the truck. The cops would soon conclude he fled and question the missing tractor. He pressed the gas pedal to the floor. He steered away from the jet, the cops, Charlotte and the team bus at the tractor's maximum speed, unsure where to go.

A loaded luggage train chugged over the concrete ahead, yielded to a taxiing MD-88, then lurched forward. He was unfamiliar with the airport exterior, and how to exit without guidance. Traynor would scoot around in circles until the cops caught on. He spun the steering wheel and veered toward the loaded luggage train, transferring luggage to baggage claim. Somewhere between the cluttered tarmac and numerous terminals, arriving passenger luggage penetrated the inner workings of the airport to be thrown upon the winding conveyors. He closed within twenty yards of the luggage train, eased up on the accelerator, and matched the moderate pace.

Half an hour later, Traynor, soaked by the rain and sweat, coiled beneath a cheap blue tarp in the bed of a pickup truck parked in the North Terminal decks. He unzipped his flight bag and found his cell phone. From memory, he dialed.

"Yeah, who is it?"

"Chet," Traynor said. "It's me."

"Torch? That you, pal? Boy, you sent that ball into orbit in St. Louie."

"Chet. I need your help?"

"Speak up. Can't hardly make out what you're saying. Did you say you need help?"

"I can't talk any louder. I'm in trouble, Chet."

"Then you called the right number. How can I help ya, Torch?"

"Listen close…."

Chapter Twenty-Eight

"I can't believe he got off that plane without being seen." Charlotte cradled a cup of decaf to warm her hands.

Pope and Cox had joined her at Houlihan's, a restaurant and bar that opened into the main terminal atrium. It was almost ten o'clock. Most of the terminal shops and fast-food eateries had closed, their storefronts sealed with security gates.

Cox chugged draft beer. "APD underestimated Traynor. They think he climbed down the catering truck."

"St. Louis cops spooked him, or cops on the runway wouldn't have fazed Bic-boy," Pope said. "He would have assumed the police were a highway escort for the privileged."

"Did St. Louis homicide question him?" Cox asked.

Pope sipped a dark Cabernet. "That's what I understand. I heard homicide detectives cornered him in the locker room. Hendricks chased the cops away before they hauled him off, then instructed Tad to hide Bic-boy until they chartered out. Or so they say."

"They?" Cox arched his eyebrows. "Not exactly a reliable source, Pierce."

"I paid hard-earned money for that account. Good gossip, but not reliable enough to put it in print. Although Lord knows how tempting it is to sling mud at my favorite celebrity."

"I'm surprised St. Louis reacted so quickly," Cox said.

"After the conference call with APD Wednesday night, they must have checked the Cardinals' schedule." Charlotte turned her attention to commotion in the atrium. A cluster of television equipment, reporters and technicians scampered toward the underground terminal train.

"Breaking news." Pope held up his wine glass like a microphone. "Braves' superstar Torch Traynor evades APD dragnet. More at eleven."

Charlotte smiled. "I guess my wild allegations go public tonight."

"Traynor becomes a most-wanted mug shot. You're right about St. Louis,

Charlotte. They wanted to detain him before Atlanta nabbed him. Atlanta wants him before the Bureau barges in. Prisoner custody is a huge factor when it comes down to who prosecutes first." Cox's phone chirped from an inside pocket. "It was St. Louis' only chance. Excuse me." He raised the phone to an ear and spun away to listen.

Pope rested a hand on Charlotte's knee underneath the tabletop. She slid a hand to his and squeezed. The discreet affection swapped flashbacks of the tarmac escape for tender images of a St. Louis hotel room and two days alone with Pope, barricaded from her woes in his embrace.

"Have you thought about accommodations in Atlanta?" Pierce whispered.

"I haven't had time. I suppose I'll check into a motel."

"Tough to find a room in Atlanta," Pope said. "Business travelers, conventions...can be a real problem."

She put her elbow on the table, rested her chin on her hand, and leaned into him. "Oh my. Maybe you can help me with this dilemma."

"It just so happens I can. It's not much. Small two-bedroom brick on Collier Road. Of course, I converted the second bedroom into a home office."

"Of course—"

"That was APD," Cox burst into their private conversation. "Good news."

Charlotte blurted, "They caught Traynor!"

Cox's chin drooped. "Well, no. That was Dickson, the homicide detective on Liz's case. They identified a suspect. He wanted to know if the name Chester Suggs is familiar. Goes by Chet, I think he said."

"Chet Suggs!" The color drained from Charlotte's face. "Yes, I know him. Well, I met him. Nasty sort. He grew up with Traynor in Rome...." Her words froze. She recalled the Ford pickup truck streaking by in the fog, determined to run her off the rural highway. "It was him."

"Huh?" Cox said. When he received no response he continued, "With all the cops in the neighborhood after Liz's death, a do-good citizen reported a suspicious-looking truck parked on the street close to the time of the crime. Turns out the vehicle belonged to Suggs. Another neighbor saw a man matching Suggs's description going up the stairs around eleven thirty Tuesday morning."

"Charlotte, you look sick," Pope said.

"I feel awful." She licked her lips. "Remember when I went to Rome, Sunday. I asked questions about Traynor. I riled Suggs. He must have followed me. I led him to Liz." Her eyes panned to Cox. "He wanted to shut me up, not Liz."

"Are you saying he was protecting Traynor?" Pope asked.

"Maybe," Charlotte replied in a puny voice.

"Two questions. Were you his intended victim and Liz just got in the way?" Cox touched Charlotte's forearm. "And second, did he act on his own or after consulting with his lifelong pal, Torch?"

Traynor peeked beneath his droopy eyelids. "Where we at, Chet?"

"You fell asleep before we got on the interstate. I was wondering when you was gonna rally." Suggs pointed at the windshield. "Coach Al's fishing camp, 'bout fifteen miles west of Rome. He stocks a little pond out yonder with largemouth bass. Few brim, too."

Pointy shadows of knee-high grass, bathed in the headlights, crept along the faded green house-trailer siding. Illuminated beams shot up through rusted holes in the awning like a Chevrolet dealer's grand opening spotlight. A combination lock, threaded through a sturdy hasp, secured a dented door.

"Ain't much to look at." Traynor unbuckled his seatbelt and stretched his arms.

"Holiday Inn it ain't. Not even a Motel 6, but it's got power, that is, if I can coax that old generator into cranking. But no one will come looking for ya here, unless Coach Al wanders up here to fish tomorrow. Course, he'd never turn his prize student over to the law."

"You know the combination?"

"Nah." Suggs pressed his belly against the steering wheel, reached to the floor, and fiddled with tools under the seat. He grinned and held up bolt cutters. "Don't need no numbers with this baby."

"We're breaking into Coach Al's place?"

"Just messing with him, Torch. Every time I come up here I snap the lock. Coach Al finds it, cusses like he's arguing balls and strikes with a blind ump, and then he sends me up here with a new lock. Drives him bonkers. He thinks a pack of hoodlums is ransacking his place, all the while it's me funning him. We even spent a night out here in woods 'cause he had a hunch they'd show up. Ol' Coach Al was right, I reckon, since I was with him."

Suggs shut off the lights and killed the engine. No streetlights, no electricity, and rain clouds blotting out the moon and stars—Traynor couldn't see his hands in the blind country darkness.

"Hope you got a flashlight."

"Yep." The interior lights glowed when Suggs opened his door. He followed a weak light beam, trampled high grass, and traipsed toward the trailer. Suggs clamped his teeth around the flashlight, spread the bolt cutters, and grunted. The high-strength steel yielded and fractured. A metallic screech shattered the black tranquility.

Suggs hollered, "Grab something out of the back and come on in, Torch.

I'll try the generator."

He climbed down from the cab, put his flight bag over his shoulder, and lifted a cooler from the truck bed. He hoisted the heavy cooler to his shoulder. "What the hell you got in this thing anyway?"

"I chilled a quart of Jack Black and iced down a couple of cases of tall boys to chase it with," Suggs responded from the shadows. "Ought to last us 'til morning."

The generator spit and coughed after Suggs pulled the cord twice. Traynor saw a light bulb flicker through the smudged window, dim, and brighten to full illumination as the power flow stabilized.

Traynor tugged the flimsy door open and climbed the stacked concrete block stairs. The trailer floor trembled when he set down the cooler. A ratty couch and chair with ripped upholstery bordered a dusty rug. Plastic plates and cups cluttered the cheap kitchen counter veneer. He lowered his bag to the floor, sat in the chair, and closed his eyes. He led the majors with thirty-eight saves, made six million dollars a year, and here he was, holed up in a flea-infested trailer. Not even a double wide flea-infested trailer. How fast fame flames out....

Suggs lumbered up the stairs, squeezed through the door, toting a weathered footlocker, and dropped the trunk next to the cooler. "Just you and me, Torch, like when we was kids." He threw open the cooler lid, grabbed the liquor bottle, and took a long swig. "Son, that'll take the edge off what ails ya. Want some?" He offered the Jack Daniels to Traynor.

Traynor wiped the bottle and tilted back the bourbon for a shot while Suggs popped open two sixteen-ounce Budweisers.

"There ya go, bud." Suggs handed him a beer. "This'll put out the fire in your throat."

Traynor washed down the bourbon. "I appreciate your help, Chet."

"They mess with you, they're messin' with me. You know that."

"This ain't no barroom brawl. There could be a heap of trouble for helping me."

Suggs sat down on the footlocker. "You dozed off before you told me why the cops is chasing you."

"They think I killed a woman in Tampa. Maybe another one in St. Louis."

"That's deep shit. Don't matter to me." Suggs sipped his beer. "Did you do what they is saying?"

"Hell no. All I'm guilty of is tying on a helluva buzz and trying to talk a fine-looking woman to roll in the hay with me."

"Man's entitled to some pussy. She the one that got herself killed?"

"I met her in a bar in St. Pete the night I blew the Devils Rays game."

Lifting himself with the chair armrests, Traynor rose, walked to the kitchen area, and sorted dishes and glasses. “This place is a pigsty.”

“What happened to her, Torch?”

“Showed up dead in Tampa the next morning. Her sister’s been hounding me ever since the bartender blabbed that he saw me hitting on her.”

Suggs spun on the trunk toward Traynor. “Her sister been up here pestering you? She a reporter?”

“Yeah, or so she said. How’d you know that, Chet?”

“It’s that damn Gordon woman, ain’t it?”

“Right. Charlotte Gordon.”

“Damn bitch. Knew I should’ve shut her up for good.” He fell to his knees and unlatched the footlocker. Traynor’s attention drifted from the kitchen disarray to his friend, throwing camouflage clothing and camping gear on the floor.

“Here it is.” Suggs withdrew a Smith & Wesson .357 magnum revolver. He spun the cylinder and examined the blue steel six-inch barrel. “It ain’t too late to seal her lying lips…forever.”

“That cannon loaded?”

“Not yet.”

“Keep it that way,” Traynor said. “Where did you see her?”

“She strutted into the ballpark one afternoon, asking all kinds of questions about you, what riles you, and such. I could tell she was trouble from the get-go, but old Al rambled on, telling stories ’bout you like she was your long-lost cousin Annie.”

“Well, whatever she knows, she’s got the cops believing her. I got to find a simple way to show this lynching party that they’ve treed the wrong cat. Fast. The Braves are in a pennant race and I don’t want to miss out.”

“Like I said, I’ll shut her up for you, Torch.”

“Too late now, but I appreciate it. Since I vamoosed from that airplane, every cop in Georgia is out to bag ole Torch. Anything happens to her will just make it worse.”

Suggs, passed out on the couch, snored. An unfinished beer lay on its side and soaked the plaid fabric of the sagging sofa. As the beer and bourbon flowed, Suggs had waved the unloaded revolver, spewing threats toward Charlotte and various National League hitters, renown for tormenting Torch. No one exhibited loyalty like Chet Suggs, but Traynor insisted that his friend bury the weapon within the old trunk.

Only a swallow or two remained in the bottle. Traynor squinted his eyes to keep the trailer walls from scrolling like a television screaming for a vertical hold adjustment. No television, radio, or chatter from Chet, only his thoughts occupied him.

Why had Margaret been in a dump like the Hatch? She wasn't the type. If only she found some other bar that night, he would be sleeping it off in his Buckhead condo instead of hunkering down in this roach trap. Charlotte Gordon wouldn't be snipping at his heels like a teething beagle pup. Hell, she wouldn't back off now until they stuck him with a lethal needle. Who was that lawyer? The one that sprung O.J.? Damn, what was in that file of hers that kept her coming after him, wave after wave, ignoring the casualties as she charged? The file.

Traynor unzipped his flight bag and retrieved the file she had flung across the bar Tuesday night. He opened the folder and squinted at the words. Newspaper articles and plain paper printouts were stapled together. He dug for Charlotte's link to him among the clippings. If he could discover how all this writing made her so damn sure he killed Margaret, or the others, then maybe he could construct sure-fire alibis and discredit her accusations.

He thumbed the file contents. Six thin packets, paper clipped. Atop each segment were vivid memories from Philadelphia, Chicago, Tampa Bay, San Francisco, Atlanta and St. Louis. All six of his blown saves, the six low points of his season, and six ensuing hangovers. He remembered each pitch, each batter, and how the magic abandoned him in each bad outing, stranded him to confront club-swinging apes and screaming hordes with a cowhide ball and no zip in his arm.

All the pitching obituaries came from *The Atlanta Journal-Constitution*, except the St. Louis disaster. The colorful picture of him hitting the home run and the St. Louis article looked like an Internet printout. The story of Megan Rivers's murder was paper clipped to Monday's game recap. Likewise, he found the report of Margaret Gordon's murder in Tampa attached to a game story.

He closed one eye and deliberated over every blurry word from *The Tampa Tribune* article describing Margaret Gordon's death. He blinked and tried to recall the photograph Charlotte showed him, or an image of the natural beauty that attracted him to Margaret at the Hatch. The story didn't expand on police theories and only reported her injuries as multiple blows to the head and probable defense injuries. He finished reading, closed the file, and set it on the floor.

"To you, Margaret." He chugged the last swallow of bourbon and wiped his mouth. Staring at the Jack Daniels label, he connected pieces of the newspaper articles in a subliminal matching game.

"Shit." He lunged forward. The bourbon bottle toppled off his lap, bounced on the linoleum and spun. Traynor fell to his knees, ripped open the file folder, and used a finger to re-read the story of Margaret's death. He combed the St. Louis article describing Megan Rivers's death with care. His finger stopped, and his face burst into a smile. "That's it."

He snatched the photo of his home run stroke from the pile and kissed it. "Ain't you beautiful, Torch, you sorry excuse for a closing pitcher?"

Chapter Twenty-Nine

Traynor woke to the waft of crackling grease and corn meal, browning in the frying pan.

"It's almost noon. 'Bout time your lazy ass woke." Suggs stood over the stove with a beer.

"Smells good. What you cooking?"

"Fresh bass and hush puppies. A little after sunup, I caught a three-pounder with a Rapala." He reenacted the top water lure cast, and the fight the fish put up after it struck. "Son-of-a-bitch hit it like Shamu. Damn, it was a pretty sight."

"Hope it tastes as good as it smells. I'm so hungry I'd could eat raw opossum."

"Damn, Torch. I wasted all that time hooking this lunker, when I could've drove down to the highway and scraped up road kill."

Traynor leaned forward in the chair and spotted the open file folder. "How long before the fish is ready?"

"Ten minutes."

"I think I found a way out of this jam." Traynor removed the cell phone from his flight bag. He stood and walked toward the open door. "I need to make a quick call, then I'll be ready for the catch of the day."

He hustled down the stairs into the clear day, and turned on his phone, hoping for a strong signal. His head hurt, and his tongue felt swollen. He dug Pope's card from his pocket and dialed.

"Pierce Pope," he answered after one ring.

"Hey, Pope. Earl Traynor, here."

"Bic-boy! You finally made the front page, and you didn't lose a game to do it. The cops are turning Atlanta inside out looking for you. Where are you hiding?"

"I'd be bed sore on a cell bunk if it weren't for you, but I got a sneaky feeling trusting a reporter with my whereabouts would be all over the papers before the line went dead."

"Then I suppose you're not proposing to surrender to me, including an exclusive interview prior to turning you over to Atlanta PD?"

"You said you'd help me, Pope."

"That I did. Within the realm of the law, what can I do?"

"I didn't do what the cops are saying," Traynor squinted at the blazing midday sun, "killing those women and all."

"Tell it to the jury. Listen Bic-boy, I could care less whether or not you're guilty. You're news, lines of black and white print to me. By helping you, I escalated a simple arrest into a daring escapade and major media magnet. Man, *Headline News* plastered your photo nationwide this morning. By helping you, if I become your conduit to the press, then I help myself."

"I ain't stupid enough to think you'd lend a hand out of the goodness of your heart. I'll talk through you, if that's what you're asking. And whatever story there is belongs to you, although I'm hoping this'll be over with quick."

"Good. What do you want?"

"I need to meet with Charlotte, and I don't know how to find her. I figured you'd know where she's staying in Atlanta."

"I might be able to contact her. What should I tell her?"

"Tell her I can prove I didn't kill her sister or the Rivers woman in St. Louis."

"That should intrigue her. Want to share how you would accomplish that?"

"Charlotte's the one pointing a finger, whipping the cops into a lather, so the way I see it, she needs to be the one to call off the hounds. If she wants you there it's fine by me."

"Face-to-face meeting," Pope said. "Where do you want to meet?"

"I haven't worked that out, yet. Lots of people. No cops. Outside. Plenty of roads in and out," Traynor thought aloud. "You got any ideas?"

"Hang on." Traynor heard Pope ruffle paper. "There's a football game. Clemson plays at Georgia Tech tomorrow at noon. Grant Field seats over fifty thousand at capacity."

"That's plenty of folks. Do you know your way 'round the Tech campus?"

"I'm familiar with it. I usually go to the game when North Carolina comes to town."

"Is there an open area where Charlotte and me could meet?"

"The closer to the stadium, the more cops for crowd control and traffic," Pope said. "West of the stadium, up the hill, there's a clearing between the library and Tech's student center. After the game, mobs of fans parade to the perimeter parking lots along that path."

"And this area is wide open."

"I'm working from memory here, but what I remember are a few trees, and a grassy patch, crisscrossed with sidewalks. The student center and a couple of classroom buildings border the field."

"Sounds like it will work. Tell her I'll meet her there 'bout twenty minutes after the game ends. Is there somewhere, a landmark, I should look for her?"

"There's a fountain. They built it for the '96 Olympics."

"Tell Charlotte I'll meet her at the fountain, twenty minutes after the Tech game ends."

"And how can I contact you with her approval?"

"I'll call you tonight. Have a good one, Pope." Traynor shut off his phone and pounced up the stairs for a serving of fried fish and hush puppies.

Chapter Thirty

A night-long drizzle had dissolved the muggy humidity. Charlotte sped south on Peachtree and allowed the rain-cleansed air to rush in the window of Pope's black Lexus. Liz's fleece kept Charlotte warm as she admired hardwoods mottled in fiery red, shocking yellow, and burnt orange.

Cox's call woke her before seven. He told her that the Floyd County police could not find Suggs. After coffee and a toasted bagel, she decided to shop for new clothes, tired of wearing the same jeans and sink-washed panties. The thought of returning to Liz's apartment for her clothes revolted her. Chet Suggs had converted her belongings into a urinal. She doubted if a washbasin of super-concentrated bleach would clean Suggs's filth from her wardrobe.

She turned right on Collier Road. A Parisian's bag, full of cosmetics and undergarments, tumbled to the backseat floor. She looked over her shoulder at the Abercrombie & Fitch bag, and the brown paper sack from the Peachtree Industrial Thrift Store. Her big sister never bought a stitch of clothing at full price and would have wooed over the bargains Charlotte found—a jeans jumper, print skirt, faded denim jacket, and scratched leather clogs all for thirty-three dollars.

Charlotte steered into Pope's driveway and shut down the engine, relieved she had returned his vehicle undamaged. She balanced the shopping bags, climbed the stairs, and freed her pinky to ring the doorbell.

Pope swung the door open. He wore a starched white Hilfiger button-down, gray pleated slacks, and black polished wingtip loafers. "There you are. I was afraid I'd be gone before you returned."

"I have your car."

"Details, details."

She leaned forward and kissed him. "I had such fun. And I can change my clothes. I'm sure the gray fleece and denim look was tiresome. Hope you'll like the new me. Thanks for loaning me your car." She held out the keys and dropped them into Pope's palm. "No dings, no dents. Your car is gorgeous. Call me nosy, but just how do you afford a Lexus on a sportswriter's salary?"

"Ha," he laughed. "I bought it *pre-owned* and restored the faultless ebony exterior and creamy tan upholstery to showroom condition with my own two hands."

"Sorry. It's really none of my business."

"I have nothing to hide...from you. There are a few side perks from covering the Braves. As their beat writer, I become an expert by association. It opens doors to supplement my income with various freelance opportunities. Currently, I'm working a deal to write a biography on Frank Houseman in the off-season." He lifted the bags out of her arms.

"Oh, if you'll be gone all day," Charlotte said. "I might need a vehicle to get around."

"Where's your rental?"

"Carlton returned it for me while I was in St. Louis and negotiated a deal on the damages." Charlotte reached into a jeans pocket. She dangled a key. "I thought I'd borrow Liz's Jeep. Will you drive me there on your way to the *AJC*?"

"My pleasure, Charlotte. Now, come on in. I have a lot to tell you before I go into the office."

She followed him in and closed the door. The ceiling fan twirled in slow revolutions and drafted an agreeable breeze from the open living room windows. Violin music with an Oriental flare played from Bose speakers embedded in the wall.

"The music is beautiful."

"I'm glad you approve. Vanessa-Mae from her *China Girl* album. 'Fantasy for Violin and Orchestra on Puccini's "Turandot".' I believe the Royal Opera House Covet Garden Orchestra accompanies."

She settled on the red leather sofa. "You continue to surprise me, Pierce. You write about grown men that scratch their crotches and spit for a living, yet you can recite the ensemble from a classical piece."

"Mystery nurtures infatuation. A slow revelation of my inner self adds anticipation. You become intrigued with what facet of my complex yet adorable personality will surface next," he sat down next to her, "until you're addicted and can't live without me."

Pope kissed her cheek.

They came in so late the night before she hadn't noticed the room's decor until now. Rich leather furniture coordinated with a lavish Oriental rug. Contemporary novels, classics, and an impressive collection of coffee table books from museums and art galleries throughout the country stocked elegant walnut bookshelves.

"This room is so peaceful. How do you ever leave?"

"Only to fund my indulgence. Regardless how hectic the day will become, I know that tomorrow I will be here, relaxed, absorbing a venue of my choice. This is my favorite place, my favorite time of day. And today, I'm privileged to share my oasis with my favorite person."

Charlotte threw her arms around his neck and pulled him tight. "Don't go today, Pierce."

"I have a wad of expenses to submit, and a game tonight." He removed her hands from his shoulders and lowered them between them. "I assure you what I want to do and what I must do today severely diverge."

She studied his handsome features, pried her hand loose, and touched her wrist to her forehead. "Rejected again."

Pope laughed.

"We need to talk before I go, Charlotte."

"If seducing you is out of the question," she rubbed his chest, "then I suppose rousing conversation will have to suffice until you return."

"Traynor called."

"What! Why didn't you say so?"

"Floating on a magic carpet through Shangri-La with you was exceedingly more pleasurable than discussing a crotch-scratching, tobacco-spitting ballplayer."

"What did he say? What did he want?"

"He wants to meet with you."

"No. Absolutely not. I refuse to be anywhere near Traynor. I'll consider speaking with him, but I will not under any circumstance go toe to toe with that killer again."

"He claims he has proof that he didn't murder your sister. He'll share with you and only you."

"What? What could it be, Pierce?"

"I'm his number one critic. He wouldn't dare trust me with any more than the essentials."

"When?" Charlotte rose and paced from the Oriental rug to the hardwood floor and back.

"Tomorrow afternoon following the Clemson, Georgia Tech football game. He suggested the grassy area in front of the Tech student center. He wants to rendezvous at the Olympic fountain twenty minutes after the game ends."

"No. It sounds too risky."

"Couldn't hurt to see what he has to show you. Even Traynor isn't stupid enough to hurt you in the middle of a liquored-up football crowd."

"I'll ask Carlton to call his APD contacts. Then whatever Traynor has to offer, he can release it to the world."

"He explicitly demanded no cops," Pope said. "If he smells a trap, he could disappear, and Margaret's murder might remain unresolved indefinitely."

Charlotte bit her lip. Closure—her fixation, her only aspiration, the gateway to a future beyond Margaret's death. If Traynor showed conclusive proof of his innocence, he would eradicate the mounting suspicion thrust upon him. If she didn't agree to the meeting, only Traynor's arrest and conviction would abolish Charlotte's uncertainty.

"Pierce, I can't believe I'm going to do this." She sighed. "I'm still skeptical. Drat, what choice do I have? I'll meet him. How do I contact him?"

"He wouldn't leave a number. Not that I blame him. He said that he'd confirm the arrangements with me tonight."

Charlotte's face wrinkled. "Why did he call you, Pierce?"

"Association, I suppose. You don't have a local telephone. After the confrontation at Adam's Mark, he surmised that I would know how to find you."

"I suppose," Charlotte responded, still bewildered.

"Do you ever straighten your work area?" Pope asked Cox, leaning against the cubicle.

"A neat desk is a sign of no work being done. Speaking of desks, do you need a broom to sweep the spider webs off yours?"

"Funny, Cox. I'm just passing through to get reimbursed for my extravagant travel expenses." He sipped coffee from a Styrofoam cup. "Traynor contacted Charlotte."

Cox dropped his hands from his keyboard and looked up from the monitor. "What did he want?"

"He wants to meet with her."

"That's insane. Hell no."

"I concur. But Charlotte insists. Traynor convinced her that he can prove his innocence."

"I don't give a shit if he shows her that he's fricking George W. Bush himself. Traynor is a killer, and he's killed more than once. What will prevent him from killing again? No way, I don't want her near him!"

"My sentiments exactly…at first." Pope rolled a chair from the cubicle across the aisle and sat.

"At first? What are you up to, Pope?"

"Suppose Charlotte meets with Traynor. And further suppose the arrangements leak to APD. Now imagine, APD surveillance, perhaps a tactical sniper, and plainclothes cops for protection, the ensuing capture and incarceration of Bic-boy. No more threats. No more murders. No more danger to Charlotte. Could you not orchestrate such a scenario?"

"Yes." Cox tapped a cigarette filter on his desk. "And Charlotte is willing to bait the trap?"

"I didn't say that. As adamant as she is about seeing Traynor, she is vehemently opposed to police intervention. She's afraid their presence will spook him."

"Endanger Charlotte without her permission? I won't do it without her consent, Pope."

"It's for her own good. You know as I well as I do that she's obsessed with these murders. We have a chance to rid her of the screaming meanies whacking away with their misery sticks. It's up to you and me, Cox. She'll meet with him, regardless. Call it insurance."

Cox coughed out the first puff of smoke. He turned to a blank page in his notepad and reached for a number two pencil. "All right, I'll run it by APD. How? When? Where? Did she happen to entrust you with details?"

Pope reached inside his blazer pocket and pulled out a leather-bound notebook. "Georgia Tech. In front of the student center. They'll meet at the Olympic fountain, twenty minutes following the football game."

"Too many people. The cops won't like it. Accidental victims. Liability."

"According to Charlotte, Bic-boy dictated the location. Non-negotiable. A crowd should provide an extra layer of safety insulation for Charlotte. Traynor will be careful of his actions amid a throng of football fans."

"I don't like it." Cox inhaled a deep breath, and lifted his telephone. He punched in the number for APD homicide and waited for an answer. "May I speak with Detective Roger Chawk, please?"

Chawk. Roger Chawk. Pope logged the name into his notebook. While Cox held, Pope stood, and rolled the chair across the carpet. "If you speak with Charlotte, not a word."

"I'll think about it."

"She'll worry. Her anxiety could tip Traynor off, and this episode might never end."

"I said, 'I'll think about it.'" Cox turned his attention to the call when a voice squawked through the receiver. "Roger. Carlton Cox here. How'd you like a chance to corner Torch Traynor?"

Chapter Thirty-One

Minutes past seven, Cox loitered on the lawn fanning out from the Georgia Tech student center like a river delta. He spotted only an occasional Friday-night student, trudging along the concrete sidewalk network outfitted with backpacks and laptops. He wandered toward the fountain where Charlotte would meet Traynor.

He had asked a student for directions to the fountain when he entered the Tech campus. "You mean the shaft," the kid responded, and he pointed him toward the structure. He stood before the Kessler Campanile, an artistic tower silhouetted against a hazy sunset, and appreciated the nickname. He waited for Chawk to arrive and read from the plaque. Richard Kessler had spearheaded the funding efforts of the classes of 1943 and 1953 to build the pointy edifice named in his honor. The futuristic tower and surrounding fountain were constructed prior to the 1996 Atlanta Olympics and added an arty inspiration to the otherwise urban campus hosting the Olympic village.

Four men exited from the student center and turned toward him. He recognized Roger Chawk, accompanied by three men in uniform. They descended through the concrete amphitheater to join him.

Chawk extended his hand. "Carlton, good to see you again." He nodded to the left. "Carlton Cox, this is Captain Richard Bishop and Sergeant Sam Mitchell from APD's tactical team." Cox shook their hands. "And I'd like you to meet Lou Gundy, Georgia Tech police chief."

"Chawk explained you're privy to information regarding Earl Traynor," Bishop said. "He's coming out of hiding to meet this Charlotte Gordon woman, tomorrow."

"That's right," Cox answered. "Right where we're standing, twenty minutes after the game."

Bishop turned to the sergeant. "How's the layout, Mitch?"

Sunlight reflected in Mitchell's Oakley sunglasses. He pivoted in a thorough survey of the building tops. "Not bad, Captain. What time will it be?"

"Game time is noon," the Tech police chief answered. "Should be over by three thirty. The meeting should take place by four o'clock."

Mitchell pointed at the sun and drew an arc upward. "Sun should be about there. Weather calls for rain tonight, but Saturday's forecast is clear. A sniper in the stairwell." He leveled his finger at a brick-encased staircase attached to the student center. "That portal at the top will make a nice perch. And there, on top of that building on the arch above the stained glass."

"The old bookstore," Chief Gundy added.

"Sniper two up there, with the sun to his back," Mitchell said.

"Clear line of fire, Mitch?" Bishop asked.

"Yes, sir. Seventy-five yards tops. We could shoot a plum out of your hand from there. Captain, I'm concerned about the pedestrian traffic."

"I understand, Mitch." Bishop looked at Chawk. "Can the time be rescheduled?"

"My understanding is that the arrangements are non-negotiable. Isn't that right?" Chawk asked Cox.

"I'm just a messenger, but that's what I've been told."

"Let's pray we grab him without a shot. Chief, we'll need your boys to restrict access to the stair towers," Bishop said.

Gundy jotted a note.

"Mitch, go check out the stairwell."

"Yes, sir." Mitchell climbed the amphitheater seats toward the student center.

Bishop's eyes combed the terrain. "Chief, what kind of traffic flow should we expect?"

"Grant Field is east of here," Gundy waved his hand at the sidewalk that separated the Tech library and the Skiles Classroom building. "After the game, a continuous mob of fans will come down those stairs, split at the fork in the sidewalk, and plod toward parking lots to the northwest and west of the student center. The flow of people will then disperse across this open area toward numerous parking lots," he pointed to the grassy area before them.

"We will deploy a task force of patrolmen in uniform and plainclothes observing the crowd as they penetrate the perimeter. Photos of the suspect will be distributed in the tactical briefing tomorrow morning. Hopefully, an alert eye will identify Traynor and he will be apprehended prior to convening with Miss Gordon." Bishop rubbed his chin. "In the event the situation escalates, there will be two SWAT tactical officers with MP5 sub machineguns in the northern most staircase, and two in a van over there." He nodded at the parking lot that border the grassy area. "In addition, three SWAT officers in plainclothes, Glock secondary weapons only, will mill around within ten yards of Miss Gordon.

"Mr. Cox," Bishop said. "Does the suspect know Miss Gordon?"

"Yes."

"No chance to substitute a female officer then. And I understand Miss Gordon will not be aware of our presence?"

"That's the plan," Cox answered. "I've been told she'll back out if the police are involved."

Bishop grimaced. "I sure would like to suit her in body armor. We'll do what we can to keep her safe. Mr. Cox, do you have a photo of Miss Gordon?"

"No. But, I can identify her for you. What time should I be here?"

"We'll deploy after kickoff, oh, twelve fifteen, sharp. Meet me over there." He pointed to the Bunger-Henry Building. "We'll set up the command post on the roof."

Pope peered down, his arms folded in disgust, at the Turner Field groundskeepers hustling in the rain to roll the massive tarp over the infield. Another rain delay, another race to the deadline, and possibly, another write-through. He fumed.

"Pope," he barked when he answered his cell phone.

"Will she be there?"

"Bic-boy." Pope looked both ways to check if anyone overheard him. The press box was almost empty as the reporters searched for diversions to endure the rain delay boredom. "She'll be there."

"Good. No cops, right?"

"If you're innocent, why are you so worried about the police?"

"I ain't kidding, Pope. No cops."

"Neither Charlotte nor I have divulged your arrangements to the police."

"Will you be there?"

"Nearby. Wouldn't miss it for the world. Ted Benson said he'd cover the Braves beat for me tomorrow night."

"Hell, if it goes as I plan, I'll be suited up in time for Benson to write up my thirty-ninth save."

"You sure are cocky for Georgia's most wanted." Pope sipped a Diet Coke. "What do you have that's so conclusive? Photos? Video? Charlotte's pretty headstrong, I can't see you stopping her crusade to imprison you without dramatic evidence."

"Ever play Monopoly?"

"Not recently."

"Got me a get-outta-jail-free card. In black and white." Traynor paused.

"How are the boys doing tonight?"

"It appears they don't miss you in the least. Bottom of the seventh, they're up three zip on Pittsburgh. Rain delay."

"Good. Hope they can hang on 'til I get back. See ya tomorrow afternoon, Pope. Georgia Tech, twenty minutes after the final whistle."

"Get your shit, Chet." Traynor closed his cell phone.

"Where we going, Torch?"

"Hot-lanta. Sleep in a soft hotel bed. Chase women. We'll wake up, grab some eggs and grits, and go to a football game. My treat."

"What if someone recognizes you?"

"Won't matter after tomorrow afternoon." Traynor dug through his flight bag. "Shit, my razor is in my suitcase."

"You gonna shave?"

"Without my goatee, I'm just another baby-faced redneck."

"Coach Al keeps a razor in the head."

"Pack up, bud." Traynor walked toward the bathroom. "Chet. Is there a store between here and Atlanta where I can pick up some clothes?"

"There's a twenty-four-hour Super Walmart outside of Cartersville."

"Perfect. Let me scrape off this stubble and we'll hit the road."

Chapter Thirty-Two

Charlotte found Cox hunched over the bar at Manuel's Tavern. He stared at another muted episode of *The Andy Griffith Show*, broadcast during the rain-delayed Braves telecast. She brushed her hand across his shoulders. "I was hoping that I'd bump into you here."

"Pull up a stool," he said without looking at her.

"I tried to call you." She reached for his cell phone. The readout was dark. "Dead battery?"

"Doesn't work unless I turn it on."

"You hiding from me, Carlton?"

Cox spun on the stool. His eyes were glazed and red. "What makes you say that?"

"Sorry." Charlotte held up the palms of her hands and backed away. Maybe he *was* avoiding her. "A bit sensitive, aren't we? I can leave if you'd rather be alone with your longneck."

"Sit down." He forced a smile. "Please."

Charlotte eased onto the barstool. When the bartender approached she ordered a Miller Lite.

"How's the game?" she asked.

"Atlanta's up three to nothing. Umpire stopped it a few minutes ago because of the rain."

"I wanted to buy you dinner. I dropped by here earlier looking for you. Busy night?"

"Working a story." Cox spoke in snippy, concise sentences. His caustic demeanor reminded her of his gloomy disposition at the airport the previous night.

Charlotte asked, "What did I do wrong this time?"

"Nothing, Charlotte. Nothing. I'm in a raunchy mood. Can't an old grouch mope without an inquisition?"

Charlotte sipped her beer, unsure what to say, or whether she should even stay.

"With Pope at the stadium, how are you getting around?" Cox broke the silent stalemate.

"I borrowed Liz's Jeep."

"Right." Cox crushed his cigarette in a plastic ashtray. "So, what will you do when they capture Torch? That is, if the cops nab him."

He fumbled with the cigarette package. His gaze shifted away from Charlotte.

"Have you heard something about Traynor, Carlton?"

"No. Just trying to make conversation. Traynor is too high profile to hide forever. For Pete's sake, his mug shot was plastered on *Sports Illustrated* in August. Someone will spot him before too long."

"The sooner the better." She resisted the urge to divulge the plans to meet Traynor. She yearned to test the unorthodox arrangements with his streetwise skepticism and crime experience. She promised Pope she wouldn't. Untold knowledge, part truths, wasn't the same as lying…was it? Charlotte washed down a knot of guilt crawling up her throat with a swallow of beer.

"So, will you stay in Atlanta?"

"I'm not sure. I haven't thought that far ahead. If indeed they catch him, then I have a few personal fires to put out. Mourn appropriately for Margaret with my parents. I have an apartment lease in Dallas to wiggle out of. Unfortunately, my portfolio is not sufficient to lead a life of leisure much longer, so I'll have to deliberate, and quickly, where and what I'll do to support myself."

"You're a decent snoop. Can you write?"

"Business communications—you know, one run-on sentence after another, chocked full of non-descriptive verbs, and big words no one ever uses. Three paragraphs to say what could be said in two sentences."

"Never too late to learn how to write."

"You don't actually think I could be a reporter?" She smiled. "Why, Carlton Cox, that might be the nicest thing you've ever said to me."

"Oh, don't go getting sentimental on me."

Holding a portable telephone, the bartender called out, "Hey, Carlton. Chuck Stennett from *The Charlotte Observer* wants to talk to you."

"Tell him I'm yakking with a friend," Cox replied above the tavern clatter.

The bartender spoke into the phone and hollered to Cox again. "He says you ain't got no friends."

"Then obviously I ain't here."

"Is he still trying to bet on the Falcons game?"

"Chuck's a persistent cuss. Every time I talk to him, I lose money. The Falcons could be undefeated and I'd still lose money to Chuck." Cox looked up at the television. "The tarp is coming off."

Charlotte glanced at the illuminated Anheuser Busch clock hanging at the back of the bar. It was ten forty. "What inning is it?"

"Seventh, I think."

"It'll be midnight before they finish the game."

"At least," Cox answered. "You'll probably leave Atlanta and never look back."

Charlotte noted Cox missed the opportunity to chuckle at Pope battling another deadline—one of Cox's true joys. She was certain, now, more than ever, something was going on that distracted him beyond the contents of their conversation.

"You won't get rid of me that easy, Carlton. Now that I've become accustomed to your endless ridicule, I find it somewhat addicting."

He laughed. "Bring us two more, Cody," Cox yelled.

Porch light illuminated the darkened living room when Charlotte entered Pope's house. She flipped a light switch, closed the front door, and locked the bolt.

"Pierce," she called out, wishful Pope had slipped away from Turner Field early.

Only her echo answered.

Charlotte and Cox had watched the Braves' bullpen blow a four-run lead in the ninth. An hour and twenty minutes after midnight, the Pirates rallied to win the game in the thirteenth inning.

She flopped on the leather sofa and glanced at the VCR digital clock. Romance, murder, and beer—her weary thoughts swirled like a waterspout scooting across white-cap wave crests. She needed to be alert, well-rested and agile to meet with Traynor. When would Pope be home? She wanted to wait up for him, greet him in an outpour of affection. A mild beer buzz muddled the simple decision if and when to go to sleep. Deliberating, wondering, worrying, she blinked hard to relieve her burning eyes. Her eyelids refused to spring open as if superglue mascara lined her eyelashes. She slumped over, her indecision overrun by fatigue.

Charlotte slept hard, coiled on the rich leather, the lights blazing. At first, her subconscious ignored the gentle jingle. The ring intensified from a fingertip dinner bell to a raging fire alarm clanging on the walls of her dreams until the persistent noise woke her.

She staggered to the desk, fumbled with the telephone, and swept hair from her face. She pressed the talk button. "Pierce. Is that you, Pierce?"

"Yes."

Her legs weak, she dropped in the desk chair. "Are you all right?"

"I've been better."

"Has something happened?"

"No, Charlotte. Nothing like that. Just another long night at the ballpark." His sullen voice lacked the typical confident arrogance that dripped from his words.

"I tried to wait up for you. I must have dozed off. What time is it?"

"Almost four."

"Where are you?"

"I'm." Pope paused. "I'm in my car."

"Are you coming home?"

"Eventually."

"Come home now." Charlotte rubbed sleep from her eyes. "I'll cheer you up."

"Now isn't a good time. I called so you wouldn't worry. You need your sleep for tomorrow."

"You woke me, to tell me to sleep well!…I'm sorry. When my mind is groggy, my tongue misbehaves. Please come home. I want to see you."

"I said, not now!"

Charlotte bit her quivering lip. "I see."

"I shouldn't have snapped at you, Charlotte. I wrote through two deadlines and I'm wired. I need to unwind." He chuckled. "I never thought I'd say this, and if you quote me I'll categorically deny it, but if Bic-boy hadn't flown the coop I'd be under the sheets with a beautiful woman, dreaming about waking up next to you."

"Where are you going? I'll come meet you."

"Rest, Charlotte. I need to hack out a column for next week, then I might swing into Waffle House for an omelet and hash browns. I'll be home before you leave for Tech."

"You need some sleep, too."

"I'll power nap at my desk. I'll be fine."

"I want to be with you, Pierce. Please come home."

"Charlotte, listen to me. Being together this week has been special. Do you agree?"

She mumbled, "I do."

"Well, I'm afraid if you see me in this atypical state, I'll ruin precious infatuation with ugly realism."

"I can help you unwind. If we want to go any further than a week in the sack, we have to share our whole selves. I want to know the real you, all of you."

"In time, Charlotte. In time. Until then, will you do me a favor?"

"Yes, anything."

"Trust me."

Charlotte's head spun. Trust. Five little letters. "Of course, Pierce. I'll be here. Wake me when you get here?"

"I will."

"Hurry home."

She hung up. What a strange night. Charlotte massaged her face with both hands. First Cox, now Pope. Supportive and protective, strong and wise, within hours her rocks crumbled into a shaky rubble piles. Did she have this unnerving effect on everyone she met?

Chapter Thirty-Three

An occasional roar from the distant stadium interrupted the Saturday afternoon tranquility. Bright sunshine wrestled with a nippy wind to balance Atlanta's thermostat. Charlotte followed Pope to a remote parking lot three blocks north of the city campus while less than a mile away over fifty thousand fans watched Georgia Tech and Clemson bang helmets.

She wasn't sure why Pope insisted that they drive separate vehicles. Thankful he had returned safely, Charlotte held her tongue, refused to question him, fearful she would convert pettiness into conflict. As much as she wanted to riddle him with inquiries, she sidestepped her inquisitive instincts, satisfied to be with him. He would share his inner self when he was ready. They strolled, her arm locked around Pope's, through crammed parking lots haunted by the smoldering charcoal and stuffed trash containers, tailgate carnage abandoned as festive parking lot parties transformed into caravans of game-goers.

"How much further?" Charlotte asked as they walked behind the physics building.

"Five minutes," Pope said.

She looked at her Timex. Ten of three. She had listened to the Tech game on the Jeep radio. Not for entertainment—she cared as little for football as she did for baseball—her ears tuned to game clock updates. Clemson led Tech by three late in the third quarter.

"There's plenty of time, Charlotte."

"I know, I know. He could be out there watching me right now. It gives me the creeps."

"Bic-boy says he's innocent. If he's not, he's either courageous or stupider than I ever dreamed. Certainly, if he was determined to hurt you, he wouldn't do it on a campus overflowing with potential witnesses."

Charlotte ducked under a car flag affixed to a car window, embroidered with Buzz, the Georgia Tech Yellow Jackets' mascot. On the sidewalk, they rounded the corner under the Drama Tech sign.

Pope stopped Charlotte. “There’s the fountain.”

Beneath maple tree branches, she saw the Kessler Campanile at the foot of a gentle incline. “I’m nervous, Pierce.”

He wrapped his arm around her. “I don’t blame you. I won’t be far away. Probably over there.” He pointed toward the student center.

She snuggled her head into his shoulder.

He lifted her chin and looked into Charlotte’s eyes. “One way or the other, meeting with Bic-boy will alleviate the uncertainty, Charlotte. I won’t lie to you. He very well could try to strong-arm you. If that is his intent, however, why not stalk you, trap you in a desolate corner and shut you up permanently? On the other hand, walk away, don’t meet with him if your intuition is screaming, *Why the hell am I here, idiot?*”

“I can’t hide from myself, can I?” Charlotte said.

“There are ways. Most are illegal.”

“You’ll be nearby?”

Pope kissed her. “Close enough to see a threatening wrinkle on Bic-boy’s forehead.” He dropped a hand to the small of Charlotte’s back and gave her a loving shove. “Go on. Never keep a killer waiting.”

Near frantic, she said, “What are you going to do until we meet?”

“I need to find a payphone.”

“Why not use your cell phone?”

“I forgot to recharge it. The battery is weak, and I want to save power in case I need it. Don’t worry, Charlotte, the call won’t take a minute or two. I promised I’d touch base with Benson before the Braves’ game. I’ll be watching over you long before Bic-boy stomps in.”

Charlotte crossed her arms. She took a few steps, glanced over her shoulder at Pope, and strode down the sidewalk into the clearing.

“There she is. That’s Charlotte.” Cox pressed his eyes against the binoculars.

Bishop raised his binoculars. “You’re sure?”

Cox observed Charlotte approach the Kessler Campanile from the rooftop of the Bunger-Henry Building. He turned to Bishop. “One hundred percent.”

“Flame has penetrated the perimeter,” Bishop announced Charlotte’s arrival using the code name assigned in the tactical briefing. “Brown hair, tied back. Jeans jacket. Khaki slacks. Pink sweater. Leather clogs. Confirm visual contact with subject.”

“One,” Mitchell responded from his sniper high in the brick stairwell. “Ten-four.”

Prone on the old bookstore rooftop, the second sniper followed in sequence, "Two. Got her, Cap."

"Three. Ten-four," confirmation squelched from the tactical team viewing her from the van in the library parking lot.

"Four. Roger that, Captain," the tactical team holed in the north student center stairwell replied. "Pretty in pink, sir."

"What now?" Cox asked.

Bishop lowered his binoculars. "You're a veteran crime writer, so I'm sure you're aware how the 'SWAT' acronym originated."

"Special weapons and tactics?"

A belt beeper chirped behind Bishop and Cox. Detective Chawk glanced at the pager readout, hit one key on his cell phone and listened.

"Technically, you're correct; however, we've adapted a more realistic interpretation—sit, wait, and talk. Mr. Cox, we lay low and wait."

Chawk held his phone and tapped Bishop's left arm. "Captain, I think you should hear this voicemail that came in a few minutes ago."

Chawk pressed a button to replay the voice message, and handed the phone to Bishop.

Cox overheard the recording. "This is…well, it don't make no never mind who the hell I is, and I ain't getting involved. I heard on the TV news you folks was looking for that ballplayer. Done seen him this morning at a Quik Trip in Atlanta. Work thar, I do, not that it matters 'cause he done hightailed it outta here hours ago. Came in here for a coffee. We got them fancy cappuccinos, you know, if you take to that creamy shit. Me, I like mine thirty weight, black and strong. Well, being a Braves fan and all, I recognized him right off. Boy howdy, they dang sure could've used that boy last night. Thar he was, other side of the counter, handing me a George Washington for his coffee.

"Well, my hands was shaking like it was purt near freezing outside and I dropped the dang dollar. That's when I seen it. When he bent over to pick up his money, his coat rode up over his belt. Plain as day, ole Torch had a heater clipped to his belt. Thought you folks should know he was carrying a peashooter. Who'd thunk it? There go the dang playoffs. Be careful y'all."

"Shit," Bishop whispered. "He's armed."

"Sounds that way," Chawk answered.

"You need to yank Charlotte out of there, now," Cox insisted.

"Could be a hoax," Chawk said without acknowledging Cox.

"Happens all the time. We wouldn't take the information so serious if we weren't running a special op." Bishop rubbed his neck. "It's not like we didn't consider the possibility of violence. That's why the tactical team is here to begin with. Best two marksmen in the squad less than a hundred yards away. If he waves fingernail clippers at Miss Gordon he'll have two three oh eight holes in his chest. We don't abort."

"It's too dangerous!" Cox protested.

"Mr. Cox, Traynor is a multiple murder suspect. If we pass on this opportunity to capture him because of an anonymous, possibly prank phone call, we all share the responsibility should Traynor kill again." The captain raised his binoculars and watched Charlotte pace. "We assessed the risks. That's why my men train rigorously for operations exactly like this. They are the best, Cox. They won't let him hurt her. We control the high ground this time. The next situation might involve escalated risks to more victims, hostages, and my unit. It's my call. The operation is a go."

Bishop thumbed a radio button. "All units. Consider suspect armed and dangerous. Repeat. Consider suspect armed and dangerous."

The sun blazed above the student center. Charlotte blocked the blinding glare with an arm and examined the glass entrance and concrete benches stationed on the concrete apron. She exhaled—a breath she hadn't realized she held—when Pope emerged from student center.

He waved. She was tempted to trounce through the fountain at a full run into his arms. She smiled instead, again conscious that Traynor could be hidden, noting her movements. Pope sat on an amphitheater seat, less than fifty yards away, toasted her with a Diet Coke can, and sipped from it.

Three thirty-eight. Her heart pounded faster. She turned east, toward the stadium. A trickle of football fans descended the stairs between two brick classroom buildings. Boisterous Tech fans outnumbered gloomy Clemson rooters clad in fiery orange shirts and caps. The crowd roared beyond the horizon followed by a hollow steam whistle hooting. The Tech campus celebrated their Atlantic Coast Conference victory.

Gold, yellow, and orange, hordes of football fans invaded the campus meadow, only moments ago sleeping beneath the Atlanta skyline. Intoxicated rowdies mixed with older alums towing children. The parade to the perimeter parking lots escalated. Charlotte jerked toward each random scream, jittery, her nerves at full alert, and studied the faces, some painted like extraterrestrials in school colors.

Then…she saw him.

Chapter Thirty-Four

Mitchell sighted the crosshairs three feet in front of Flame. The tunnel vision view through the Leopuld mounted scope would be his perspective of the world until the operation ended. The tip of his Remington .308 caliber rifle, at rest on a small black sandbag, would be visible from below, but only then by the keenest of inspections. In the shadows of the stuffy stairwell cubbyhole, the brick enclosure shielded him from baking in the direct sunlight and deprived him of the autumn breeze. His right finger resting on the trigger guard, he used his left thumb to wipe perspiration that streamed from the band of the Kevlar helmet to his bushy eyebrows.

The heat could be worse. His body armor weighed less than ten pounds without the shot plates the tactical officers on the ground inserted in their vests. He could be roasting on a blacktop roof in his black uniform like sniper two atop the Houston building.

Wait, wait, wait, then execute on command. Training and experience kept him patient and sharp. Different building tops, different emotions, different suspects, different weather—every operation was unique. The SWAT officers relied on the constants, trust and knowledge of their team's capabilities and leadership, to succeed.

Today was the same. Unsure when and from where the suspect would arrive, Mitchell would depend on Captain Bishop to formulate tactics based on the immediate situation. A former rooftop sergeant like himself, he trusted Bishop's command ability and his adept grasp of field strategy.

Today, his confidence as an expert marksman bordered on cocky arrogance if ordered to shoot from less than one hundred yards, seventy-seven he estimated when he stepped off the ground to the target area. He shouldered his customized .308 caliber Remington, Model 700 PSS, its floated barrel separated from the stock, for increased accuracy. Hours of perfect practice on the firing range, deployed in low wind conditions with the sun to his back, and armed with a weapon that Davy Crockett would have saved the Alamo with single-handed, he could not miss if Bishop called upon him.

Routine radio chatter had ceased, leaving the frequency silent for short bursts of surveillance and tactical commands since Flame penetrated the operational perimeter. "Two. Flame has a visitor."

A man dressed in outrageous Georgia Tech paraphernalia wandered into Mitchell's scope. A yellow pompom under the man's gold cloth cap looked like clown's hair. Face paint, alternating yellow and black stripes, hid the man's face. He wore a gray Tech sweatshirt beneath a leather bomber jacket. Mitchell pressed the radio button on his vest with his left hand, never relinquishing his aim. "One. Confirmed."

"Is it Firefly?" Bishop's calm voice asked by codename if the man was Traynor. "Confirm."

Mitchell wasn't sure through the face paint and yellow wig. "One. Negative confirmation."

"Two. Negative."

"Five. Commence walk by confirmation," Bishop ordered.

"Five." A female undercover officer moved toward Flame to verify the man's identity. "Ten-four."

No time to mop his brow, sweat dripped from Mitchell's forehead. Crosshairs intersected between the 'C' and the 'H' on the man's sweatshirt. He waited anxious seconds for the walk-by identification.

"Five. He shaved. Firefly is confirmed."

Bishop said, "Repeat, Five."

"Firefly confirmed. Five out."

"One and Two." Bishop remained stoic in his commands. "Acquire target."

"Two. Target acquired."

Mitchell slipped his finger from the trigger guard to the trigger. "One. Target acquired."

"Three and Four, prepare distraction devices for dynamic assault." Bishop ordered the tactical officers on the ground to ready flash bang grenades and prepare to storm the site.

"Three. Ten-four."

"Four. Roger, Captain."

"Five. Get close to Flame. On 'Go,' get her out of there. Knock her in the pond if you have to."

"Five. Douse the Flame. Ten-four."

Her nerves in fretted knots, face to face with the man she believed murdered her sister, Charlotte giggled. "You look ridiculous."

"Don't like my game day duds?" Traynor asked. "Yellow ain't my color."

"What's with the clown costume, if you're innocent?"

"February through October, my face is pretty damn familiar between the paper and television coverage. I can't risk a campus rent-a-cop waving his pistol like Dirty Harry if he spots me."

Chet Suggs ambled from the crowd and positioned himself behind Traynor's left shoulder, a Clemson T-shirt flapping loose over his beer gut, and his face striped orange and black like a bearded Bengal tiger. He looked side-to-side. "I gotta bad feeling, Torch. Let's get the hell outta here."

"Be cool, Chet. This won't take long."

A crinkled scowl etched in Charlotte's face, she muttered, "What's he doing here?"

"Chet? He came along for the ride."

"Tell him to take a hike, or I walk away and you can enlighten APD with your falsely accused sob story."

Traynor looked over his shoulder. "Give us some space, Chet."

"Bitch," Suggs hissed as he retreated.

"Do you always keep such sophisticated company?" She shifted her intense stare from Suggs to Traynor.

"He's an old friend, Charlotte. He'd do anything for me."

"Right. He'd probably even kill for you, wouldn't he, Earl?"

"What are you talking about?"

"You haven't heard, have you? Your lifelong pal is wanted by the Atlanta Police for the murder of a *Journal-Constitution* photographer, Liz Vanderwahl. My friend. My fault. Liz was an innocent victim. Liz was kind enough to share her home with a new acquaintance. Chet broke in, determined to eliminate his best buddy's nosy nuisance, me, and murdered her in my absence."

"It ain't so." Traynor shook his head. "It couldn't be. Chet wouldn't kill no one."

"Ask the cops. Or better yet, ask good old Chet himself."

Stunned, Traynor's eyes toggled left to right as he digested her tale in awkward silence.

"Pierce told me you have proof that you didn't kill Margaret."

"Why would I admit to you that I met your sister at the Hatch if I was trying to hide a murder?"

"Hold on, Earl. If you dragged me here to twist the logic that led me to you, then you're wasting my time. The police are convinced. Unless you're prepared to show me tangible evidence, rock-solid proof that you didn't kill Margaret or those other women, then this clandestine reunion is adjourned."

"I read the clippings you threw at me in St. Louis."

"Congratulations. You've advanced from Dr. Seuss. Of course, then you realize, in Tampa and St. Louis, the night you blew a save, a woman was murdered. By the way, the file I flung at you has thickened up since with additional murders in Atlanta and Philadelphia hours after bad outings by the legendary Torch Traynor. Each death, a violent death, young women beaten to death." Charlotte waved her hand over her head. "Or is the obvious association beyond your comprehension."

"I've blown six. What about the Cubs and the Giants?"

"Enough with the logic. Four out of six is a high probability. Statistically sufficient for the cops to believe the trend is more than coincidental. By the way, the articles didn't describe how the killer scrubbed the crime scene and his victims with fanatical invigoration. Ever heard of obsessive-compulsive disorder? Straightened the bullpen lately, Earl?"

"You think I'm stupid 'cause I can't string words together like you or your writer friend, Pope. I know about OCD. Surprised I could abbreviate it? Some folks say I ought be checked out, since I'm such a neat freak. Being compulsive ain't bad, fact is, it can make a fella downright good at what he does. And Lord knows keeping things straight and clean ain't a sin. The way I see it, if I got OCD, then some shrink is gonna analyze me, tell me I hated my daddy, or prescribe some medicine that could screw up my slider."

"It's a disease, Earl. There's treatment. Get help before you hurt anyone else."

"Damn it, Charlotte. I didn't hurt a single solitary soul."

Charlotte sighed. "We're going in circles here. Proof. Where's the proof?"

"You're so ate-up with revenge," Traynor reached inside his jacket pocket and pulled out rolled paper, "you can't read these here clippings without seeing blood. My blood. It's all here, plain as day."

"One!" Mitchell broadcast. "Weapon!"

"Three. Confirm weapon," Bishop ordered. "One. Two. Sniper initiated assault on my count."

A tactical officer, positioned in the bottom of the stairwell, took a sneak peek around the corner. "Three. Looks like rolled paper. Repeat, rolled paper."

"Abort sniper initiated assault. Abort," Bishop repeated.

Charlotte took the wrinkled articles from Traynor. She unrolled three sheets of paper—the report of Margaret's death, the article on Megan Rivers's murder in St. Louis, and another clipping, along with a photo of Traynor's home run swing, from the *Post-Dispatch* online sports page.

"Cops, Torch!" Suggs spotted the Kevlar helmet and goggles that popped out from behind the brick stairway. He pulled out the revolver, tucked in his belt, hidden by the windbreaker, and dashed forward.

Traynor spun left. "What? Where?"

"I knew it. Damn bitch sold us out!"

He aimed the handgun at Charlotte and charged like an enraged rhinoceros.

A female spectator screamed. The steady flow of fans reacted to the berserk Clemson supporter with a gun. Frantic cries followed. Some ran. Others dropped to the ground. Courageous parents shielded small children from the melee.

The long barrel leveled at her, Charlotte froze in disbelief. She glanced left. Twenty-five to thirty yards away, Pope jumped down the concrete amphitheater seating. She'd be dead before he could rescue her. The pond trapped her—there was nowhere to run.

"Chet, no!" Traynor hollered.

Suggs ran at Charlotte, extending the revolver like a lance.

Traynor flung both arms around Suggs's gun arm. He twisted inside Suggs's large frame, used his body as a lever, and threw him to the brick surface. Traynor collapsed on top of Suggs, their limbs entangled.

The gun discharged. The thunderous explosion rolled across the clearing as if Sherman's artillery bombarded Atlanta.

Charlotte gazed at the carnage. His large reddened hands lifted the motionless body on top of him. The gaping wound, shredded like hamburger, soaked the ripped sweatshirt in blood. Traynor's closed eyelids were fleshy islands afloat in a yellow and black striped gulf.

Suggs rose to a knee, tears in his eyes. "Nooo! He's dead." He clambered to his feet and turned to Charlotte. "You killed Torch, you bitch!"

"Shots fired, shots fired. Alert EMT." Bishop issued calm directives. "Five. Get Flame down, now."

"Five. Ten-four."

"All units. Sniper initiated assault on my count." Bishop alerted the sharpshooters and began his count. "Five, four, three."

"Die!" Suggs cocked the double-action revolver and aimed.

Charlotte stared down the gun barrel and swallowed.

Suggs tugged on the trigger.

A woman sprinted into the line of fire. Her muscular shoulder rammed into Charlotte's chest. Water splashed. Charlotte's tailbone crashed on the campanile pond bottom. The shot whistled over them.

Charlotte's gaze locked on Suggs. His chest burst twice. Sniper rifles crackled like thunder chasing lightning. Suggs bounced on his knees, his eyes wide open, and collapsed face first, heaped across Traynor.

"Police! Down! Get down! Police!" Uniformed men assaulted the pond.

The woman on top of Charlotte smiled. "I'm tactical officer Lucy McConnell. Are you hurt, ma'am?"

Charlotte sat up in the pond and rested her hands on her knees. "I don't think so." She watched the SWAT team and medical personnel swarm.

Pope waded through the shallow water. "Charlotte! Charlotte!" He fell beside her. "Please tell me you're not hurt."

"Confused. Startled. Scared to death. Wet and freezing. Nothing I won't survive."

He kissed her forehead.

Charlotte saw Cox, heavyset and gray-headed, racing across the meadow, resembling a walrus running low hurdles. "Carlton will have a coronary if he doesn't slow down."

Police officers formed a perimeter and backed curious onlookers away as paramedics attended to Traynor and Suggs. They separated the old friends and checked for vitals.

"Call in air evac," the paramedic squatting over Traynor called out. "This one's alive."

Chapter Thirty-Five

The Crown Victoria headed east on North Avenue. Charlotte saw street lamp starbursts spin, stall, and reverse direction through the windshield. Only an occasional blink or a flared nostril broke Charlotte's trance.

She was wrapped in Detective Chawk's APD windbreaker. She couldn't warm up even though her clothes had dried. She doubted whether a few seconds in the water surrounding the Kessler Campanile could cause the polar-like dampness that chilled her. She saw a man die. The bullets didn't zing or explode. Two moist thuds, no louder than a wet tennis ball thumping against cedar siding, ended Suggs's life.

Miracles happen. Traynor survived the point-blank gunshot, or she would have witnessed two deaths. The last news Charlotte heard reported that Traynor had entered the fourth hour of surgery at Grady Memorial Hospital. She often wished over the last few days that a fate equal to his monstrosity would devour Traynor. Now, her vengeful thirst and contempt faltered. Even if he had killed Margaret, the prey of her relentless hunt had saved Charlotte from certain death. She rooted and prayed silently for Torch Traynor to save one more game.

The unmarked sedan coasted to a stop. Chawk turned off the routine chatter on the police radio, put the car in park, walked around to the passenger side, and opened Charlotte's door.

"Here we are, ma'am."

Charlotte turned her head. She looked across the sidewalk and watched the Manuel's Tavern clientele. She unbuckled the seatbelt and climbed out, her fist clenching the wrinkled copies of the papers Traynor had handed her.

"Are you sure that I can't take you home, Miss Gordon?"

She scanned the parking lot and found Liz's Jeep backed into a front row space. Pope and Cox had shuttled the Jeep to Manuel's while APD finished questioning her. "My vehicle is right there." She inclined her head toward the parked automobiles. "Thank you, Detective."

Charlotte wiggled an arm loose from the APD windbreaker.

Chawk laid his hand on her arm. "The jacket looks a lot better on you than it does on me. Keep it until you warm up."

"It may be a while."

"Just send it to me when you're done."

She smiled and stepped toward the entrance. "Good night."

Through smudged door panes, the bustle inside Manuel's was silent like a muted television. She grabbed the doorhandle, pulled, faced the escaping waves of rowdiness, and merged into the festive crowd. She walked toward smoke swirling above the center of the bar.

She touched Cox's shoulder. "Hi."

He spun his barstool, swung his feet to the floor, and embraced her. "I'm sorry, Charlotte. I never should have brought in the cops without telling you. I thought I was going to die when Suggs pulled out the gun."

She leaned back and smiled. "Me, too."

"What can I get for you? Anything, you name it."

"Nothing." Charlotte climbed on the barstool next to Cox. "I'm afraid if I start, I won't stop." She observed a tumbler near Cox's elbow, half-full with clear liquid. "Where's your Budweiser?"

"Absolut, rocks. Vodka deadens the nerves."

"That bad, huh?"

Cox sipped the vodka and crunched a piece of ice.

"Me, too, Carlton."

"First, I thought you were a goner. Then seeing them gun down Suggs. Not that the redneck bastard didn't ask for what he got. Even in my line of work, it's not every day you see snipers take down a suspect…thank God."

"If you hadn't called APD, Chet would have killed me." A perplexing thought stopped Charlotte. She tilted her head to the right and asked, "How did you know I was meeting Traynor anyway?"

"Pope told me." He crushed a cigarette butt in the ashtray, and lit another. "He asked me to notify APD and keep it from you."

"Is that why you were acting so weird last night?"

"I'm not a good liar. Gets me all knotted up inside, like I'm going to explode."

She grinned. "He told me to keep it from you, too. Am I confused or stupid? Why would Pierce tell me not to call the police then tell you the exact opposite? And where is Pierce? He said he'd be here."

"Easy question first. Pope walked out of here almost an hour ago, around eight thirty. He told me to tell you that he's cooking for you tonight. Scallops and some kind of pasta, I think he said."

"When?"

"He said dinner's on twenty minutes after you arrive." Cox paused. "As for the contradictory approach from Pope, I guess it was for your own good. If you knew the police were there, you might have accidentally spooked Traynor. If Traynor didn't show, who knows when the cops would have had another shot…opportunity to apprehend him."

"Suggs killed Liz, and Traynor is in custody. One dead and another on his way, Pierce's plan worked, but the consequences were steep." Charlotte's eyes scrolled up the bar to the television. The Braves batted against the Pirates. "Have the broadcasters mentioned his condition?"

"Last I heard he's out of surgery, but he's critical."

She watched the ballgame and asked, "How are the Braves doing tonight?"

"They look like zombies. Twelve to two, Pittsburgh." Cox nodded at Charlotte's hands. "Are those the papers Traynor gave you?"

"Yes." She unrolled them and spread them on the bar. "Three articles from the file we put together. These are copies. The police kept the sheets he gave me this afternoon. Margaret's death. Meg Rivers's death. And his home run in St. Louis."

"Suggs shot him before he could explain?"

"Yes. He believes something in these articles clears him of the murders. I've read them over and over, but my mind is so fried, nothing I see exonerates him. The police are looking, too. Maybe Traynor will survive and solve the puzzle for us."

Cox waved to the bartender and pointed at his empty tumbler. "You sure you don't want a drink?"

"No thanks."

He used the lit cigarette to light another.

"You smoke too much, Carlton."

The bartender set Cox's Absolut in front of him.

"And you drink too much." Charlotte slid off the barstool.

"Is there anything else you don't like about me?"

She gave him a surly grin. She twirled a stray gray hair above Cox's ear around her finger. "Well, you could you use a haircut."

Cox grunted.

"It's your fault, you know." Charlotte kissed his cheek. "I wouldn't care if I didn't love you so, you old grouch."

He chuckled. "Women. Get out of here and leave me with something I understand." He raised his glass.

Chapter Thirty-Six

Saturday night traffic crawled north along Peachtree Street toward Buckhead, renowned for sprawling nightclubs and restaurants, and notorious for early-morning pedestrian accidents and occasional gunfire. Charlotte checked the green and white street signs at each intersection until she found Collier Road. She jammed the Jeep's accelerator to the floor and squirted through a gap in the oncoming headlights.

Streetlights leaked through the maples lining Collier Road. She slowed and studied the older brick homes to her left. Darkness cloaked the distinguishing shrubs and porch furniture, reducing each home's individuality into cloned angling shadows. Pope's car, parked under a drive-through canopy, the black sheen reflecting moonbeams, guided her in like a lighthouse slicing ocean fog. She turned left, stopped behind the Lexus, and shut off the engine.

She grasped the rolled articles, stepped across well-groomed fescue and ascended painted concrete stairs to the front door, her arms crossed to combat an incessant shiver. Charlotte fiddled with her key ring until she found the door key Pope had entrusted to her. She inserted the key in the deadbolt.

The door sprang open before she could turn the key. Holding tight to the key ring, she bounded through the doorframe with the hardwood door.

"I was about to think you stood me up." Pope greeted her with a bleached white grin. He held the doorknob in his right hand, and a glass of red wine in the other. "For you, Farrese Sangiovese Dauvic, ninety-eight."

Charlotte eased up to him, wrapped her arms around his waist, and laid her head on his shoulder. He removed her keys, swung the door closed, and lowered his free arm around her.

A log crackled in the small living room fireplace. Embers burst from the flame and drifted up the flue. Through Pope's sound system, a pianist performed a melancholy melody, lifting sad and poignant notes out of dark orchestral shading. Charlotte inhaled the aroma of baked bread and garlic, unleashing the hunger she had neglected over the last few hours. She couldn't remember when she had last eaten.

She craned her neck, turned her face, and kissed him. "This is nice, Pierce. Thanks."

"You've had a hell of a day. I wanted to whisk you away into a world of fantasy and whims." He handed her the wineglass. "Are you hungry?"

"Famished. Whatever you're cooking smells wonderful." She looked at the wineglass. "I don't drink anything I can't say. What is this?"

"Chianti. Robust and inexpensive."

Charlotte sipped the wine, and closed her eyes. "I hate to admit a dependence on alcohol, but I needed that."

Pope held out his hand. When Charlotte gave him her hand, he led her to the leather couch in the living room.

She kicked off her clogs, sat, and curled her legs on the sofa.

"You relax while I finish dinner." Pope opened the shutters between the kitchen and living room. "Scallops sautéed in garlic butter. Spinach linguini, Alfredo. Garlic bread and salad."

"Sounds delicious."

He walked into the kitchen.

"I like the music, Pierce."

"Rachmaninov's 'Piano Concert No. 4 in G-Minor.' Performed by Jean-Yves Thibaudet and the Cleveland Orchestra." Pope whirled around the kitchen. The sizzle from the stovetop increased. "Scallops in the pan, and the pasta is boiling. Can you wait fifteen minutes?"

"I'm starving. You wouldn't lie to me, would you?"

"Never."

"You mean, never again, don't you? Pierce, why didn't you tell me that you asked Carlton to call in the police?"

Wiping his hands on a dishtowel, Pope returned from the kitchen. "I didn't really lie. Call it a little slight of hand. To protect you."

"I was an eyelash from dying."

"Would you have met him if you knew the police were there?"

"Well, yes."

He sat down next to Charlotte. "Then you would have been *an eyelash from dying* whether you knew SWAT was there or not. Right?"

"I guess so, but—"

"There's no way in hell would I let you face him without protection. You wanted the cops there, although you didn't know they were. Without knowledge of the APD operation, you played your role to perfection. You didn't have to fool Traynor. Deception is not one of your strong points, is it

Miss Freelance Journalist?"

Charlotte smiled. "I guess I'm not much of an actress."

"I knew meeting Traynor could be dangerous, Charlotte. But when Bic-boy offered to come out of hiding, I had to think fast. All I wanted was to end this horrible nightmare for you. It's over. You're safe, here with me, and the boogey man and his redneck sidekick are gone forever. By the way, how is Bic-boy?"

"Carlton said he's out of surgery, but in critical condition at Grady. I hope he makes it."

"Uh, yeah, me, too." Pope was sluggish to reply. He tilted his head toward the rolled papers in Charlotte's lap. "What did he want to show you?"

"Suggs shot him before he told me. Traynor believed these articles prove he didn't kill Margaret. I've read them until my eyes watered. Word by word. I found a few typos, but no revealing evidence." She tossed the papers to Pope. "Maybe you'll see the obvious that I'm missing."

Speed-reading, Pope scanned the articles with casual interest. "Nothing jumps out at me. Odds are it was all a ploy to divert your efforts or worse. It's entirely possible Suggs and Bic-boy planned the rendezvous simply to eliminate you."

"Then why did Traynor tackle Chet?"

"Murderers are people, too." Pope crumbled the papers in a wad, and tossed it toward a wastebasket. The airborne trash hit the wall and rolled over the hardwood floor. "Maybe he was overwhelmed with a sudden wave of guilt. Most likely, when he saw the cops Traynor wanted to look like a hero. We may never know."

"He could survive."

"Right." Pope rose from the couch. He bent over, picked up the discarded articles, and dropped them in the wicker wastebasket. "Unless he lives. I'd better check on the scallops."

Charlotte placed her wineglass on the beveled glass coffee table. She stood, ambled across the Oriental rug to the pass through counter, and watched Pope stir linguini. "Can I do anything to help?"

"I'm a selfish chef. The accolades are all mine. Two cooks in my kitchen is one too many. Dinner will be served in five minutes." He turned from the stove. "You could light the candles in the dining room."

She entered the small dining room to her left through parted French doors. Lenox china and polished silverware bedecked the mahogany table set for two. She slid open the drawer of the matching sideboard to look for matches. She rummaged through cloth napkins, pewter napkin rings, and serving utensils before she called out, "Pierce, I can't find any matches in here."

Tending to the scallops, he answered, “Sorry, Charlotte. Look in the living room. Try the cabinet under the museum books.”

Violas, French horns, and cellos wove a dark ambiance from within Rachmaninov’s composition. In a spine-tingling build up to the “Fourth Concerto” finale, Charlotte envisioned delicate fingers coaxing eloquent notes from ivory keys as Thibaudet played in parallel with the staccato percussion.

She lifted *The Philadelphia Museum of Art: Handbook of the Collections* from the pinnacle of the publication pyramid and turned toward the kitchen, again admiring the book collection. She flipped through the glossy pages of the cloth-covered edition. “Your books are wonderful. I could mull over the museum collections for hours.”

“The only thing better than studying the pictures is to stand in the presence of the masterpieces—see the ridges, flow, and shadow of every brush stroke.”

“You’ve seen all of these collections?” Charlotte asked. “In person?”

“When you write about animals begot from prehistoric caveman, it’s imperative to cleanse oneself with culture. Art reminds me that civilization flourishes beyond the baseball diamond. On a road trip, there’s plenty of downtime. Some writers drink, sleep, or go to the movies. I seek the fine arts. A dash of Renoir somehow negates an overdose of Bic-boy. The blend is a suitable balance.”

“You’re amazing.” Charlotte shook her head and placed the book on top of the arty publications. “Or a practiced and intriguing liar. Which is it?”

“I’ll never divulge my deep dark secrets,” Pope feigned a Dracula imitation. “If my vast and worldly knowledge impresses you, then does it matter?”

“Intelligent.” Charlotte squatted and opened a floor cabinet. “And humble, too.”

She grabbed a matchbook off a shelf, stood, and pushed the cabinet door closed with her big toe.

“Humility is one of my foremost attributes.” Pope rotated a knob to decrease the heat under the sauté pan. “I rank it right up there with my modesty, meekness, and all-round gentle nature.”

Palm up, Charlotte unfolded her fingers. Her shoulders tensed. Her lower jawbone fell in sudden shock. A single word was engraved in a brushed script font—VINOY.

“No sarcastic comeback,” Pope rambled on. “You must be awed by my sincere tenderness.”

Her hand trembled. Sportswriters travel with teams. Had Pierce Pope, her lover, stayed at the hotel a meager hike from the Down the Hatch Pub? The last place her sister was seen alive. Was he in St. Petersburg, registered at the Vinoy, the night Magaret died? Her phone call. Did she call Pope? Was she waiting for *him*?

"Of course, if you're enthralled by my kindheartedness, my culinary astuteness will stun you."

Charlotte's eyes swept to the museum books, ascending by size with the precise positioning of laid brick. She read and catalogued the titles: *The Philadelphia Museum of Art: Handbook of the Collections*, *Art Institute of Chicago*, *Bay Area Figurative Art 1950-1965*, *American Paintings at the High Museum of Art*, and in a crimson hardcover, *DALI*. She knew Pope was in St. Louis when Megan Rivers died. Cox told her the Cobb County schoolteacher disappeared after a visit to the High Museum in downtown Atlanta. This book proved that Pope had traveled to Philadelphia. Was he there the same night the flight attendant was murdered?

And *DALI*. The hardback book chronicled the Salvador Dalí Museum collection in St. Petersburg, Florida. The museum was minutes from Tropicana Stadium, Down the Hatch Pub, and the Vinoy Hotel. Margaret, an eager art connoisseur, frequented the Dalí Museum.

"We're moments away from five-star cuisine. Did you light the candles, Charlotte?"

Where would Margaret ever meet Earl Traynor? Her sister would never be interested in the country boy ballplayer. This assertion bothered her from the moment she learned that Traynor had flirted with Margaret. Meeting Pierce Pope in a favorite museum knitted a far more plausible scenario. She could see Margaret with him. Sophisticated, conversant, and handsome—Margaret could fall for him.... Charlotte had.

"Charlotte?"

"Uh," she mumbled. "Not yet."

Charlotte's heart out-thumped Thibaudet's quickened piano tempo. *Get a grip, girl*, she thought. Free-falling through an unfamiliar haze of deceit, suspicion, and brutality, she worried that her capacity to trust, believe in others had shredded into scraps of incredulity. Was her imagination intruding on truth, misguiding her actions, her thoughts, her emotions with irrational injections? Like the log in the glowing hearth, a matchbook and a hodgepodge of museum books, inanimate circumstantial clues out in the open, unhidden, fueled the blaze of accusation engulfing the man she... loved?

Earl Traynor murdered Margaret. Sure, he killed her, and the evidence convinced the police, too. His willingness to risk capture to clear his name formed her lone doubt. Five more minutes with Traynor and she would have appraised and surely dismissed his defense. The proof of his innocence, the key to the encrypted pages Pope tossed in the wastebasket, were buried within Traynor's fragile comatose and would never be revealed unless the ballplayer awoke.

The articles. What had Traynor seen that she couldn't interpret?

She bent and retrieved the crumpled pages. She spread and smoothed the wrinkled papers on the desk. Again, she read of Margaret's death. Her background. No suspects. Defense wounds on her left arm. Apparent cause of death—head wounds inflicted with a blunt object.

Defense wounds, left arm? Her eyes shot back to the sentence. She held Margaret's story and reached for the St. Louis murder report. The attacker had broken Megan Rivers's left arm.

Charlotte breathed in short, rapid bursts. She examined Traynor's home run swing. His *left-handed* home run swing. She remembered Albert Haggard's story. The left-handed boy had prolonged his baseball livelihood by learning to throw right-handed. Charlotte watched Traynor autograph children's baseballs…left-handed. One of the most dominant right-handed pitchers in Major League Baseball was a lefty. The string of evidence Traynor wanted to reveal. The murderer bludgeoned his victims with lethal strokes from the right.

She spun toward the door.

"There are no matches in the desk, Charlotte." Pope stood between her and the door. He twisted the deadbolt and shoved the key in a trouser pocket.

Chapter Thirty-Seven

"Carlton," the bartender waved the phone at him, "It's that Chuck Stennett guy again."

Cox rolled his eyes. "Tell him... What the hell, I'll talk to him."

The bartender brought the phone and another vodka to him.

"Thanks, Cody." He took a long swallow of Absolut, then raised the phone. "You want cash or can I send you a check?"

"Carlton Cox," Stennett said. "You're harder to track down than Eric Rudolph in a North Carolina forest. I was beginning to think you were dead, or even worse, that you were on the wagon. You don't owe me any money... yet."

"I'll pay my gambling debt in advance, then I can enjoy watching Carolina stomp the Falcons tomorrow. Otherwise the Falcons might actually take an early lead, fortifying my hopes with the rationalization that the odds are someday I'm due to beat Chuck Stennett at least once. Then as my expectations peak, the Panthers will intercept, run back a punt, recover a fumble, yanking the carpet from under my feet, and I'll land on my ass once again. How much do I owe you, Chuck?"

"Fifty bucks. And I'll give you the spread. Six and a half points."

"Whatever. Now, if you've finished ruining tonight and tomorrow afternoon," Cox swirled the ice in his drink, "I think I'll spend my money on another vice. Goodbye, Chuck. The check's in the mail."

"Guess y'all have been busy in the Big A today. I saw the CNN story on Traynor. What a mess. Were you there, Carlton?"

"Yeah. Whatever they reported, it was worse."

"How about all this obsessive-compulsive disorder crap? Do you buy into that malarkey?"

"It's true, Chuck."

"Are you on the inside of this story?"

"Closer than I want to be."

"A Major League serial killer is big news. Maybe you could spoonfeed an old drinking buddy a few juicy tidbits for a follow-up in the *Observer*?"

"Not now. Call me at the office Monday and I'll fill in the gaps and give you background."

"You really believe Torch Traynor's OCD is so severe that he kills for relief?"

"It looks that way. Chuck, I got to go."

"I saw an obsessive-compulsive get violent once, but I didn't realize a neurotic hand washer would resort to murder." Stennett chuckled. "We had this neat-freak at the *Observer*, about six years ago. For laughs a couple of boys rearranged his files and ransacked his desk, you know, mixed the paper clips with the pushpins. The guy went whacko and beat the shit out of both of them. He resigned before the *Observer* fired him. Damn shame, he was a hell of a writer. In fact, you probably know him. After he left the *Observer*, he signed on with the *Journal-Constitution*. Pierce Pope."

Cox spit a mouthful of vodka on the counter. "Pope! You sure, Chuck?"

"Flashy dresser. Blazer and tie, in a golf shirt world. It's him, I've seen his sig shot online." Stennett referred to the photograph that often accompanies a writer's column. "He does the Braves beat, right?"

"Bye, Chuck." Cox turned off the phone.

He chugged vodka, and shook his head. Pope OCD? Just because he suffers from OCD wouldn't make Pope a murderer. Once Pope learned of Traynor's malady, why hadn't he spoken out? Then he remembered Kenneth Daniels saying that obsessive-compulsives often hide their disorder and seldom volunteer for treatment. OCD and murder—a rare combination according to Daniels. But Pope had exploded at the *Observer*. Was it a one-time occurrence or a brutal trend?

"Shit!" Cox exclaimed when the next link developed within his vodka-clouded hypothesis. Tampa, St. Louis, Philadelphia, and Atlanta. Pierce Pope traveled with the Braves on most road trips.

The file. The *AJC* game articles were in the file that he compiled with Charlotte. He could see it plain as day, to the right of his keyboard under a black-stained coffee cup. He needed the file.

With Charlotte dining at Pope's house, he didn't have time to drive to the *AJC* and research the file. He might be overreacting, but to risk another minute could be catastrophic.

He grabbed his cell phone and dialed the *AJC* copy desk.

"*AJC*."

"Nolan, is that you?" Cox recognized the copy editor's weary voice. Two years out of University of Georgia, the English major could spot a dangling participle from miles away, but in Nolan Fletcher's twenty-three years Cox doubted he had experienced an original creative idea. "It's Carlton Cox."

"Evening, Carlton. Are you transmitting an article? Kind of late for the Sunday edition."

"No story. I need a favor."

"I'm kind of swamped."

"Are you doing the Sunday crossword, or playing FreeCell on the computer? It's important, damn it!"

"What do you need?"

"There's a file folder on my desk. It's under my coffee cup. I need some info, and I don't have time to come get it."

"All right. I'll transfer you to your desk. Hang on." The phone rang four times before Fletcher picked it up. "I'm here, Carlton. Are you farming penicillin in this cup?"

"Adds flavor and fights infection. Open the file." Cox waited. "What do you see?"

"Clippings. Murder stories, fastened to articles from Braves games."

"Read the city and game bylines to me." Cox ascertained if Ted Benson had written any of the game stories, then Pope did not travel with the Braves on that road trip. If Pope remained in Atlanta as the team played in Tampa, St. Louis, or Philadelphia then he could not have murdered those women.

"San Francisco, written by Pierce Pope. Tampa Bay game, Associated Press. Philadelphia, AP again. Chicago, Pierce Pope. St. Louis, AP. And the last one, Atlanta, Associated Press. Why would AP do a local game?"

Ted Benson wrote none of the articles. The *AJC* had printed Associated Press game stories the nights women were murdered in St. Louis, Atlanta, Tampa Bay, and Philadelphia. Why not Chicago or San Fran?

"Look at the photos from San Fran and Chicago," Cox said.

"Okay."

"Can you tell from the pictures if it's day or night?"

"There's a shot of a Giant outfielder robbing a home run. He's wearing Oakleys so I suppose the sun's out. The Bleacher Bums at Wrigley Field are soaking up rays. It appears it is afternoon in Chicago, too."

"Damn, that's it." He slammed into the treacherous truth as if he had banged his head against low-hanging pipes in a dark basement. Cox had ridiculed Pope for years about coming unglued at deadline. All in fun, ill-spirited reverie at Pope's expense.

"What's *it*?" Fletcher said.

Cox turned off his cell phone.

The whole time, Charlotte and Cox assumed Traynor's obsessive-compulsive inclination escalated to violent retaliation as a result of his imperfect performance. They never considered the extended consequences of Traynor's bad outings. Never considered the impact of one obsessive-compulsive's imperfection on another with a similar disorder. Blown saves shattered the predictable outcome Atlanta fans, and writers, expected, depended on from Torch Traynor and the Braves.

No murders occurred after Traynor blew day games against the Giants and the Cubs. Deadline would have been hours away, plenty of time to reconstruct a polished game account. Under the lights, moments before the witching hour, to meet the *AJC* deadline Pierce Pope would be pressured to re-craft a game script in mere minutes. His perfected work, like shattered Waterford crystal, could not be reshaped, recreated in minutes. Unable to satisfy the obsession with perfection, compulsive behavior sought relief.

"Charlotte," he mumbled.

He punched in four-one-one, listened to the recording recite Pope's home phone number, and dialed. Pope's memory call service picked up.

"Pope! It's Carlton Cox. You goddamn son-of-a-bitch! If you touch her I swear I'll kill you!"

Cox shut off the call. He threw two twenties on the counter, ran for the door, and jammed the nine-one-one buttons.

Chapter Thirty-Eight

"I…I couldn't find matches in the bookcase, so I thought I'd try the desk drawer."

He nodded at the worn articles. "You should let the past go."

"My thought exactly." She tried to smile, balled up the papers, and dropped the wad in the wastebasket. "So is dinner ready?"

"Yes. As soon as the candles are lit." He pounced forward and grabbed her wrist.

"What are you doing? Let me go, Pierce." She struggled to break the grip. "You're hurting me."

"Perhaps," one by one, he peeled back the fingers of her clenched fist, unveiling the Vinoy matches, "we should use these."

Pope released her.

Charlotte ran to the door. Frantic, she pulled the doorknob, then rammed a shoulder into the sturdy wood.

"It won't open, my dear Charlotte."

The phone rang.

"Aren't you going to answer the phone, Pierce? I'll get it for you."

"Who would be so rude to interrupt such a glorious Saturday night? Tonight is our night, Charlotte. I won't let anyone or anything ruin the mood."

The telephone rang three times and stopped. The violas and French horns wailed. Thibaudet raced across the keys to the final haunting stanzas.

"Let me out!"

She looked over her shoulder at Pope. He calmly lifted his briefcase to the desk and ripped open a Velcro-fastened pouch. He withdrew a red, slender souvenir bat, engraved with the St. Louis Cardinals' logo. He grasped the bat handle in his right hand and slapped the club against his open left palm.

"How did you find out?" He advanced in a slow, deliberate approach.

Charlotte backed away from him, circling into the living room.

"No, Pierce. Please. Think about us."

"How did you know?"

"Margaret's defense wounds…the St. Louis woman, too. Traynor is left-handed. When he was a kid, he injured his left arm and taught himself to throw right-handed."

"The Rome junket?"

"Yes. His Little League coach told me."

"Good research." Pope pounded his bat into his hand with the rhythm of the "Fourth Concerto." "Unfortunately, you dug too deep."

Charlotte mirrored his calculated steps, in a defensive crouch, as if they waltzed to the piping music. "Carlton knows I'm here."

"I'll call him as soon as we're finished. 'Carlton, have you seen Charlotte? What? She left for my place? Good heavens, Carlton, she never arrived.'" He made a sudden sidestep left. Charlotte slid left and bumped against the couch back. "No place to go. Nowhere to hide."

"You won't get away with killing me."

"Traynor is their serial killer. Why do you think I had Cox call in SWAT? To protect you? Traynor was no threat to your safety, as you are now keenly aware. What you don't know is that SWAT was warned Traynor had a weapon—an anonymous tip from a concerned citizen. It was pure luck that Suggs shot Bic-boy first. Otherwise, I hoped he'd make a wrong move or become agitated or violent and draw sniper fire. John Wilkes Booth, Lee Harvey Oswald—dead suspects become convicted legends. If he dies, the hunt ceases. If he lives, well, with you out of the picture, no one will ever believe him. Even if they do, who else would they suspect?"

"They will connect my…*death*…to you."

"They haven't before. You saw your sister's house. OCD does have its merits. I won't be able to stop scrubbing until every trace that you graced my humble dwelling is sanitized. My plans didn't include housecleaning tonight, but we must adapt. Don't you think?"

Cornered between the couch and a wall, Charlotte braced to fight—another victim, her arms battered as the last line of defense.

"Why did you kill her?"

"I didn't want to, Charlotte. I loved her." Pope halted. His eyes lowered to the floor in a brief display of shame, then bounced up to her face. "Almost as much as I love you. After the game, she begged me to come over. If Bic-boy had done his job…one, two, three, in perfect order, Margaret would be alive. His lackluster pitching wrecked my gorgeous writing, crafted to perfection.

"You and I would have been good together, Charlotte. Margaret was a free spirit. She couldn't help it. Her sweet hands cluttered everything she touched. You, however, much like me, appreciate the necessity of order. She broke the Cabernet bottle and giggled. The dust, paper everywhere, stacks on top of stacks. I could endure no more. I warned her it wasn't a good night. She insisted. I ended sweet Margaret's suffering. I saved you from a like fate the other night. I endured the onslaught and waited until the demons slept before I returned to you."

"You're sick. You murdered her and cleaned her house."

"That's right. I bathed her, combed her golden hair, and tucked her in forever. Wouldn't you do the same for someone you loved?"

"Let me get you help, Pierce. Doctor Daniels. I have his card in the Jeep. I'll get it."

"No shrinks. No treatment. Asylum filth and stench would transform me into a raving lunatic. No, I'm content with who I am. I'll beat the demons when the time is right."

The music ended.

"I'll always think of you when I hear Rachmaninov's fourth."

Pope cocked his arm and leaped at Charlotte. He swung.

The bat whistled. She threw her shoulders back. A red streak flashed by her eyes. Charlotte rolled over the back of the couch. His second swing, a backhand stroke, split the leather upholstery.

She slid down the cushions, the crown of her head in a nosedive for the floor. Charlotte tucked at the waist and flung her feet over her head. Lower body momentum threw her torso upward, preventing the headfirst impact.

Pope pressed his midsection against the couch back and flailed at Charlotte's head. The bat whisked above her scalp, tangled in a lock of her hair, and tore the roots free.

Her knees crashed. The coffee table shattered into thousands of jagged beveled glass shards. The wineglass bounced and the stem fractured. Chianti stained the Oriental rug maroon.

Charlotte bounded up from within the empty wrought iron table frame, slivers of glass protruding from her knees. She trampled through glass splinters, gouging her bare feet, stumbled, and landed at the base of the walnut bookshelves.

She brushed hair from her face. Anticipating Pope's next blow, Charlotte cringed and glanced over her shoulder.

Pope glared at the rug, his mouth agape. Glazed with fury, his eyes strayed to Charlotte. "My magnificent rug. I'll never get Chianti out of it."

She sat up to face him. Blood from her knees and feet smeared the blond hardwood floor. Charlotte screamed, "Stop, Pierce!"

"What is it with you Gordon girls and red wine?" He rubbed his chin with his left hand. "Club soda. Maybe I'll try hydrogen peroxide—it removes blood stains, you know."

Charlotte wiped bloody glass from her feet. She used a shelf for a ladder rung and scaled the bookshelves, never moving her eyes from Pope. He rounded the couch in slow, methodical steps, inch by inch, creeping closer as if she were a ladybug snared in a brown spider's web.

"Surrender, Charlotte. The more you fight, the more the pain. Look at your knees. It must hurt. Fortunately, you won't have to worry about scarring."

She didn't look down.

"And the stains on my floors. Let's end it, dearest. Quick and merciful. No more pain, Charlotte."

Without looking, Charlotte probed a shelf with a hand. She lifted the Philadelphia Museum book and hurled it at him.

He ducked. He stopped, picked up the book, closed it, and placed it with care on the couch arm.

She flicked her wrist like a paperboy flinging the Sunday *Journal-Constitution*. One at a time, she skipped the books across the glass-littered rug like stones on calm mountain lake. The sharp edges of the table remains sliced the book covers.

"Stop!" Pope yelled. "You're being hateful."

Charlotte grabbed *DALI*. She stooped and rubbed her knee with her right hand. She held up her hand, painted bright red in her blood. Her stare blazing at Pope, she held the Dalí collection by the binder and let it fall open. She lowered her bloody hand toward vulnerable pages.

"No!" he screamed. "It won't come off."

Charlotte finger-painted on the art book canvas. She dropped the open book to the floor and stomped the cover with her bony heel. She fingered a tower of compact disks and toppled it from the shelf. Jewel cases split. Unprotected CDs strewn across the mounting debris, she stamped slivery disks with her bloody footprint.

He readied the bat above his head. His nostrils flared with each deep breath. Pope skulked forward, a vein bulging in his neck.

Charlotte backed along the shelf front. She swept novels and knickknacks to the floor. "Did any of those women fight back, Pierce?"

"They wanted me. Lust and suspicion are at opposite ends of the emotional spectrum. They never knew what hit them. They died fast. They died happy."

"Not me. *If* I die." She threw *Taming of the Shrew* at him. "I'll die angry.

You'll need a bulldozer to clean up after me."

She bumped into a wall.

"Bye, Charlotte!"

He chopped down at her head.

Charlotte collapsed to her knees.

The bat stuck, impaled in cracked plaster.

She scrambled to her feet and dashed for the kitchen door. Before the door swung closed, she spotted the chopping knife on the cutting board, speckled with diced onions. Charlotte wrapped her fingers around the Chicago Cutlery wooden handle and pointed the blade toward the door.

Pope slammed the door against the wall and leaped into the kitchen.

Charlotte stabbed at him.

She misjudged the distance. She lacked the power to plunge the knife tip into his chest, the dagger stopped short of Pope. She drew back to lunge again.

The swift downswing smashed her fingers against the wood handle. She had heard the same sickening sound the night Pope disarmed the mugger outside Turner Field. The chopping knife twirled out of her broken fingers, bounced and scored the linoleum.

Charlotte screamed. She grasped her hand and spun away from Pope. She faced the oven. Garlic-scented smoke drifted up from the burnt brown scallops and onions stuck to sauté pan. Boiling water lapped over the edge of the pasta pot, and the foamy spill sparked the gas flame.

She closed her eyes, pinned against the stovetop. *My poor parents,* she thought. *Will they ever know the same sick man murdered their angel daughter and the other one, the stupid one, the one that couldn't stop until she had all the answers?*

She heard a hollow wooden pounding from the living room. Pope crept forward to strike again. The knock seemed light years from saving Charlotte.

"Help!" Her damaged hand fell limp to her side. She braced her left hand on the stove and pleaded, "Don't do this! There's someone here."

"It's too late, Charlotte." His eyes lacked life. Pope's mission was on autopilot.

She leaned away and her arm brushed against the pasta pot handle. The scorching copper singed flesh on her forearm.

The knocking stopped.

Pope bent his knees and cocked his arm above his shoulder.

A welt blistered Charlotte's skin. She slid her arm along the pot handle toward her hand.

The head of the bat came down.

Charlotte snatched the pot handle. The handle branded its imprint on her hand. She ducked, twisted right, and launched boiling linguini and frothing water at Pope's face.

The bat bashed her shoulder, clanged against the stove, fell to the floor, and rolled.

Pope clawed at the boiled pasta clinging to his face. Deep pink streaks marked his cheeks. He staggered backward and slipped on the wet surface. His right foot rolled over the bat. His feet shot out from underneath him, and he crashed to the floor. Squirming and kicking, Pope scratched at his charred face as if he could peel off the intense pain.

"I can't see! Oh, God, I'm blind!" He thrashed side to side.

Charlotte stared, aghast at the dreadful carnage. Cut, burned, and bruised, adrift in each breath—breaths she doubted she would ever inhale—she was thankful to be alive.

Nine-one-one. She eased away from the oven to find the telephone. She stepped over Pope, lightheaded and weak in the knees.

Pope's guttural moan stopped.

Charlotte pulled the door handle.

A strong hand shackled her ankle. The swift echo of displaced air followed the bat's descent. Snap. Bone splintered above her ankle. Charlotte dropped like fallen timber, chopped down, hinged at the ankle by his powerful grip.

On his back, Pope dragged Charlotte, hand over hand, as if her leg was a tug-of-war rope.

Her shoulders and head landed through the doorframe in the living room. She stretched her arms and clung to the doorjamb.

He gave up pulling her and pounded her lower leg with repeated blows. She winced. Her vision blurred. "Hold on, Charlotte," she said aloud. "Faint and die."

Her entire focus confined to eight feet of blood-stain flooring. The car engine revving outside Pope's house sounded miles away. Metal scraped concrete. A loud explosion like a tire blowout resonated from Pope's porch.

Charlotte glanced at the front door. Wood crunched as if King Kong sized termites munched on the structure. The engine revved again, this time closer. The wall bulged, then the front door blasted open. The grill of Cox's Chevrolet Lumina pierced the plaster, wall studs, and painted trim debris.

Cox shoved his door open, shedding the rubble, sprinted into the living room, and rolled over the couch.

"Carlton, help!" she cried out.

Charlotte bent her free leg at the knee and kicked. Her back kick smashed into Pope's face. Her heel splattered the bridge of his nose. His nose cartilage caved in and blood sprayed. Pope released Charlotte's battered leg. She crawled beyond his reach.

Sirens screeched, and tires squealed outside.

Cox leaped over her.

"You fucking bastard!" he chanted and stomped Pope's arm with size twelve penny loafers, grinding the heel into Pope's wrist until the Cardinals' bat rolled from his fingers.

Chapter Thirty-Nine

"You don't have to do this." Cox pushed Charlotte's wheelchair.

"Yes. Yes, I do. I have no choice."

Charlotte had been under observation in a semi-private room since Saturday. Cox tried to call in favors to arrange a private room for her, but beds were sparse on a Saturday night in Atlanta's premier trauma unit—Grady Memorial Hospital. Traynor recovered two floors below in ICU.

She could star in a first-aid training documentary with her second degree burns wrapped in gauze, her right hand and lower left leg set in plaster casts, and both knees and feet stitched. The nagging injuries and spurts of sharp pain were tolerable, even desirable, when she considered the bat-wielding attack she had survived.

"Don't expect a warm reception." Cox halted the wheelchair.

Charlotte examined the empty chair outside the room. An Atlanta police officer had been stationed there around the clock until Sunday morning, when Traynor's status elevated from suspected murderer to wounded hero.

"He saved my life, Carlton. And I ruined his. Earl Traynor deserves my apology, welcomed or not."

Cox spun the wheelchair, backed against the door, and guided her into the room.

His sleeves cuffed at the elbow, Tad Smithurst blocked them. "Get out." He pointed and snipped in harsh whisper. "You're the last person on the planet Torch wants to see."

Traynor coughed.

"See! Your intrusion has upset him. For the last time, leave!"

"Let her in," Traynor's scratchy voice demanded.

"The nurse said to limit your visitors. You need rest, Torch."

The tubes attached to an intravenous needle jiggled when Traynor raised his right arm and leveled it at the door. "Haul ass, Tad."

Smithurst, flustered, retrieved his suit jacket from a chair back and flitted to the door. "I'll be reporting your insubordination to Mr. Hendricks."

"Knock yourself out, dipshit."

Charlotte giggled as Smithurst stormed from the room.

"Come on in," Traynor said.

Cox wheeled her toward the bed. In the dim overhead lighting, she surveyed digital monitors plugged to Traynor through multiple electrodes. Clear liquid dripped into an opaque tube and delivered painkiller.

"Can we talk?" Charlotte asked.

"I ain't going nowhere no time soon."

She looked up at Cox. "I'll be fine."

"I'll be outside if you need me."

The door swung closed after Cox exited.

"You look like hell," Traynor said.

"It could have been worse."

"Will ya heal?"

She lowered her eyes to the leg cast. "Except for the leg, it's all superficial. The doctor told me multiple compound fractures typically require extended rehabilitation therapy."

Charlotte used her hand cast and the heel of the hand on her burned arm to rotate the wheels a turn closer to the bed. She noted traces of the yellow and black face paint along his jaw and temple. "Next time you see a nurse ask her to wash that ridiculous paint off your face." Charlotte raised her arms. "I'm all thumbs or I'd wash it off myself."

He snickered with a lopsided grin. "I looked pretty stupid, didn't I?"

"Yes," she smiled. "But I'm grateful you were there. I only wished you had explained the articles before Chet charged me. I must be dense, but I couldn't find the connection between the articles until it was almost too late." She glared at the bandages shrouding Traynor's left shoulder. "How bad is it?"

"The slug nicked a lung and burrowed a gully all the way to my shoulder. Somehow it missed my heart, if I got one. Doc said the arm will be about twenty percent disabled. Can't pitch with it anyway, so what good is it? Not a scratch on my throwing arm. If I ever get out of this damn hospital, I'll be in shape by the time pitchers and catchers report for spring training."

Charlotte touched his hand. "Good, Earl. I'm so glad." Tears welled. "To tell you the truth, I wasn't expecting a civil conversation today. You're making this too easy for me."

"I don't blame you, Charlotte. If someone murdered my sister, I reckon I would do the same. Besides, the fireworks would never have begun if Chet hadn't flipped his lid." Traynor shook his head. "Don't know what came over the boy. I'll miss him. As good a friend as there is." His eyes turned to

Charlotte. "I'm sorry for what he did to your friend."

"Another deep regret I'll have to live with. If I'd left Margaret's murder to the appropriate authorities, Liz would be alive, and you'd be striking out Mets, or Phillies, or whoever the hell you pitch against. I'm sorry for the pain I've caused you, Earl."

Charlotte began sobbing, ending the self-imposed moratorium on crying.

"Cut it out, Charlotte. That damn reporter out there will think I'm roughing you up."

Tears streaked down her cheeks. She tried to smile.

"When I finally came out of the coma, I thought about what Pope had done. Let me ask you this, if you hadn't stuck your nose in and chased down this lunatic, how many more women would he have killed? When I look at it in that light, I figure it was a worth a few days in the Grady Hilton to help you flush that skunk. How is the varmint anyway?"

"In the burn ward, under heavy sedation and maximum security. They're not sure yet how much permanent damage there is to his eyes."

"Won't make a difference where he's going. Boiling water in the face. Remind me never to get sideways with you…again."

"My options were limited." Charlotte inhaled and sighed. "I came here to say I'm sorry."

"Accepted."

"And to thank you. You could have let Chet kill me. So long, Earl."

Charlotte struggled to spin the wheelchair and rolled for the door.

"No, I couldn't," Traynor said.

She made a half turn and looked at him. "Couldn't what?"

"Even if I'd killed all those women, no way in hell would I let Chet hurt you."

"I believe you," Charlotte said, and she burst into a joyous smile.

"If you're ever in Milwaukee, or wherever Hendricks offloads me, holler at me and I'll scrounge up some tickets for you."

"I'll come see you, Earl—in Atlanta. Whatever Austin Hendricks might be, he isn't stupid. The team is falling apart and right out of the pennant race without you. The *AJC* is drawing comparisons to 1964…. Who was it?"

"Phillies blew a huge lead to the Cardinals."

"Right. You'll be on the mound at the Ted, with forty thousand adoring fans chanting, 'Blow 'em away, Torch.' And Torch Traynor, the Atlanta Braves' closer elite, will straighten his uniform, adjust the brim of his cap, and mow them down, one, two, three."

*